JOURNEY TO THE SUNSET

GLYNAE L. DESCHENE

©2025 by Glynae L. Deschene

Published by hope*books
2217 Matthews Township Pkwy
Suite D302
Matthews, NC 28105
www.hopebooks.com

hope*books is a division of hope*media

Printed in the United States of America

All rights reserved. Without limiting the rights under copyrights reserved above, no part of this publication may be scanned, uploaded, reproduced, distributed, or transmitted in any form or by any means whatsoever without express prior written permission from both the author and publisher of this book—except in the case of brief quotations embodied in critical articles and reviews.

Thank you for supporting the author's rights.

First paperback edition.
Paperback ISBN: 979-8-89185-299-0
Hardcover ISBN: 979-8-89185-309-6
Ebook ISBN: 979-8-89185-310-2
Library of Congress Number: 2025945288

All Scripture quotations, unless otherwise indicated, are taken from the Holy Bible, New International Version®, NIV®. Copyright ©1973, 1978, 1984, 2011 by Biblica, Inc.™ Used by permission of Zondervan. All rights reserved worldwide. www.zondervan.com The "NIV" and "New International Version" are trademarks registered in the United States Patent and Trademark Office by Biblica, Inc.™

ENDORSEMENTS

"Glynae Deschene's *Journey to the Sunset* takes readers back to the confusion and uncertainty of early biblical history. Through vivid imagery and emotion, Deschene paints a compelling picture of a world on the brink of transformation. The characters wrestle with their faith, navigating doubts while seeking God's direction. With each turn of the page, the suspense builds, making it a book you can't put down. As an avid fiction lover and author, this is my kind of read; an inspiring journey of faith and perseverance that is a must-read for anyone seeking a story of hope in the midst of uncertainty."

—Carrie Watts, RN, BSN and author of
Crisis of Faith, Speaker, *Saved and Strong*
Podcast host, and writing coach

"A beautifully written and emotionally rich story set in the shadow of Babel. Glynae Deschene brings a rare era of biblical history to life with tenderness, depth, and quiet power."

—Naomi Rawlings, USA Today
Bestselling Author of *Echoes of Twilight*

"Glynae Deschene's *Journey to the Sunset* sweeps readers into a richly imagined world where timeless truth meets ancient adventure. Her vivid prose and soul-stirring dialogue breathe life into the biblical landscape, inviting us to walk alongside Shana and her family as they seek purpose, belonging, and the God who goes before them in those days—and before us today. This is a story that awakens the senses, stirs the spirit, and leaves you hoping for a sequel!"

—Thalia L. Polk, Biblical Mentor and Author of
*Finding My True Father: My Journey of Overcoming
Parental Abandonment and Becoming Beloved*

"*Journey to the Sunset* is a moving and inspirational journey of faith, family, and the God who keeps His promises."

—Lucio Berumen, Pastor

"*Journey to the Sunset* is a beautifully written novel blending historical imagination with timeless spiritual truths. Readers are guided through an enduring story of hope to an understanding of how God keeps His promises. This book will resonate with fans of biblical fiction and lovers of redemptive journeys alike."

—Annette Peterson

"A beautiful blend of biblical history and imaginative storytelling, *Journey to the Sunset* is a must-read for fans of redemptive fiction."

—Vanita Berumen

DEDICATION

To Elohim who spoke the world into being,

who sees all things,

and for whom all things exist.

Colossians 1:16

For in him all things were created: things in heaven and on earth, visible and invisible,

whether thrones or powers or rulers or authorities;

all things have been created through him and for him.

ACKNOWLEDGMENTS

To my husband—thank you for drawing me deeper into the world of hunting and animal encounters. Your insight shaped scenes I never would have written on my own.

To my family—your love and support have held me steady throughout this journey.

To hope*books—Brian Dixon, Hope Dover, Angela Abbott, Amanda McMullen and the entire staff—for your incredible guidance, encouragement, and commitment to excellence.

To hope*writers—thank you for Tuesday Teaching, the community, and Zoe Shaw, whose wisdom helped me press forward when the path felt uncertain.

To my early morning writing cohorts, Carrie Watts and Thalia Polk—your presence, accountability, and shared passion made the quiet hours shine with purpose.

To my Facebook encouragers, faithful beta readers, and generous launch team—your voices cheered me on when I most needed it. This story has your fingerprints on it, too.

With deep gratitude to all who believed in the message and helped carry it into the light.

TABLE OF CONTENTS

FOREWORD

Dear Reader,

I have to tell you about a book that really touched my heart. I think you'll enjoy reading it, too. It is written by a Christ-following author, Glynae L. Deschene, and it follows a girl named Shana and her family as they travel through the wilderness and face hard days and challenges.

But the amazing thing is, even when they feel tired or unsure, they keep trusting God. They believe He is leading them somewhere good, even when they do not know exactly where that is. What really stood out to me is how real their struggles feel. There is a mix of adventure and discovery. There is also faith, prayer, and those small, quiet moments when the reader feels God's presence. The way the characters in Glynae's book lean on each other and on God reminded me that we are never alone, even when life feels uncertain.

One of my favorite Bible verses came to mind while I was reading: "The steadfast love of the Lord never ceases; his mercies never come to an end; they are new every morning; great is your faithfulness" (Lamentations 3:22–23, ESV).

That verse fits this story so well. The characters are learning to trust in God's provision, just like we are. They pray when they do not have answers. They sing when they need courage. They listen for His voice when they do not know what is next. Through the book and in life, as followers of Almighty God, we see that His mercies never end.

If you've ever wondered what it means to trust God with your life, real choices, fears, and dreams; this book shows what trust in God looks like in such a beautiful way.

—*Dr. Faith Marie Nava, CEO of Sunset Familia*

CHARACTERS AND RELATIONSHIPS

Elohim—God, supreme power, might and rulership

Yahweh—Personal covenant name translated as "Lord"

Shana—"Shawnah"

Mikael—"Mik-ael"

Johanan—Father of Shana

Sarah—Mother of Shana

Eldad—Brother of Shana

Tobiya—Became friend at gathering

Tabitha—Wife of Tobiya

Bathshua—Daughter of Tobiya

Lemuel—Son of Tobiya

Hadassah—Daughter of Tobiya

Jairus—Father of Johanan

Martha—Mother of Johanan

Jared—Father of Mikael

Elizabeth—Mother of Mikael

Mikah—Brother of Mikael

Malaki—Brother of Mikael

Chapter 1

THE WHISPERING HILLS

The morning mist still clung to the hills like a soft blanket as Shana stepped outside, barefoot and quiet. The earth was cool under her feet, and a chorus of birdsong echoed from the trees that ringed their little village. Sheep were baaing from somewhere behind the house, and she could already hear Eldad laughing with one of the neighbor boys.

She didn't join him yet. Instead, she climbed the short path to the hill behind their home, where wild thyme grew between the rocks and the sky always seemed bigger. From there, she could see across the low plains and catch a faint glimpse of the far-off tower—not the structure itself, but the strange shimmer in the sky above it, a haze that danced like heat above a fire.

Shana didn't know why, but she had started watching that shimmer every morning. She'd ask her father questions he couldn't quite answer, and her mother would brush her hair and say, "Best not to think too hard about what men build when they think they're greater than Elohim."

But Shana did think about it. She wondered what it would be like to stand where the sky touched the stone, or to speak with someone who had seen the top. She didn't want to build towers. She just wanted to understand the feeling inside her that there was something more beyond the hill, the plain, the loom, and the daily bread.

She drew her knees up and rested her chin on them.

Maybe it was enough to sit and wonder.

Eldad's voice called up to her, breaking the quiet. "Shana! Come! Yofet found a baby dove fallen from its nest!"

She scrambled down the hill, feet slipping on the dew-slick rocks. Eldad met her halfway, cheeks flushed with excitement, a small bundle cradled in his hands. "It's still warm, I think it can live," he begged.

Shana looked at the tiny creature, heart fluttering. "We should bring it to Mother."

They hurried back to the house where Sarah was kneading bread by the hearth. The scent of yeast and woodsmoke filled the air. She looked up, wiping her hands on her apron. "What have you brought me?"

Eldad gently opened his palms.

Sarah's brow furrowed, then softened. "It's too young to be alone. We'll keep it by the hearth until we see if it survives."

She nodded toward a basket in the corner. "Line it with wool, Shana. And Eldad, go tell your father where you found it. He'll want to check the nest."

As Shana prepared the basket for the dove, she glanced at the bread rising in its bowl. There was comfort in the rhythm of the day. Bread in the morning. Fire at night. A father who told stories beneath the stars, a mother who sang softly while she worked, a brother who still believed every small thing mattered.

And yet...

Even as she cupped the fragile dove in her hands and felt its tiny heartbeat against her skin, her thoughts drifted beyond the village, beyond the hills, and beyond even the shimmer in the distance.

Something was coming.

She could feel it, like the stirring of wind before the sky changes.

Chapter 2

WHEN WORD BROKE

"What did you say? Wait, what's happening? I can hear you, but I don't understand a word!"

The man's voice rose above the clatter of tools, but the foreman only stared at him, lips moving, eyes wide. Around them, workers dropped bricks and shouted words that made no sense. Familiar faces now spoke in unknown words.

The tower loomed overhead, casting its shadow across the city of Babel. All eyes had once been on the towering structure. It was the pride of a united people. The bricks, hardened in fire and laid with tar, were ready for the next layer. But building required more than material—it required direction, rhythm, and understanding.

And now, that was gone.

A mason shoved his apprentice, shouting something sharp and urgent. The boy flinched, then blurted back in a stream of strange syllables. Others stopped, stared, confused, and then they were angry. Someone screamed. A tool crashed. Another man ran, arms flailing, calling for his friend in a voice that no longer matched his friend.

The air thickened. Voices overlapped like waves in a storm, clashing and breaking. It wasn't just noise; it was *wrong*. The kind of wrong that made your skin prickle and your legs want to run.

Children cried. Mothers shouted the names of their children and wrapped them in tight embraces, unwilling to let them go. Friends, lifelong companions, looked at one another like strangers.

Confusion spread like wildfire.

And then chaos erupted.

Families scattered. The city broke apart, not brick by brick, but voice by voice.

And in the shadow of the unfinished tower, the world as they had known it fell apart.

Words fractured into fragments. People grouped by sound and by whatever speech still made sense. Some wandered. Some waited. And some… Johanan came running to his home. There, he found his family huddled together in their small village. "What is happening?" Sarah asked.

"Shana, Eldad, go get your special things. Put them in your leather bags. Hurry." The children looked at him with wide eyes but released their hold on their mother and moved to retrieve their belongings. "Sarah, we must leave. Elohim has enacted His command for us to fill the whole earth. We will start our journey, and Elohim will guide us. Pack only what is necessary. I will get the animals." He wrapped his arms around her, trying to soothe the fear in her face. He stood still for a moment, thinking, steadying himself. "Wait. Shana and Eldad, come listen! We leave in the morning. I need you to go to the river and fill some waterskins. Then return and help your mother pack. We will take the tent down first thing in the morning."

The children nodded.

Shana whimpered, "We get water every day, but it is scary today."

Johanan wrapped his arms around them, "It will be okay. Take the path you usually take. If someone tries to talk to you and you don't understand, smile, wave, and move on."

They trudged to the river and filled the waterskins. As they climbed the uneven hill from the riverbank, Eldad stumbled, his sandal catching on a root. He lurched forward, but caught himself with a grunt, knees bent, arms out like a goat regaining balance on a rocky ledge. His frame was compact but sturdy, built for scrambles like this.

Shana, just ahead, glanced back with a frown. Though she was ten and two years older, she stood barely taller than him, her slight figure almost lost in the cascade of dark brown curls that swayed down to her waist. Her eyes, deep brown like dates ripening in the sun, glinted with displeasure.

Eldad shook the dust from his tunic, revealing a few loose curls on his head that caught the sun with hints of chestnut. His hazel eyes flicked up at her, wide and sheepish.

"Oh, be careful, Eldad. We don't want anything else to happen today."

As they came to the neighbor children, they tried to speak, but the words tangled and faltered. In the end, they could only shake their heads. The children embraced one another as tears ran down their faces, then turned away, glancing back before hurrying home to help their own mother.

Shana and Eldad burst through the flap of the tent, breathless.

"Mama, we can't understand our friends!" Shana clutched her tunic, her face pale.

Sarah pulled them close. "We will find people we can understand!"

***

Javan, son of Japheth, grandson of Noah, sent out a call: "Tribe of Javan, come to Mount Urartu, to the place of the ark. Let us remember the beginnings. Let us remember Elohim."

No one knew exactly how the word spread. Maybe it traveled in fragments, or in looks and gestures, or in the silent hope shared among broken families. But it moved like water finding a streambed.

Families gathered their belongings. Not all spoke the same language anymore, but some found others they could understand. And more than that, they shared the same longing: to remember, to belong, to begin again.

5

Chapter 3

THE DUST BETWEEN US

The morning sun rose behind them, casting their shadows westward as Johanan's family began their journey to the place of the ark. Their village lay quiet in the distance, as Shana glanced back. It was softened by the mist, as if it too was trying to forget the voices it could no longer understand.

Shana walked beside her mother, the leather strap of her waterskin cutting a familiar line across her chest. Each step felt heavier than it should have, not because of what she carried, but because of what she left behind. The path twisted through the hills like a ribbon someone had tried to unsuccessfully flatten but never could. They walked with others, strangers who had become familiar overnight simply because their words made sense.

They didn't talk much.

It was not the silence of tension, but of listening, of grieving. It was the silence people shared after the world changed, when speech seemed too small to hold what was inside them.

That night, Johanan chose a clearing near the stream where the stones were flat, and the grass was dry. Eldad kicked off his sagebrush sandals and raced down to the water, calling back to Shana. "Come feel it. It's freezing!" Eldad shouted, his voice echoing off the stones.

Shana ran and knelt to splash her face. The chill snapped against her skin, jarring her from the heaviness that sorrow threatened to drag her into. As she dried her face with the corner of her hide, she looked up and saw her father by the fire, staring into it as if the flames could tell him what to do next.

Shana thought, he's like a tree that's been struck by lightning. Still rooted. Still strong. But changed.

They ate simple food—flatbread, dried meat, a handful of dates. They curled together beneath a heavy fur under the open sky. The stars blinked like ancient watchers, steady and cold.

Shana lay next to her parents.

Eldad, on the other side, was already asleep.

Sarah's arm wrapped around her shoulder.

"Do you think we'll find the ark?" Shana whispered.

"We will," her mother emphasized. "Javan said that the ark still waits. It's waiting for those who remember."

The next day, the land began to rise beneath their feet. The hills lifted slowly, as if the earth itself was drawing them upward toward something sacred. Trees grew thicker, the air cooler. Some families had joined them along the way. Others veered off when their words no longer matched.

Shana noticed her father watching each family as they passed, his eyes scanning for understanding and for kinship. Sometimes he found it. Sometimes he nodded and kept walking.

On the third day, they reached a ridge where the path flattened, and the world opened below them. There in the distance, Mount Urartu stood like a sentinel, and its peak was kissed by clouds, its base was wrapped in pine and rock. Shana caught her breath.

She had seen mountains before, but not like this. This mountain looked like it *remembered* the flood, the waiting, the promise.

THE GATHERING

Before the scattering, there was one voice.

Now, in the shadow of loss, families gather at the foot of the mountain

to remember, to listen, to begin again.

Here, among the people and stories,

the journey begins not with footsteps,

but with the echo of what was once whole.

Chapter 4

THE PLACE OF DESCENT

Despite the absence of quakes or winds, the earth had been shaken by the loss of shared language. In an instant, the world's one language splintered into many, and the people scattered in fear and confusion. What had once been a united people was now divided by sound, families and tribes fleeing in different directions.

But word had begun to spread again, and a gathering was being called.

The tribe of Javan, son of Japheth, was making its way to Mount Urartu and to the resting place of the ark, where Elohim had once acted so clearly in the lives of men. Would they be able to understand one another when they arrived? No one knew. Some believed this fracture of language was the judgment of Elohim, a breaking caused by humanity's pride and rebellion. Even so, they remembered His first command: "Be fruitful and multiply. Fill the earth."

So they would go. They would scatter with hope. Now, they must make reparation with Yahweh Elohim. And they must remember to carry His promises forward.

Noah was eager to see the people and all his children. As the forefather of everyone present, Noah was beloved by all. The gathering would need to hear the stories of Yahweh Elohim, stories that Noah wanted them to carry in their hearts as they traveled. The promises of Yahweh Elohim must be remembered and anticipated.

The village of Naxuana, Noah's home, settled quietly at the foot of Mount Urartu, where the snow-draped peak touched the sky like a finger pointing to the heavens. The village was not large. It was just a scattering of stone and clay homes with thatched roofs, built close to one another as if for warmth. The ground underfoot was hard-packed earth laced with old stones, worn smooth by bare feet. Children's laughter echoed through the paths. Set in a fertile valley, the village thrived with agriculture. Terraced fields climbed gently up the lower slopes, golden with wheat and barley in the sun, and groves of fig and pomegranate trees swayed in the gentle wind. Vineyards promised a good year's production. Shepherds tended to sheep with their bells clinking softly, and goats bleated in their pens, mingling with the low murmur of water from a nearby stream that tumbled down the mountain. It was a beautiful place, one that Noah had called home for a very long time. His son Japheth remained with him, along with their extended family.

The village had prepared for the gathering. Tent spaces were marked, livestock areas designated, and large quantities of food were readied. The villagers felt that they were the protectors of the ark. Most of the villagers would remain in Naxuana. This gathering was special, as it would mark the beginning of long journeys for most of those who had answered the call of Javan.

As people arrived in small groups, tents were quickly set up, and the gathering grew throughout the day. Among them were Johanan and Sarah with their children, Shana and Eldad. Shana was especially excited to see her forefathers, Noah and Japheth. Noah was very, very old, though he would often say he was still young compared to those in the beginning. Japheth was old, too.

Shana loved the "beget" story. She knew it by heart: Noah - Japheth - Javan - Elishah - Nathaniel - Jarius - Johanan - Eldad. She wished she could add her own name to the begets. However, she knew only boys could be named in such stories. Her brother Eldad, though younger, carried that honor. Would she be able to understand the people here at the gathering?

By afternoon, smoke from cookfires curled gently into the dusk, carrying with it the scent of roasting grain and herbs. The villagers guided everyone to the central clearing gathering area. It was a wide, flat place where the grass had been worn thin by footsteps and fire rings. At the edge of the gathering place stood a low platform made of weathered cedar beams, smoothed by years of sun and use. It was raised just enough for all to see, set against a backdrop of climbing vines and stone. At its center sat an old chair carved from a single trunk of olive wood. Its back was high and arched, worn shiny where hands had rested or leaned across it. Noah sat quietly as he prepared to speak, cloaked in wool dyed deep with indigo, his presence both commanding and gentle. At his feet lounged two hounds, their long, silky coats gleaming in the firelight. With calm, almond-shaped eyes, they watched the crowd in silence. Noah rested a hand along their backs, his fingers lightly brushing their fur.

Shana sat cross-legged beside her mother, her eyes fixed on the figure by the fire. The oldest man she had ever seen, his silver-white beard trailing to his chest and a voice that rumbled like distant thunder… Noah. Would they be able to understand Noah?

The others hushed as he looked around the gathered circle. His eyes, still clear and bright, found each face in turn. Then he spoke, not in the hurried speech of men, but slowly, like water flowing over stones.

"In the beginning… Elohim created the heavens and the earth," Noah began, his voice carrying effortlessly into the hush.

The children stopped fidgeting. Even the elders leaned in. They could understand Noah!

"The earth was formless and empty. Darkness covered the face of the deep. Yet, the Spirit of Elohim was there, moving and hovering over the face of the waters.

Then Elohim said, 'Let there be light.'

And there was light."

Wonder held Shana's breath captive. She imagined the first glimmer of light piercing an endless ocean of black, sudden and blazing. Her fingers tightened on the hem of her tunic.

"Elohim called the light 'day,' and the darkness 'night.' Evening came, and morning, the first day…"

Noah's words rolled on like a wave, shaping the days of creation with reverent clarity. The sky, the seas, the dry land. Trees bursting forth. Stars scattered across the heavens. Great creatures of the deep, flocks of birds rising into a world of blue.

"Then Elohim said, 'Let us make man in our image…'"

Noah's voice softened; its weight deepened.

"So Elohim created man in His own image—male and female He created them. And He blessed them. He gave them the earth, the plants, the animals. Everything that has breath."

Shana closed her eyes. In her mind's eye, she saw the garden, the first man and woman walking hand in hand, sunlight streaming through branches heavy with fruit.

"And Elohim saw all that He had made. And, it was very good.

Evening came, and morning—the sixth day."

Noah leaned forward slightly, his eyes gleaming in the firelight.

"And on the seventh day… He rested."

The last words fell into silence — like creation itself had exhaled. The fire crackled. A breeze stirred the hair at Shana's temples.

Noah sat back, letting the hush linger.

Shana drew in a slow breath. For a moment, the world seemed new again, as if she were hearing it all for the first time. She glanced at her mother's quiet smile, then back at Noah, whose eyes now rested not on the crowd, but on the mountain where the ark stood, silent and enduring. The ark still waited up there, weathered by time and memory. And now, so did the journey.

"This is the story of our beginning and our Creator, our invisible Elohim. He is revealed in creation," Noah declared. The large group was silent for a moment and reflected on the awesomeness of their God, Yahweh Elohim.

Shana turned, "Father, isn't it great to hear Noah's stories?"

"It sure is, Shana. Let's get something to eat."

They moved towards their tent to get ready for the evening meal. Sarah and Shana began to set out what they would need for supper. Shana got the wooden bowls out of the reed basket and set them on the meal cloth.

Sarah directed, "Johanan, please take Eldad and get some of the red deer meat—hart, I think they call it, or hind—from the campfire pit." Sarah got out the onions and cucumbers and sliced them up while Shana got out the bread.

Johanan and Eldad returned with the meat. They sat down around the cloth by the fire to eat. Johanan prayed, "Thank You, Yahweh Elohim, for our food and the safe trip that we had getting here. Guide us as we prepare to continue our journey to wherever You want us to be."

They ate and talked about who they had seen so far.

Johanan requested, "Shana, why don't you and Eldad go fill the waterskin so we have it full in the morning?" Shana and Eldad retrieved the waterskin and then headed to the river.

Johanan spoke gently to Sarah, "We must talk about us moving on. We must obey Elohim's command to fill the earth. We must find people of our language or start our own clan. There are many languages here. Yet, we can all understand Noah and the forefathers. What happened far to the South has affected all of mankind. Please think about it now. After the gathering, we will start."

"Johanan, I am afraid. When will we know to stop?"

"Continue to pray about it, Sarah. We will know."

Chapter 5

IN THE BEGINNING

The night deepened around their tent, but the stories were not yet done. Sarah cleared the meal cloth and readied things for the morning. "Mama, will we be able to hear more stories tonight around the campfire?" asked Shana.

"Yes, for a little while," Sarah said. "Grab some hides, it'll be cooler tonight."

"Tonight, we will hear an expanded story of the creation of man and woman and how Elohim made them," Johanan remarked, as the four headed towards the campfire, as many others were doing. When they got to the campfire, they spread their hides out and took a seat. Shana had some extra hides in case it got too cool.

As everyone settled themselves around the crackling fire, Nathaniel arose. "Tonight, we'll hear more of our beginnings," Nathaniel said. "These stories tell of our great God, Elohim. Many of us may never come this way again. That is why we speak, so you carry these truths wherever you go. We do not understand how, but you can all understand those of us from the older generations. Japheth will start with a story now."

Japheth took his place in the ancient chair. The fire glowed on the people's faces as they sat in anticipation. "Look into the starry sky and see the greatness of Elohim. This story expounds on the creation of man."

Japheth's voice was low and steady. His words carried weight, like stones placed one by one to build something strong.

"In the beginning, Elohim formed the man not from the heights of heaven, nor from the depths of the sea, but from the dust beneath our feet. The earth itself gave him shape. Then Elohim bent low and breathed into the man's nostrils the breath of life. The man opened his eyes. And so the dust became a living soul."

Shana leaned forward, elbows on her knees, chin in her hands. She smiled at her mother and whispered, "We can understand Japheth." Eldad sat cross-legged, fidgeting only a little.

"Elohim planted a garden for the man, eastward, in Eden. There, He made every tree grow—trees pleasing to the eye and good for food. In the middle of the garden, two stood apart: the tree of life, and the tree of the knowledge of good and evil. Rivers flowed out from Eden, dividing into four: Pishon, Gihon, Tigris, and Euphrates, giving life to the world beyond."

Japheth's eyes drifted toward the horizon, as if he saw it all.

"He gave the man a task: to tend the garden and keep it. And He gave a command: 'You may eat of every tree. But of the tree of the knowledge of good and evil, you must not eat. For in the day you eat of it, you shall surely die.'"

A soft wind stirred through the grass.

"Then Elohim said, 'It is not good for the man to be alone.' And He brought every beast of the field and bird of the air to him, for the man to name. But for him, no companion was found."

Japheth drew a breath.

"So Elohim caused the man to sleep. A deep sleep, like the stillness of night before the dawn. And while he slept, Elohim took from the man's side a rib and from it, shaped the woman. Not from the dust this time, but from the very body of the man. Flesh of his flesh. Bone of his bone."

"And when the man awoke and saw her, he said:

'This at last is bone of my bones
and flesh of my flesh;
she shall be called Woman,
because she was taken out of Man.'"

Japheth's voice softened. "And so the two became one flesh—naked, and unashamed."

A hush lingered over the gathering, the crackling of the fire filling the quiet as everyone absorbed the story's weight. Shana drew her hide closer, feeling the cold that had settled in, a reminder of the ice creeping over the north and mountains. Japheth's voice broke the silence. "It is colder now with the glaciers forming north of here. The water from the flood had to go somewhere, so Elohim put the water into storage in the ice." He chuckled softly, pulling his own hide tighter. "So, everyone, bundle up. It'll get colder tonight. Let's end with some songs. Nathaniel, think you've still got a voice left? Mine is all used up."

Nathaniel laughed, his breath visible in the cold night air. "I don't know how much of a voice I have left. Everyone, join in your own tongue."

As he spoke, the soft notes of a reed pipe drifted through the air. A small harp joined in, followed by the plucking of a lyre's strings, and a flute's melody wove itself into the mix. The gathering warmed their hands while firelight flickered across their faces. The first notes of the hymn took shape. The sound of voices, some high and soft, others deep and rich, merged with the melody of the instruments, the gentle tones of the harp and flute weaving into the tones of the reed pipe and the lyre. They began to sing the familiar hymn to their Creator:

In the beginning, Elohim's Word did speak,
Light from the darkness, day from night, unique.
Waters He gathered, heavens He stretched wide,
Earth brought forth life where His glory abides.

Oh, sing to the Maker, the heavens declare,
The stars and the oceans proclaim He is there.
From dust He formed us, His breath gave us life,
Oh, praise the Creator, in Him we delight.

Sun, moon, and stars to mark every day,
Seasons and rhythms, His wisdom displays.
Creatures that swim, that fly, and that roam,
All find their place in the world He calls home.

From Eden's garden, rivers did flow,
Man and his helper, made to know,
The Lord of all who walked in the breeze,
Perfect in purpose, the world at peace.

Holy Creator, we lift up Your name,
Alpha and Omega, forever the same.
All of creation joins in this refrain,
Oh, glory and honor to You ever reign!

The different languages all blended in harmony along with the instruments as the singing continued. For a moment, it was as if the curse of Babel had lifted: many tongues rising together, not in confusion or fear, but in peace. Shana could feel it: the music bridged what words alone could not.

Not long ago, the sound of unfamiliar speech stirred fear. Mothers were clutching their children tighter, and friends were turning into strangers overnight. Many still struggled to communicate, relying on gestures and guesses. Through this song, those fears fell silent. The harmony didn't erase the differences. It held them woven together like threads in a single cloth.

For the first time since the scattering, they felt like one united people again. They were gathered not by words, but by fire and song.

"Let's close for tonight with a prayer of guidance," Nathaniel said, his voice steady beneath the hush of settling campfires. "Dear Yahweh Elohim, guide us as we prepare for long journeys to unknown lands. Help us with this confusion of languages to bring peace, which can only come through You. Watch over us in dangers seen and unseen. Strengthen our hearts to obey Your command. Amen."

He stepped down from the platform, and the quiet murmur of the crowd swelled again. There were gentle voices in many tongues, families gathering their cloaks and baskets, the flicker of firelight catching in tired eyes. Smoke drifted low in the cool evening air, laced with the scent of roasted grains and damp earth.

Johanan stood and offered his hand to Sarah as she said, "Tomorrow I will bring my harp." Then Johanan reached out his hand for Shana, her small frame drooping with weariness, while Eldad rubbed his eyes with grubby fists.

Johanan lifted a burning branch from the communal fire. "Sarah, you would enjoy playing with others. Come. Let's light our way home."

Their tent was not far, just beyond the curve of a small ridge where other families from Javan's tribe had pitched their shelters. The ground was hard-packed from many footsteps. Shana stumbled once, and Johanan reached out to steady her.

"You walked a long way today," he said.

"I didn't have to carry anything," she murmured.

"You carried yourself. That counts."

Inside the tent, Sarah brushed dust from the children's hair and tucked them into the layered hides. She knelt beside them and whispered a prayer—one of protection, of trust, of hope. Shana clutched a worn leather pouch close to her chest as her eyes slipped shut.

Outside, the stars had begun to emerge, sharp and brilliant in the dark sky. Johanan sat beside the fire, staring into its glowing heart. Sarah joined him, wrapping her cloak tighter.

"Johanan… do you think we're ready?" she asked quietly.

He didn't answer at first. The fire popped. Distant voices murmured. They were soft words in languages they couldn't yet understand. But not all were unfamiliar. People still laughed. A child cried out and was hushed. Somewhere, a flute played a few slow notes.

"We'll never feel ready," he declared. "But the time is now. We'll need supplies, yes—but more than that, we need faith. We're not the only ones going. Others are getting ready, too. Maybe we'll travel together… for a while."

She nodded. They didn't speak again. The fire burned low. The tent flap rustled as they entered and lay beside their children, the four of them curled in the quiet dark, held by the silence between stories—and the promise of the journey ahead.

Chapter 6

THE PROMISE
AND THE PATH

"And I will put enmity between you and the woman,
and between your offspring and hers;
he will crush your head,
and you will strike his heel."
Genesis 3:15

As the sun rose, it cast a golden hue on the river's surface, making the cold water shimmer like sunlight on polished stone. The gentle rush of the river blended with the distant calls of morning birds, creating a tranquil backdrop for the camp's early stirrings. At the bank of the river, Johanan bathed. "Does it feel good to wash the journey off of you?" Sarah stepped onto a rock, her laughter skimming across the water.

The water was glacial, biting into his skin with a chill that lingered even after he had dried off. "It sure does. The water is straight from the glacier. You'll want to heat some water for the children.

"I think I will heat a little extra for me, too. Will you help me carry some water?" asked Sarah.

"Of course, we will want extra for tomorrow anyway."

The children were waking as Sarah and Johanan returned. Johanan kindled the family fire while Sarah set a pot of water over it. Smoke curled skyward, mingled with the scent of sage and wood ash. Shana and Eldad licked honey from their fingers as they finished their bread.

"There is a meeting of the men this morning," Johanan said. "I will need to go to that in a little bit. Is there anything else you will need this morning?"

"Not that I can think of."

"All right, I will look for you at the gathering place."

***

As the men gathered, Noah turned to Japheth, his voice a low murmur against the morning's stillness. "I wish I could journey with some of you," he said, his gaze softening as he looked at the surrounding hills, "but I must remain here. I'm too old to take a journey now, and someone must guard the truth of the ark."

Japheth gave a nod. "Well, I am too old also. I will stay by your side to help guard the truth of the ark."

Noah's eyes swept over the land beyond, tinted gold by the early light. "Where do you think they will go?"

Japheth glanced at the clusters of men murmuring among themselves. "I believe they will go west. We'll see what the men say." He placed a gentle hand on Noah's shoulder. "Be in prayer with me as we discuss these journeys."

Japheth raised his voice. "Good morning, men. Today, we have an opportunity to work out details of the journeys many of you and your families will undertake. The first question: how many think they would like to go south?"

A rumble of disapproval stirred through the men. "Nay, the trouble with our language all started down there. They are a godless bunch," one muttered.

"What about further north?"

The men shuffled uneasily, casting wary glances toward the distant northern mountains, their peaks shrouded in a frosty blue haze. "The glacier seems to be growing to the north," another said, his voice rough and wary. "Nay, nay, not north; it's an inhospitable land beyond the great sea."

"What about to the east?" Japheth asked.

A hush."Nay, there has been no leading that way," a man finally replied, looking around as others nodded. "Most of us feel led to go west, to the setting of the sun."

A satisfied murmur rippled through the gathering. Javan, who stood among them, raised his hand. "That is what I have felt also." He looked over the men. "We believe this gathering is of my people, the tribe of Javan, the clans: Elishah, Tarshish, the Kittites, and the Rodanites. Now, let's spend some time organizing by language. Find men you can understand besides us elders; it may help to form groups that can travel and perhaps settle together."

Excitement crackled through the group. Men began speaking in quick, animated tones, testing their languages, marveling at the similarities and differences. Gradually, four distinct groups formed.

Japheth nodded. "This is good. Now we need one man from each clan to make an expedition to Mount Urartu. If you can see the ark, it will strengthen your faith. Choose someone today for the expedition."

"We'll prepare for the expedition on the first day. I am curious, though, are these languages divided by clans?"

Johanan answered, "It does seem so, Japheth."

A mix of excitement and nervous anticipation rippled through the crowd. Javan addressed them, his voice deep and steady. "It would be best if some of the younger men went on the expedition. It has been quite a while since I was up there, but the ark… it is truly awe-inspiring, a testimony to Elohim's direction. Are there any volunteers?"

The men exchanged glances, each waiting for the other to speak.

Breaking the silence, Johanan stepped forward. "I would be privileged to go for the clan of Elishah." His voice held a blend of humility and resolve. Tabel, Eliezer, and Bezalel followed, volunteering for the clans of Tarshish, Kittem, and Rodanim, respectively.

"If anyone else wishes to join, let me know," Javan continued. "Gather warm clothes—thick furs for your feet, hands, and bodies. Bring ropes and enough food for the day. We'll go for a brief trip and see what we can find."

***

As dawn brightened, Japheth motioned to the men, "Then let us get ready for the women and children to join us. Today, we will hear the story of mankind's fall."

Families joined together, children with wide eyes, mothers carrying younger ones. Javan settled into the ancient chair. The people leaned forward, hungry for the next part of the story.

"In the garden of delight," Javan began, "Elohim placed the man and the woman, whom He formed with His own hands. He breathed life into them. He walked with them in the cool of the day. He gave them every tree, every fruit. All was theirs, except one."

A hush fell.

"In the center stood two trees. One was the Tree of Life. The other was the Tree of the Knowledge of Good and Evil. And Elohim said, 'You may eat of any tree, but not that one. For on the day you eat of it, you shall surely die.'

"But the serpent came, more cunning than any creature Elohim had made. He said to the woman, 'Did Elohim really say you must not eat of any tree?'

She replied, 'We may eat, except from that tree. If we do, we will die.'

The serpent said, 'You will not surely die. Your eyes will be opened. You will be like Him, knowing good and evil.'"

Javan paused.

"The woman looked. The fruit was beautiful. She desired wisdom. She took it and ate. And gave some to her husband. And he ate."

The fire popped. Shana's hand reached for Eldad's.

"Their eyes opened. And shame fell like a shadow. They hid, no longer able to walk with Elohim. Elohim called, 'Where are you?' The man said, 'I was afraid… so I hid.' Elohim asked, 'Did you eat from the tree?' The man said, 'The woman you gave me, she gave me the fruit.' The woman said, 'The serpent deceived me.'"

Javan's voice steadied.

"So Elohim cursed the serpent. There would be enmity between his seed and hers. One day, her seed would crush his head. To the woman, great pain in childbirth. To the man, the ground cursed with thorns. He would labor until he returned to dust."

Javan looked upward.

"Elohim made garments of skin for them. And He sent them out of the garden. They went east of Eden. And He placed cherubim with a flaming sword to guard the Tree of Life."

Javan's voice fell to a whisper.

"But still… Elohim did not leave them."

The silence lingered, heavy with meaning. Children clung to their mothers. Shana leaned against Sarah.

Japheth rose. "Our stories remind us who we are, and of the promise woven through them. One will come to conquer the serpent and restore what was lost. Every child may carry that hope. Noah's name means rest, a hint of peace we long for. Though he was not the promised one, Yahweh used him to save mankind. Let us keep this hope alive, a hope in the One who will come to restore our relationship with Yahweh.

Tomorrow is the seventh day, so prepare today so we may rest."

The men nodded. Families drew into quiet circles. Children watched with wonder. They could understand the people in their circle! Shana's chest swelled with something warm. Maybe it was hope. For once, their words connected.

Johanan turned to Sarah and the children. His voice was hushed but hopeful. "Isn't it great that our clan speaks our language!" He paused, looking over his shoulder at the gathered clans. He explained the expedition. "I volunteered to go, Sarah. Seeing the ark will deepen my faith, even if we don't reach it. It's an adventure few of us have taken. These glaciers are a mystery, shifting and growing since our elders first saw the climate change." Sarah nodded, understanding the significance of his words.

Noah stood near Japheth, his lined hands clasped. "These families carry the seeds of our history and our future. Wherever they go, let them carry the truth."

"I believe they will," Japheth replied. "Each journey will be its own testimony." He looked toward the sunset, where the light glowed warm and full of promise.

He turned back to the people. "The first day, we'll arrange for a group to visit Mount Urartu. A final glimpse of the ark is a reminder of our covenant."

Anticipation rippled. Several men placed hands over their hearts, a silent vow of reverence. The children, sensing the solemnity, huddled closer to their parents, their young eyes wide with curiosity and awe.

As the sun dipped low, Javan lifted his arms. "Let this gathering be blessed. May Yahweh guide our steps into the lands beyond. Be our strength, and our hope."

An echo of "Amen" rose from the people.

Slowly, they returned to their tents, carrying with them the stories, the blessings, and a sense of purpose— toward the sunset, where promise still waited.

Chapter 7

THE SPARK OF BELONGING

The morning after the blessings, small fires kindled to life again across the camp. The promise of departure still hovered in the air, but today would be a day of preparation and belonging. A crisp wind stirred the grass outside their tent, carrying the scent of ash and dew.

"Tonight is the group meal; I'm baking bread for it. Eldad, is the fire ready?"

"I think so, Mother! I will check." Eldad's eyes sparkled with enthusiasm.

"Shana, are we ready with the dough?" Sarah asked.

Shana's eyes crinkled in a smile. "Yes, Mama. The bread should be ready to bake now." She moved quickly, lifting the dough to test its softness, inhaling the familiar yeasty warmth.

"Good. Let's have a light lunch—just bread and dried meat." Sarah suggested, smoothing a lock of hair behind her ear as she turned to Johanan. "How many of us are there now? Will we be able to travel as one?"

"There are about 50 men in each clan, plus families," Johanan replied thoughtfully. "Javan suggested we start by traveling with our clans. It'll help us stay organized, and we'll learn from each other as we go."

Turning to Eldad, he added, "Eldad, check our flock, will you? Look for a lamb fit for sacrifice tomorrow. I'm not sure if we'll offer one, but it's best to be prepared. Bring a little dried meat with you."

***

Sarah and Shana moved to the rock oven, placing the risen loaves inside. The scent of baking bread filled the air. It was rich, earthy, and comforting. As they worked, they spoke in low voices, their hands moving in a quiet rhythm.

Johanan fetched waterskins and sorted furs and hides, selecting the toughest ones for his feet. His bear wrap, scarred, well-worn, gave him a small sense of comfort.

"Father!" Shana called. "The bread is ready."

The family gathered, tearing pieces from the crusty loaves, savoring the soft insides and the taste of cured meat. Sarah poured warm herb tea into pottery cups, the steam curling upward in delicate spirals.

The oven's warmth continued to chase away the lingering chill.

Meanwhile, Johanan walked to the pasture where Eldad crouched beside a young lamb, his face solemn.

"How are the lambs and kids, son?"

Eldad looked up, pride lighting his face. " Good, Father. Two new ones today!"

Johanan knelt, running his hand over a goat's coarse fur. "Let's count them. Grandfather Jairus's goats—the buck, four does, two with twins, and one with a single kid. Another close to birthing. How many?"

"Five grown ones and three kids… eight!" Eldad beamed.

"Quick with numbers," Johanan chuckled. "You'll need your mother's magic when the flock grows even more."

They turned to the sheep. "Start with the ram, then five ewes. One set of twins, two singles."

Eldad tallied. "Ten!"

Johanan gave his shoulder a light squeeze. "Well done. Now, let's look for one for sacrifice. Are the twins strong?"

"They're perfect. Either could be used… but I don't want them to be killed." His voice dropped. "They're just babies."

Johanan's smile softened. He placed a hand on his son's back. "That's the heart Yahweh wants from us. A lamb is offered not in cruelty, but in faith. Trust that Yahweh will one day send One who will take away sin forever."

Eldad's small hand curled into Johanan's. "Will you tell this to Shana, too?"

"Of course, son. She should know, just as you do."

Johanan looked toward the setting sun. "Come, it's almost time for the feast."

As the final loaves came out of the oven, Sarah and Shana wrapped them in damp leather and set them on sun-warmed rocks. Then they turned to prepare themselves.

Sarah sat Shana down and began untangling her hair with a wooden comb Johanan had carved. As she smoothed Shana's thick locks into rows, she wove in a red strip of leather. "It's lovely."

Shana's eyes sparkled; wearing her hair this way made her feel special, as if the celebration was for her.

"Mama, are you going to wear your rainbow dress?" she asked.

Sarah smiled. "Yes, I think it would be perfect. And you may wear your special dress as well."

Sarah cherished the colors around her—the reds, greens, and ochres of the earth. She had learned to capture them from plants and soil as dyes for her leatherwork.

When Johanan and Eldad returned, dust clinging to their clothes, Johanan called, "Two new lambs! How are things here? We're starving! Is it almost time to go?"

Sarah laughed. "It is, but not until you're clean. Go wash and change. This may be the last time we get to wear these for a while."

She moved to untangle Eldad's hair, but he squirmed away. "Just let me wash my face, Mama!"

Shana stepped out in her special dress, colors swirling softly. "Hurry up, Eldad! Once you're ready, we can go!"

Eldad and Johanan quickened their pace, washing up with water from the pot and skin. Laughter followed the chilly splashes. Sarah returned to the tent to change, and Johanan followed.

Eldad, momentarily distracted playing in the water, prompted Shana to give him a gentle push. "Come on, Eldad, let's go!"

He splashed at her, but Shana dodged, protecting her dress. She nudged him toward the tent to change. Soon, the family re-emerged, joyful and vibrant in the late afternoon light.

Shana looked around wide-eyed. "Oh, we all look so nice. Let's go.

***

The gathering place was alive with movement and warmth. A rich, savory aroma wafted through the air. Villagers had roasted a hart, a sheep, and a goat over the fire pit since early morning. Large boards were ready to hold the evening's feast.

Jairus raised his hand. "Let's all gather. Once everyone has arrived, we'll begin with a prayer to Yahweh Elohim. Take some time to visit with one another." He added, almost to himself, "These new words still feel strange on our tongues. We may not yet know all the ways we once spoke, but we will learn."

Nearby, a small group of children stood hesitantly apart. Shana tugged her mother's sleeve. "May we go see if we can understand them?"

Sarah nodded, her smile encouraging. "Yes, but come back when they're getting ready to pray."

Shana and Eldad approached slowly. The children looked wary but hopeful. Shana broke the silence with a gentle, "Hello, how are you?"

The children paused, then the tallest girl responded, "Hello, what are you called?"

Shana gasped. Her eyes lit up. "We understand you!"

The girl smiled. "I am Bathshua, and I am nine. This is my sister, Hadassah. She's four, and my brother, Lemuel. He's seven. We haven't understood anyone besides our family in days."

"I am Shana. I'm ten. This is my brother Eldad."

Eldad jumped in. "I am eight, but I'm taller than you."

Unable to hold back his excitement, Eldad grabbed Lemuel's arm. "Let's wrestle!"

Shana laughed and pulled him back. "Not in your special clothes! Mama wouldn't like that. We'll have plenty of time to play. Let's just talk for now."

"I agree," Bathshua giggled. "It's wonderful to finally talk to someone we can understand! Where is your tent so we can find you?"

"Near the olive trees," Shana replied. "You can't miss it."

Lemuel, still eyeing Eldad with a mischievous grin, pointed. "Our tent is over by the cow pasture."

Shana beamed. "We'll come find you." Shana's voice carried a note of wonder, as if something long-lost had just been restored.

Bathshua leaned closer. "I'm glad we found you. I was starting to feel like the only ones left in the world with our language."

"My father says the languages are divided by clans. If there are fifty men in each clan, then that's about fifty families with our language!" Shana said. "I'm so glad we found each other. I had a friend before the journey whose language I couldn't understand. We hugged and cried, but we couldn't talk."

Bathshua nodded. "The same for me."

Eldad and Lemuel exchanged a few words of boy-talk, their connection instant.

Hadassah clung to Bathshua's side. Shana knelt. "Hadassah, what about you? Can you tell me how old you are?"

Hadassah looked up at Bathshua. "Four."

Just then, Shana noticed movement near the platform. "Oh, we need to go. Jairus, our grandfather, is getting ready to pray."

Bathshua reached for her hand. "We need to go too. Can we look for you when we start to eat?"

Shana's face brightened. "Please do! We'll look for you, too. I bet our parents would enjoy talking as well."

The children parted with cheerful waves, promising to find each other again. Shana looked back. In the midst of strangers, the spark of friendship had lit, and it warmed her more than the fire ever could.

Chapter 8

WHEN SIN CROUCHED

The feast had begun, and the air was thick with the scent of roasting meat, herbs, and baked bread. Around the fire, laughter and new connections blossomed as families found others they could finally understand.

Near the center of the gathering, Jairus stepped back toward the ancient chair, lifting his hands to call the crowd together. His voice rose above the mingled conversation. It was rich and steady.

"Tonight, we have another story after everyone settles in—the story of Cain and Abel. But first, let us give thanks. Dear Yahweh Elohim, we thank You for the bounty You have provided. We are grateful for this gathering of families and friends. Please bless this food and our fellowship as we celebrate. So let it be."

He turned and nodded to Noah. "Why don't you begin? Lead the way as the feast begins!"

The people rose and moved toward the tables, the scent of roasted meats and herbs wrapping each step in invitation. Laughter rolled gently through the gathering as villagers passed platters with cheerful hands and eager smiles. For many, this would be the last feast before their journey westward. The village's sturdy homes stood behind them like guardians, flanked by the temporary shelters of travelers.

As Johanan guided his family toward a quiet spot, Shana's eyes lit up.

"Father!" she called, tugging his sleeve. "There are the children we met earlier! We can understand them. Can we sit with them?" Eldad was already craning his neck, searching for familiar faces.

Johanan exchanged a glance with Sarah, who gave a quick nod, her eyes dancing. "Lead the way," he said. "Just stay where we can see you."

Bathshua clutched her father's tunic. "There they are—the ones we told you about!"

Their families converged in the twilight.

Johanan approached the man beside Bathshua. "Would it be alright if we joined you? Can you understand me?"

The man's face lit up. "Yes! Perfectly. Please, sit with us!"

They spread furs on the soft grass and settled in—parents to one side, children forming their own lively circle.

"I'm Johanan," he said warmly, "and this is my wife, Sarah. We've only met a few others we could speak with since arriving. This is a joy."

"Tobiya," the man replied, "and my wife, Tabitha. Our children have been hoping to find friends who understand them." He nodded toward the cluster of laughing children. "Looks like they've succeeded."

Sarah leaned forward, her voice eager. "Where did you come from?

They traded stories. There were long roads, and the shock of language splitting—like a river breaking into streams. With it came the pain of leaving, and the quiet relief of being found.

Tabitha's voice softened. "My daughter cried herself to sleep the first night. She didn't understand why the world had changed."

Sarah touched her hand. "So did mine."

Meanwhile, the children swapped names and memories, giggling over misheard words and wild gestures. Eldad offered a strange-looking fruit to Lemuel, who sniffed it and made a face.

"It smells like a goat," he smirked.

"No, it doesn't!" Eldad laughed. "It's sweet, 1 promise."

Lemuel snatched a fig. "Let's trade."

"Hey!" Eldad protested.

"Share," Shana said gently, dividing it between them.

Bathshua leaned over. "Do your brother and you fight like that too?"

"Sometimes," Shana sighed. "Mostly about nothing."

Bathshua rolled her eyes. "We fight all the time. But I love them. And I'm so glad we can talk again."

"You're right."

The parents laughed as the children played, the echo of conflict faint as smoke. It was a whisper of what was to come in the story.

Just then, Jairus climbed back onto the platform and whistled.

"Please, continue eating," he called as the crowd quieted. "Tonight's story is a somber one—the story of Cain and Abel, a reminder of the darkness that sin can bring."

The gathering was silent. Parents pulled children closer. Even the little ones hushed, sensing the shift. Laughter faded like embers falling silent, but warmth lingered, stitched into the hush of expectant hearts.

Javan stepped forward as Jairus settled into his seat. The hush deepened, like the stillness before a storm. He didn't climb the platform but stood at its foot, close to the people. The firelight played across his face, lending a grave warmth to his expression.

"This story," Javan began, "is not a happy one. But it is true. And it has been told from the beginning."

He looked across the crowd, locking eyes with no one and yet everyone.

"Adam and Eve had two sons: Cain and Abel. Cain worked the soil, plowing and planting under the sun. Abel tended the flocks, gentle and watchful." He paused, letting the rhythm settle. "In time, both brothers brought offerings to Yahweh. Cain brought fruits of the ground. Abel brought the firstborn of his flock. It was the best he had."

Javan's voice dropped.

"Yahweh looked with favor on Abel's offering, but not on Cain's. Not because one was grain and the other meat. No. Because Abel gave with a heart that trusted Yahweh. Cain gave only what he must."

A murmur stirred among the listeners. Shana, nestled between Bathshua and Hadassah, leaned forward.

"Cain saw the difference in Yahweh's response. He was furious. His heart twisted with jealousy. His face fell, darkened. But Yahweh, in His mercy, came to him."

Javan raised his hand, mimicking Yahweh's gentle approach.

"'Why are you angry, Cain? Why is your face downcast? If you do what is right, will you not be accepted? But if you do not… sin is crouching at the door; it desires to have you, but you must rule over it.'"

He let the words ring.

"But Cain did not listen. His pride drowned out the warning. He invited his brother into the field. There, with his own hands, he struck Abel down. The first murder."

The air grew colder.

"Yahweh came again and asked, 'Where is your brother, Abel?' And Cain said, 'I do not know. Am I my brother's keeper?'"

A sharp breath swept through the crowd.

"But Yahweh knew. 'Your brother's blood cries out to Me from the ground,' He said. And He cursed Cain. No longer would the soil yield for him. He would become a restless wanderer, carrying the weight of what he had done."

Javan's eyes lifted toward the stars.

"And yet, even in justice, Yahweh showed mercy. He did not strike

Cain down. He marked him—to protect him from vengeance. Because only Yahweh gives life. Only He may take it."

He turned back to the people.

"Abel gave his best, with a heart full of trust. Cain gave only what he must. Let us remember what happens when jealousy takes root and when sin is not addressed but rules us."

Javan stepped back in silence.

Jairus remained seated for a moment, letting the story settle over the gathering. The firelight flickered across his face, deepening the gravity of his gaze.

"Yahweh Elohim is still with us," he said quietly. "Not with us in the same way He walked with Adam, but He is near. Imagine being driven from His presence altogether. That is what sin does. But even then, Yahweh promised One who would come and restore what was lost."

He looked over the many people who would soon depart westward.

"As you journey, remember this promise. Yahweh Elohim does not dwell in things shaped by human hands. He reveals Himself through what He has made. And He draws near to those who obey Him."

He scanned the faces before him—quiet now, many solemn. Then a smile softened his features.

"Now, return to your meals. Visit with one another. We'll have music and another story before the night ends."

The gathering stirred to life again. Plates were refilled, conversations resumed with fresh energy, and families moved among friends both new and familiar.

Johanan and Tobiya stood together, drifting back toward the serving tables.

"So," Johanan asked as they walked, "what do you think tomorrow will bring? We usually keep a day of rest. Perhaps there will be a sacrifice."

Tobiya considered this. "We rest as well. I've heard of sacrifices… but I've never been part of one."

Johanan nodded. "Jairus spoke of obedience. A sacrifice that is not payment, but devotion. A way to remain in Yahweh Elohim's presence."

Tobiya's brow furrowed, then brightened. "If there is one tomorrow, I'd like to witness it. You're going to the ark, yes?"

"I am," Johanan confirmed. "I'll represent the clan of Elishah. But others are welcome. You're welcome to come."

Tobiya smiled. "I might. I'd like to see the place where the world began again."

Nearby, Sarah and Tabitha lingered near the fire.

"How did you bake your bread?" Tabitha asked, brushing a wisp of hair from her face.

"Johanan built an oven with river stones," Sarah replied with a grin. "It took some trial and error, but now it works. Did you gather the asparagus yourself?"

Tabitha nodded proudly. "The children spotted it while we were walking. It only grows at the beginning of summer—I was surprised to find it here!"

The children sat cross-legged in a wide circle, passing pebbles and shells like treasures, each one sparking laughter or a story. For the first time in many days, they had found companions who understood their speech. The conversation buzzed with the joy of connection.

As the sun dipped behind the mountains, the central fire grew bolder. Families drew closer. Someone plucked at a stringed instrument, and a soft rhythm of drums joined in—music rising like a heartbeat.

Sarah drew out her harp. Tabitha grinned and pulled out her lyre. Together, they began to pluck out a gentle harmony.

Light danced on every face. Laughter echoed. Smiles passed from one circle to the next.

In the firelight, stories were no longer just words. They became threads, binding strangers together as they stepped into the unknown, united by shared faith, fragile hope, and the memory of Eden.

Chapter 9

NEVER AGAIN

"Whenever I bring clouds over the earth and the rainbow appears in the clouds, I will remember my covenant between me and you and all living creatures of every kind. Never again will the waters become a flood to destroy all life."
Genesis 9:14-15

Jairus raised his hands, calling for quiet as the crowd settled, their anticipation thick in the cool night air. "There is one more story tonight, one that will help us understand our beginnings. Noah himself is going to share this incredible story, one close to his heart. You may continue eating as we listen. Noah, are you ready to begin?"

Noah nodded, drawing a long breath as if steadying himself against a tide of memories. His voice was low and resonant, edged with sorrow. "As ready as I can be. My people, this is a hard story to tell and a hard one to hear."

His eyes scanned the firelit faces, and something in him clenched. He carried this story like a stone. It was worn smooth by time, but never light. The words began to flow, soft but firm, soaked in memory and loss.

"Yahweh Elohim saw that evil was out of control on the earth," Noah said, his eyes clouding not just with memory, but with anguish that never fully left him. He had watched friends, neighbors, and entire communities sink into violence. "People thought evil, imagined evil, and wickedness filled their hearts, from morning to night. Yahweh Elohim's heart was deeply grieved. It broke Him..."

His voice caught slightly. And it broke me too, he thought, though he didn't say it aloud. To witness it. To survive it.

A hush settled over the crowd as Noah's voice carried, steady yet sorrowful. "Yahweh Elohim decided to cleanse the earth. He told me, 'I will rid My creation of corruption. I'm sorry I made them, for their hearts have turned dark, like shadows over the earth.'"

Noah paused, the firelight casting flickering shadows across his face. "Then Yahweh Elohim came to me," Noah said, his voice quieter, reverent. "And I felt His presence was like a voice inside my own heart, firm and sorrowful."

He hesitated, the memory sharp as if it were yesterday.

"I remember feeling the weight of it, not just the task, but the grief behind the command. The ache in Yahweh's voice... it mirrored my own."

For a moment, he closed his eyes. "I was just a man. A father. I did not feel ready. 'Noah,' He said, 'you are a good man, but this world is filled with violence. Build yourself an ark.'"

The people listened, entranced, as Noah described Yahweh Elohim's instructions in detail about the massive structure of the ark, the pungent smell of pitch, the exact measurements of the beams and decks.

"He told me to bring animals, two by two," Noah continued, "each kind, creatures that crawled, that flew, that ran wild and free. And all the food we'd need. It was a long, hard task, but I did all that Yahweh Elohim commanded." His voice softened, carrying a hint of reverence.

"As the time grew near, Yahweh Elohim spoke again: 'Gather your family and prepare to board the ark.' I remember how strange it felt to look at the clear skies, to hear birds singing as usual, and yet know that soon, all would be washed away."

The crowd murmured, casting uneasy glances at one another. They could imagine the scene. It was the quiet before the storm, the ominous certainty of Noah's words.

"Seven days later, the flood came," Noah said, his voice heavy, hollowed by memory.

He stopped briefly, his jaw tightening. He looked away, voice almost lost to the crackling fire. "And then… Yahweh Elohim shut the door behind us. I didn't even touch it. It was His doing. And that, somehow, was harder. The skies opened, and rain poured, falling so thick and fast it hid the mountains. I heard the cries, those outside, pounding on the ark's walls. I heard them. I still do, sometimes in my dreams."

Noah's voice grew quieter, almost as if speaking to himself. "For forty days, the rain fell, and the waters rose until even the highest mountains disappeared beneath the waves. The earth was silent and empty. All life outside the ark was lost, swept away in a terrible cleansing."

A somber silence blanketed the gathering. Some of the listeners gripped their cups or sat with hands folded, as though the very telling of it brought them closer to the dark waters of that time.

"But," Noah continued, a soft light entering his voice, "Yahweh Elohim did not forget us. After 150 days, He caused a wind to blow over the earth, and the waters began to recede. Inch by inch, the waters lowered, revealing the mountaintops like islands emerging from a vast sea."

Noah described sending out the raven, then the dove, his words painting a vivid picture of those anxious days. "When the dove returned with an olive leaf, I knew the earth was alive again, ready for us to begin anew."

The crowd breathed a collective sigh, eyes bright with wonder as they pictured the ark resting on dry ground, surrounded by quiet mountains.

"When we left the ark," Noah said, voice trembling slightly, "I fell to my knees. The earth was dry under my feet again. It felt like a miracle. I built an altar and offered a sacrifice of thanksgiving."

His hands moved unconsciously, as if still laying stones. "And when I smelled the sweet smoke rising, I wept. Not just for relief, but for everything we had lost. For what the world would never be again."

His eyes turned upward. "And yet… Yahweh Elohim gave us hope. A promise: that He would never again destroy the earth by flood. The sweet fragrance of the offering rose to Yahweh Elohim, and in His heart, He promised, 'Never again will I curse the ground or destroy all life by flood. As long as the earth endures, there will be seedtime and harvest, cold and heat, summer and winter, day and night.'"

Noah's voice grew softer, a smile breaking through his worn face. "And He placed His bow in the sky, a sign of the covenant, a promise that rain would bring life, not destruction."

The people gazed at Noah. Some were nodding, others wiping their eyes as the weight of his faith and loss settled over them.

Noah looked out over the gathering, their firelit faces reflecting awe, sympathy, and wonder. "This story… it is not just history to me," he said, voice thick with emotion. "It is my heartbeat. My scars. My gratitude."

"It reminds me, and I hope it reminds all of you, that Yahweh Elohim is not distant. He sees. He grieves. He redeems. This story has been passed down to remind us of Yahweh Elohim's sovereignty and of His promises. Remember, wherever you journey, that Yahweh Elohim's covenant is with us, and His presence is all around."

Jairus stepped forward, a gentle smile on his face. "Thank you, Noah, for sharing this. We see Yahweh Elohim's promise whenever we look upon the rainbow, a reminder that rain will never again flood the entire earth." The musicians began playing. Jairus smiled and added, "Let's sing 'The Song of the Covenant:'"

> *As long as the earth endures,*
> *Seedtime and harvest,*
> *Cold and heat,*
> *Summer and winter,*
> *Day and night*
> *Will never cease.*

Nestled down between her parents as Sarah played the harp, Shana felt the music swell in her chest, the warmth of the fire battling the chill around them. As they sang in different tongues, the song held them together, a single prayer rising to the heavens.

> *Never again will a flood destroy the earth.*
> *The sign of the covenant is between Elohim and the earth.*
> *When the rainbow appears in the clouds,*
> *Yahweh Elohim will remember His promise—*
> *between Him and all living things.*
> *May Yahweh Elohim extend the territory of Japheth.*
> *Guide his sons:*
> *Gomer, Magog, Madai, Javan, Tubal, Meshech, Tiras*
> *Guide the sons of Gomer:*
> *Ashkenaz, Riphath, and Togarmah.*
> *Guide the sons of Javan:*
> *Elishah, Tarshish, the Kittim, and the Rodanim.*

The voices stilled and the music quieted. Jairus said, "Tomorrow afternoon, we will share another story, one that explains why we now have many languages. If anyone has more to add, there will be time for that, too. Now, let us prepare for a day of rest. We will see you all tomorrow."

The gathering slowly broke up, families whispering together, children's eyes wide with wonder as they glanced at Noah, imagining his journey and the rainbow that sealed Yahweh Elohim's promise.

Chapter 10

THE THREAD OF FAMILY

Johanan gathered his family, guiding them toward their camp by the river. The evening light cast long shadows across the path as they moved. Suddenly, he heard a familiar voice calling out.

"Wait! Johanan!" Jairus's voice carried a warmth that made Johanan turn with a smile. "I haven't had a chance to see you. Things have been so busy here."

Johanan's grin widened. "Father, come to our camp down by the river, after the olive trees, and we can finally visit for a while."

"That sounds wonderful." Jairus glanced over his shoulder. "Let me get your mother; she's been asking about you." He called out, "Martha, come! I've found Johanan and his family. Let's go visit them."

Together, they headed to the camp, where the gentle murmur of the river created a peaceful background. Johanan stirred up the coals in the fire pit, watching as tiny embers sparked and danced. Sarah brought a pot of water to the fire to warm, and Shana arranged soft hides for Jairus and Martha to sit on.

"Please make yourselves comfortable. We'll have tea in a few moments," Sarah shared, her voice warm with welcome.

Johanan's eyes sparkled as he turned to his parents. "I'm so glad you came, Father. Seeing you again brings peace to my heart. I could tell how busy you were, and I wasn't sure if you wanted to rekindle things with us, knowing we'll be leaving so soon. But truly, I'm grateful you came."

"Mother, how are you? It's been too long." He wrapped his arms around her, then gestured to his family. "You remember Sarah. And these are our children, Shana and Eldad."

Shana looked up shyly at Martha. "Hello… I know Jairus is my grandfather because of the family begets. Are you really my grandmother?"

Martha's face softened with a smile. "Yes, I am. Come here and let me hug you." She rose, opening her arms to embrace Shana, and then turned to Eldad. "And you too, Eldad. How old are you?"

"I'm eight years old," Eldad answered, his eyes wide with curiosity. "How old are you? Were you on the ark?

Martha laughed, the sound warm and full of life. "Well, I'm old, but not quite that old!" She looked at Shana. "And how old are you, my dear?"

"I'm ten," Shana replied. "What should we call you?"

"'Grandma' would be wonderful to hear," Martha beamed, her eyes shining. "Look at you two," she complimented, her voice full of warmth. "You have your father's eyes, Eldad—and I can see your mother's quiet strength in you, Shana."

As the family settled around the fire, Johanan turned to his father. "Who else is here with you? What are your plans, Father? Will you be traveling soon?"

Jairus nodded thoughtfully. "Yes, we plan to go west as well, though we're still working out the details. Perhaps we could join your group?"

Johanan's face brightened. "That would be excellent! We'd be glad to have you with us." He turned to Sarah. "Is the tea ready?"

"Almost," she replied, pouring the steaming water into carved cups that Johanan had made. She handed one to each of his parents. "Here you go, Jairus and Martha. Shana and Eldad, you two can share, and Johanan, I'll share with you."

Martha took a sip, inhaling the fragrant steam. "This is lovely. What did you use for the tea?"

"It's chamomile," Sarah answered. "I dried the flowers last season. I'll keep an eye out for more as we travel."

As they sipped the tea, Johanan turned back to his father. "Eldad and I checked on your goats earlier. We've just had a few lambs born, which will slow us down a bit."

Jairus chuckled. "Our small flock of goats has a few of them expecting soon. Thanks for watching my flock."

Johanan said with a nod, "We'll already be traveling at a steady pace. If we need to stop along the way, we'll make it work." He paused thoughtfully. "I need to get ready for the expedition to the ark. Father, what do you remember from your last visit?"

Jairus's eyes softened with memories. He rubbed his hands together slowly, as if the feel of the wood still lingered in his palms. "It's been many years, but I still remember the ark's immense size. It was a true symbol of Yahweh Elohim's provision. Seeing it is a reminder that He will be with us on this journey, too."

Martha glanced at the darkening sky, then smiled gently. "This has been such a sweet visit. I hate to leave, but I think it's time we let you rest. And I wouldn't mind some myself," she added with a chuckle, brushing a hand through her hair as she stifled a yawn.

Johanan rose, embracing each of them in turn. "We'll talk and plan more tomorrow. It's a blessing to have you with us." He watched as his parents made their way back to their own camp, their figures outlined in the soft light of the fading fire. Turning to his children, Johanan directed, "Shana, Eldad, we'll need to prepare for our day of rest tomorrow. Could you fetch some water for us?"

While the children filled the leather waterskins at the river, Johanan began sorting through their furs, selecting the warmest ones for the upcoming trek. Sarah moved quietly beside him. "Is there anything I can help prepare for the trek?"

"Yes, some dried meat and flatbread should be enough. Can you gather that for me?"

Shana and Eldad returned soon after, gripping the waterskins with both hands. Sarah smiled at them. "You've done well. Now, off to bed. You'll need your rest."

As the family settled onto their mats, they pulled thick furs over themselves, grateful for the warmth against the cool air. Night wrapped around their camp like a cloak. Tomorrow would bring its own weight, but for now, they rested in peace.

Chapter 11

THE DAY
THE VOICES BROKE

With the first light of dawn, Johanan stirred and stretched, the morning air cool against his skin.

Sarah rolled over, snuggling deeper into the furs. "Are you going to the river?" she asked, her voice thick with sleep.

"Yes, I'll be back shortly."

He stepped outside and followed the familiar path, ducking beneath the arch of trees that framed the river's edge. The water, smooth and silver in the morning light, beckoned quietly. He knelt and splashed his face, shivering as the cold rivulets trickled down. It woke him fully, a bracing clarity settling into his bones.

When he returned, the family was stirring. He knelt beside the fire pit and moved the logs, coaxing the embers until a soft glow returned. Sarah brought the pot to heat water, and Shana laid out bread and cheese for breakfast.

"All right, you two," Sarah called, smiling gently at the children. "Come have some breakfast. Shana, could you bring some herbs for tea?"

Johanan glanced toward his bag. "You prepared the food last night, and I've gathered my warm clothing for tomorrow. I imagine the glacier will still be cold, even in summer. While I'm gone, pack what you can for our journey west. It begins the day after the trek."

"We'll rest today," Sarah added. "Tonight, we'll gather for the story and the sacrifice."

They ate in a hush, the fire's warmth wrapping around them like a shared blessing. The river whispered nearby, and the trees stood silent and watchful. There was more to come before the day's end. One more story to hear, and one more gathering to share.

But for now, they rested in the comfort of each other, held by the quiet strength of faith and the nearness of family.

***

The gathering was lively. There was a hum of voices and the smoky scent of roasting herbs filling the cool evening air. Families clustered around the fire, sharing bowls of warm stew as twilight deepened. Tonight was special: a sacrifice had been prepared, and Elishah was to tell the story of the languages.

Elishah took his place in the ancient olive wood chair on the platform, his face lit by the fire's low flame. The low voices around him faded as he began, his voice steady, carrying authority. "This is the story as we have heard it. Some of you may have more to add when I finish," he predicted, glancing around the circle with a knowing look.

He paused, letting silence fill the space before he continued. "A short time ago, the whole earth spoke the same language. As people moved out of the east, they came upon a plain in the land of Shinar and settled down." Elishah's voice rose and fell, drawing listeners into the memory of the difficulties they had experienced.

They said to one another, "Come, let's make bricks and fire them well." The hiss of the fire on the damp earth echoed the memory, and a few nodded as Elishah spoke. They used brick for stone, and tar for mortar," he added, rubbing his fingers together as if feeling the grit once more.

"And then they said, 'Come, let's build ourselves a city and a tower that reaches Heaven. Let's make ourselves famous so we won't be scattered here and there across the earth.'" The air seemed to thicken with the weight of those words, a mixture of awe and foreboding spreading among the listeners.

He paused, then continued, "Yahweh Elohim came down to look over the city and the tower they had built." Elishah's eyes reflected the firelight, giving his expression a mysterious cast. "He took one look and said, 'One people, one language; why, this is only a first step. No telling what they'll come up with next—they'll stop at nothing! Come, We'll go down and garble their speech so they won't understand each other.'"

The crowd listened intently, a few of them breathing heavily as Elishah recounted Yahweh's act. "Then Yahweh Elohim scattered them from there all over the world. They had to quit building the city. That's how it came to be called Babel—because Yahweh Elohim confused the language of the whole world."

The evening air buzzed with anticipation. The scent of charred wood mingled with the faint tang of sweat and dust as a man stepped forward.

"We were there," he said roughly. "Elohim moved us. We heard of this gathering and came to remember Yahweh Elohim, and to find someone we could understand."

A few murmurs rippled through the circle. Elishah nodded and repeated the man's words so all could follow.

Another figure stepped into the firelight. He was a foreman with his jaw clenched. "I oversaw a hundred men on the southern wall. We had rhythm, calls, and shouted signals. We built fast." He exhaled sharply. "Then one morning, my words didn't land. My crew stared at me. Some shouted back nonsense. That day, we were screaming. Accusing. One man struck his partner with a hammer. I walked away and never went back."

Before silence could settle, a silver-haired woman stepped forward. "I wasn't a builder," she said. "I swept the dust, fetched water, and watched children. One day, I called to my daughter and she didn't answer. She wept, not knowing my voice. My own child." Her hands trembled. "Now I understand she spoke the language of her husband and his clan.

I wandered the streets calling out. Only one man understood. We left together. That's how my new life began."

Etan, a younger man, spoke next. "I was a trader. I knew goods, names, voices. But one day, no one understood me, not my friends, not even my servants. I tried to help a woman, but she screamed. I lost her. I wandered, hoping to hear one voice that made sense. That's how I came here."

Last came an older builder, stooped and scarred. "My brothers and I laid stone. Fired bricks. Raised walls. We thought we were building glory. But we were building silence." His eyes dimmed. "When the voices broke, we dropped our tools. Some wept. Some fought. Some drifted away like ghosts. I came here, hoping someone else remembered."

Elishah stood, his voice full of quiet reverence. "These are the stories we must carry. Yahweh Elohim scattered us. Not to destroy, but to humble and preserve. We are called to fill the earth, not to build in defiance." He looked at the gathered clans. "It is good to see the languages divided by family. We carry these memories forward, as reminders, as witnesses, as we journey to the sunset. Now, Noah and Javan will prepare the sacrifice."

Noah and Javan approached the altar, solemn and quiet, leading a lamb for the sacrifice. The people fell silent. The animal's lifeblood drained at the foot of the altar, soaking into the thirsty earth, then covered with fresh soil. A thick smoke curled skyward as the lamb was laid upon the fire, the scent of burning flesh and bone rising like a wordless prayer.

Noah raised his hands, his voice a steady murmur: "The blessing of Yahweh Elohim be upon you, as He blessed us when we came out of the ark: 'Be fruitful and increase in number and fill the earth.'"

Javan added gently, "Let's take a time of silence to ponder our repentance before Yahweh Elohim, and the mercy He gives us."

Elishah returned to the platform, a still figure in the thinning dusk. "Those of you going to the ark tomorrow, be sure to bring warm clothes and a little food for the journey. The trek will start at sunrise, so let's meet here at dawn. Take time to visit with one another," he added with a warm smile. "It may be the last before the journey begins."

Shana darted over to Bathshua, gripping her hand tightly. "Will you be able to travel with us?" she asked, her voice thick with emotion. "I don't want to lose you!" Around them, children clustered together, and the voices of Eldad and Lemuel blended with laughter and low whispers.

Nearby, Johanan wrapped an arm around Sarah as they approached Tobiya. "Are you ready for tomorrow morning?" he asked.

Tobiya nodded, though he shivered slightly. "Yes, but I wish I had something warmer. I don't know how cold it'll be up there."

Johanan's face softened, and he glanced back toward his tent. "Come by and see the furs I have. I'll bring a bear fur, but I have a couple of wolf pelts as well. Those might keep the chill off."

As the fire's warmth reached the gathered families, Sarah reached for Tabitha's hand, squeezing it with quiet affection. "I hope we can travel together for a while," she urged. "Jairus and Martha will be with us, too."

Tabitha's face lit up, and she pulled Sarah into a hug. "Yes, I hope so too! We'll all have to work hard tomorrow to make sure we're ready."

Sarah smiled, glancing over at her provisions. "I'll help in the village tomorrow as they pass out supplies."

Johanan looked around, his eyes lingering on each member of their little circle. "It's time we settle in. Tomorrow will be a long day." His words were soft, although their impact was felt in the wordless nods and lingering glances as the families prepared for the night ahead.

As they made their way back to their tents, the night air wrapped around them, cool with the weight of parting, stirred by the promise of paths yet unseen. Above them, stars glittered as silent witnesses to the journey that waited just beyond the dawn.

Chapter 12

AS LONG AS
THE EARTH ENDURES

The morning air was crisp as Johanan stirred beneath his hides, the chill creeping through even the thickest layers. Early light lent the campsite a sacred stillness. He moved quietly to the fire pit, squatting low to stir the blackened remains with a stick. One ember pulsed, then caught, and a thin ribbon of warmth rose into the dawn. He rubbed his hands together briskly, welcoming the heat against his knuckles as he considered the journey ahead. The glacier's icy grip was already looming in his mind. He reached for a strip of leather to wrap around his hands, knowing he'd need every bit of insulation against the climb's cold bite.

Sarah approached, her footsteps quiet. She placed a gentle hand on his arm. "Let me help you," she offered, her voice calm with morning hush. She wrapped his arms from the elbow down, pulling the leather snug. "We'll be waiting to hear all about your adventure tonight," she murmured, her eyes glowing with pride and concern.

Johanan pulled her into a brief embrace, savoring her warmth. "Pray for us," he whispered. "We're walking toward something incredible—the ark." With a final squeeze, he stepped back. "I'd better head out."

At the meeting place, men gathered in quiet clusters, adjusting bags and furs. Tobiya joined Johanan with a silent nod, and Jairus raised his hands.

"This is Kenan, from Naxuana," he said. "His people are guardians of the ark. He'll lead the way. I hope you brought hides. The mountain gets cold quickly." He paused, eyes solemn. "Observe the ark closely. Store every detail. This journey may strengthen your faith when you need it most."

They set out in a single file, the trail narrowing as forest gave way to rock. The rising sun cast a pale glow behind them, but the air stayed sharp, each breath a bite of cold.

At the snow line, they paused to pull on thick furs. Frost crunched beneath their feet. Johanan's breath coiled white in the mountain stillness.

Jairus stopped a final time, drawing them into a circle. "Yahweh Elohim, guide and protect these men. Let them feel the depth of Your love as they witness the ark." He nodded once, then turned back, his figure swallowed by trees.

As the path steepened, the air thinned. Breaths came harder. Fingers stiffened despite the leather wraps. They stopped only briefly to eat, their hands red with cold.

"We must reach the ark by the sun's peak," Kenan urged. "That's the only way we can explore and descend safely."

The climb pressed on in silence until, suddenly, a collective breath escaped the group.

The ark.

It rose from the slope like a monolith, a mass of dark timber stark against snow and sky. The hull, weathered and immense, looked both ancient and alive.

"Oh! It's massive," Tobiya exclaimed, awe thick in his voice.

Kenan stepped forward, gesturing up the length of the structure. "Spread out. We have limited time. Cover as much as you can. It's five hundred feet long, eighty feet wide, and forty-five feet high. Built with cypress wood, coated inside and out with pitch."

Johanan walked its length slowly, taking in the sheer scale of it. "How did Noah find the courage to bring his family here?" he wondered aloud, tracing the timber walls. "His faith in Yahweh Elohim must have been tremendous."

He stepped cautiously onto the lower ramp. The wood creaked beneath his foot coverings, a low hollow resonance that vibrated in his chest. The surface was smooth in places, splintered in others. Some worn down like stone, others rough as bark. Splinters caught briefly in his calloused skin.

Inside, the air was heavy with a scent like old pitch, aged wood, and something earthen and preserved. It felt like the memory of thunder still lingered in the beams.

They moved through the first level—thick beams, animal stalls, remnants of hay. Dust lay thick across the wood. In the alcoves, Johanan could almost sense motion, as if beasts once silent in the dark had just stirred. He touched a feeding trough, its edge gnawed smooth by mouths long gone.

On the middle level, smaller stalls and storage rooms lined the passage. The layout was deliberate, precise—evidence of Noah's careful preparation.

On the upper level, they found the living quarters. Sparse but thoughtfully designed, the rooms held built-in chests and benches. Angled slats in the roof allowed light and fresh air to filter down, golden shafts stretching across the floor.

Johanan ran his hand along a timber beam, feeling the grooves and knots smoothed by time. He paused at the window, gazing at the glacier beyond, its blue-white surface gleaming like a blade.

"Will the glacier consume the ark or preserve it forever beneath the ice?" he whispered.

Tobiya joined him, wide-eyed. "Noah and his sons built this by hand? Every beam? Every wall?"

Johanan nodded slowly. "It's the largest structure ever crafted by human hands… and it was built by faith."

Kenan's voice called them back. "We must begin our descent."

The men turned for one last look. The ark stood silent and massive, unmoved—a witness to obedience and promise.

"Yahweh Elohim," Kenan prayed, "may these men carry the encouragement of this day. Let them remember this journey, and strengthen the hope of others. Your promises endure."

The descent was quicker. The air thickened and warmed. Furs were loosened, steps grew lighter. But no one spoke.

The ark lingered in their thoughts, like a question, a promise, and a command.

Chapter 13

THE ARK AND
THE ROAD AHEAD

Dusk draped its veil over the mountains as the men descended into Naxuana, the Place of Descent. The air was cool and still, carrying the low tones of the night ahead. Shadows stretched long over the rocky path as firelight flickered to life below. Kenan bid the group farewell; his silhouette briefly illuminated by the golden glow of a nearby fire before slipping into the dark.

As their footsteps crunched on the gravel, a murmur rose ahead, eager, expectant voices carried on the evening breeze. The air was laced with the rich aromas of roasting meat and herbs, awakening hunger even in the most tired bodies. Sparks from the fire spiraled into the dimming sky, the glow reflecting in the excited eyes of those preparing for the night's gathering.

Shana and Eldad rushed forward, faces bright with excitement.

"Father, what did you see?" Shana's voice rang out like a bell.

Johanan chuckled, scooping both children into a warm embrace. "Let me catch my breath first. You'll hear all about it at the feast. Where's your mother?"

"She's at our campsite preparing food," Shana replied, her voice bubbling with energy.

"Then let's go fetch her. We'll share everything once we're all together," Johanan suggested, slinging an arm around Eldad's shoulder.

At the tent, Sarah embraced Johanan with a mixture of joy and relief. "You're well?" she asked, scanning his face.

"Fine, but tired," he replied. "Let's eat, there's much to tell."

Together, the family joined the stream of others moving toward the gathering. The aroma of roasted meat, warm bread, and fragrant vegetables deepened, stirring every appetite.

Jairus stepped forward, lifting his hands. "Let us pray," he announced. "Yahweh Elohim, bless this food, those who prepared it, and all who partake. May we honor You as we embark on our journey. Amen."

"Amen," the people echoed, unified in reverence.

"Those who visited the ark, please, eat first," Jairus continued. "We'll hear your stories while we finish."

Johanan and Tobiya stepped forward, bowls in hand. Friends clapped their backs and asked questions, but Johanan only smiled. "Soon, you'll hear everything."

They found a place near the fire, and Sarah and Tabitha joined them with the children. As they all ate, the women murmured appreciatively about the meal, while the conversation gradually turned toward the journey ahead.

"Tobiya's family will be traveling with us," Johanan began, glancing between the others. "And my parents as well. We'll be a strong group."

Sarah looked up from her bowl. "Stronger still if we share more than supplies. We'll need one another's gifts."

Tabitha nodded. "And voices. For the little ones, especially."

Soon, Noah rose from his carved wooden chair, flanked by Japheth and Javan. His hounds lay at his feet, silent and watchful.

"We will listen to the men who visited the ark," Noah announced. "I will add what I can. Elishah will interpret for all."

Kenan began, describing the ark's massive size and precise construction. Then Johanan stepped forward.

"I am Johanan, of the clan of Elishah," he said. "The ark is overwhelming in size, five hundred feet long, eighty wide, forty-five high. But more than its size, what struck me was its purpose. Elohim instructed Noah to build with obedience, not just skill."

Others followed, describing its levels, its water-tight pitch, the care in every detail. One man spoke of the stalls for animals, another of the clever systems for storage and health.

Then Japheth stepped forward, his voice calm and thoughtful. "We lived in that ark for months. It was quiet at times with just the groaning of the wood and the wind. But when we left it, we soon heard new cries: fawns, chicks, cubs. Yahweh had not only preserved life—He multiplied it. Each of our wives bore children in the months after. We were not just survivors—we were the beginning of something new."

Elishah turned to Noah. "Father, what more would you have them take with them to the sunset?"

Noah rose slowly. "There was one window. I released a raven and then a dove. The second time, it brought an olive leaf. The third time, it did not return. That's when Elohim opened the door He had sealed. Remember His covenant. The rainbow is His sign. One day, He will send a Descendant to conquer evil and restore all that has been broken."

Then, Noah lifted his hands. "Most of you leave at first light. I offer a blessing."

Japheth and Javan stood with him, arms extended.

"Bless these people, Elohim," Noah prayed. "Guide them where You have called them. Let them know when their journey ends. Watch over them, Yahweh Elohim."

Japheth added, "We may not see you again, but you are in our prayers."

Javan looked out over the crowd. "Please, share what you know as you go. Knowledge is being lost."

As the fire died to embers and the hush of night deepened, Shana tugged at her father's arm. "Can we meet Noah? Please?"

Johanan smiled. "All right, but respectfully."

Noah welcomed the children with a warm smile. "And who are these young ones?"

Shana stepped forward. "I'm Shana, and this is Eldad. We want to remember everything about Yahweh Elohim. And you, Noah."

Noah laid his hands on their heads. "May you carry truth with you and bless the earth."

Later, the families returned to their tents. Johanan stoked the fire while Sarah washed the bowls. The children curled into their hides. The sounds of the night crept in: the distant hooting of an owl, the crickets chirping, the gentle burbling of the river…

For a few sacred days, this place had been their home. A sanctuary. A reminder of the One who brings order from chaos—and of the promises that still guide them into the unknown.

***

Predawn light cast a faint glow on the horizon when Johanan and Sarah rose. The air was still cool. Johanan called softly to the tent. "Children, time to get ready."

Shana stirred. "Mama… how far are we going?"

Sarah handed them bread and cheese. "We don't know yet. But we know how to make camp, and we know how to take it down. We will do that as long as Yahweh leads us."

Father and son worked quickly, dismantling the tent in rhythm. The sheepskin released the earthy scent of leather and warmth. They secured it onto the travois they had made with two poles joined together with crossbars lashed between with sinew and rope. The sun began to rise, painting the sky in warm streaks. Tobiya's family arrived, followed by

Jairus and Martha. "Gather poles as we go," Johanan said. "We'll take turns pulling."

Sarah handed Shana a bundle. "Take the children to the main gathering place. We'll follow."

Shana spotted a tree and ran ahead. "Here, by this one!"

Soon, Noah approached along with Japheth and Javan. At his side stood two sleek young dogs. "May I speak with you?" Noah asked Johanan, who nodded. "These are Baluchi hounds. They are from the pair I have now. I have had a pair since leaving the ark. They're six months old, ready to keep up. I'd like to give them to your children." Shana and Eldad gasped. The dogs wagged their tails that curled at the end and stepped forward, sniffing their new companions. "Would you like to care for them?" Noah asked. "They'll need food and love. In return, they'll guard you and walk beside you."

Shana knelt, stroking the female. Eldad laughed as the male nuzzled his chest. "Can we, Father?" he asked.

"Yes," Johanan smiled. "It'll be good for you to have something to care for."

"Thank you, Noah!" they cried.

"This is Affie," Noah said of the female. "And this is Kubal. They'll stay close if you let them know that you are their people." He looked at the other children. "Perhaps, if you all help, there may even be puppies by the time your families part ways."

A whistle pierced the morning air. "Let us pray before you depart," Nathaniel called. Heads bowed.

"Yahweh Elohim, guide and protect these families. Help them trust You wherever the path may lead. Amen." Elishah raised his hands. "Farewell to those who journey west. We who remain will guard Naxuana, the Place of Descent." With a final glance at the ones they left behind, the travelers hoisted their bundles, called their animals, and stepped forward, toward the unknown, toward the sunset.

THE JOURNEY

From the foot of the mountain, they turn to the sunset.

The land stretches wide with wonder and silence,

a path unmeasured by time or distance.

Here, steps become stories,

and the trail itself begins to shape the soul.

Chapter 14

AS THE SUNSET BECKONS

Hugs and tears filled the early morning air, the warmth of farewells mingling with the first blush of sunrise cresting over the mountains. The procession moved slowly, with Johanan urging the sheep forward. Their soft bleats mingled with the shuffle of hooves and the crunch of gravel underfoot. Tobiya nudged the cows onward with his walking stick, each tap gentle but firm. Ahead of the flock, Shana and Eldad held tightly to Affie and Kubal's leashes as the dogs sniffed the fresh morning air, eager to explore. The children's excited chatter and laughter echoed ahead, momentarily lifting the somber mood.

"Don't get too far ahead!" Johanan called to them. "It's easy to get lost with so many people around." He adjusted the travois strap over his shoulder, feeling its weight, while Sarah, Tabitha, and Martha brought up the rear, keeping a watchful eye on their group..

Those without livestock moved more quickly, and the group began to spread out as they passed through an alpine meadow. Bright wildflowers dotted the landscape, nodding in the gentle breeze among tufts of grasses and volcanic scree. Johanan looked out at the distant mountains, their jagged peaks etched against the sky. "We'll push on until the sun's overhead," he said, glancing back. "Let me know if anyone needs a break. There's no rush. We're not meeting anyone at the end of this journey."

As the sun climbed, warming their backs, the travelers descended into a forest of mixed trees, the scent of pine and juniper rich in the air. Dappled light wavered beneath the canopy of deciduous and coniferous trees. Tobiya paused, looking up at the towering oaks and beech trees, their silvery bark gleaming in the sunlight. "These giants are familiar," he remarked, gesturing toward a nearby beech. "But these needle-leaved ones are new to me."

Jairus nodded, his gaze traveling over the evergreens. "The pines and junipers—they stay green through all seasons, even in the cold."

Meanwhile, the children played with the dogs as they walked, Shana keeping a firm grip on Affie's leash. She leaned toward Eldad. "Let's keep them close for now. We don't want them running back to Noah."

Eldad pulled a rope from his fur wrap and fastened it to Kubal's leash. "If we tie him up with this, I can throw sticks for him to chase without him running off."

Lemuel joined in, a grin on his face. "Let me throw the sticks, and you can let him chase them on the leash."

The girls watched the boys' game, giggling as Kubal eagerly chased each tossed stone. "Affie's more of a lady," Bathshua crooned, patting her soft fur. "She prefers to stay with us girls."

Not far behind, Sarah watched Martha spinning wool as they walked, her spindle twisting with practiced ease. Tabitha was fascinated, too. "Martha, when we stop, would you show us how it's done?"

Martha smiled; her hands steady. "It all starts with shearing the sheep, which I see yours have already had done. What did you do with the wool?"

Sarah nodded. "I tried matting some of it, but I'd love to learn to spin. Maybe Johanan can make me a spindle."

Tabitha chimed in, "Our family kept cattle, so this is all new to me. We'll share what we know. We make cheese from cow's milk, but I'd love to learn about using goat's milk, too."

Around midday, Johanan stopped and looked around. "Let's rest for a bit. There's a small lake here, and the animals can drink." The sun shone high above, casting a warm glow over the landscape. "Boys, fill the water skins. Girls, gather some sticks for a fire."

They spread out, each taking up their task. Sarah smiled, setting her bag down. "It'll be nice to have a fire. We can toast the bread and make tea."

The girls returned with bundles of dried grasses and twigs. Johanan struck two volcanic stones together, the spark catching on the dry tinder, sending a thin curl of smoke into the air before the fire sprang to life. Sarah set a clay pot of water over the fire. "Shana, can you grab some sage for the tea?"

With the animals grazing contentedly, the group sat in a circle around the fire, enjoying the warmth and the sight of the sheep nibbling on soft grasses, while the goats browsed on shrubs and low-hanging branches. Johanan glanced at Tobiya. "What about the cows? Do they graze all day?"

Tobiya laughed. "Yes, they'll likely be hungry again by nightfall. They're not ones to skimp on eating."

As the water boiled, Sarah ladled out tea for each of them. "Try some sage tea," Sarah said, handing Tabitha a cup. "Shana and Eldad love it."

She took a cautious sip, surprised by the earthy warmth. "It's different; nice! I use sage in cooking, but I'd never thought of it for tea."

"We've got some honey, too, if the children want to sweeten it a bit," Sarah passed a small pot. The toasted bread, slathered with honey, was appreciated by everyone.

They rested around the fire, savoring the peaceful moment. Across the meadow, other groups spread out or continued onward. Jairus looked out over the terrain, his gaze thoughtful. "We may reach those mountains by nightfall. Let's hope there's a valley path, but if not, those glaciers will be challenging to cross."

Johanan nodded. "Some may attempt it, but we'll see what feels best for us. Our animals may struggle on the ice."

Nearby, Hadassah lay curled up with Affie nestled beside her, both of them dozing in the warm sun. Kubal stretched out beside them, eyes half-closed, keeping watch.

Martha glanced at the sleeping children, a fond smile on her face. "While they're resting, I can show you the spinning technique. Johanan, do you remember when I used to spin?"

Johanan grinned. "I do, though I couldn't explain it to Sarah. Now that I see your spindle, I can make one. Jairus, think you can help me find the right wood?"

Jairus chuckled. "I'll look for a bush that blooms this time of year—'spindle bush' we called it. My father taught me to make these a long time ago."

The children perked up, each wanting a spindle. "Make one for me too!" Shana shouted, while Bathshua, Hadassah, and Tabitha chimed in with excitement.

Johanan stood, stretching. "Not every day will be this kind," he said, glancing at the sky. "Let's use the good weather while we have it." Shana gently roused Hadassah, who mumbled sleepily, "Why do I have to wake up? Can't we stay here?"

Tabitha put an arm around her. "This is just the beginning of many days on the road."

Johanan looked over the animals, then called to the children, "Let's try for the mountains in the distance. Keep an eye on the animals. We may need to stop if one of the goats gives birth soon." He whistled to the sheep, leading them forward, their woolly forms falling into line. Jairus and Tobiya took their places, urging the goats and cattle along.

"Come on, let's get moving," Shana grinned at Hadassah. "We don't want my father poking us along!" Shana and Bathshua took Hadassah's hands, swinging her a few steps to get her going, while Eldad and Lemuel wrangled the dogs, who leapt with excitement, eager to run.

The women trailed behind, with Martha spinning as they walked, while Sarah and Tabitha kept a keen eye out for edible plants. The dense tree cover thickened as the sun began to dip, tinting the forest floor with shifting bands of light and dark.

As the trees thinned, Johanan's group emerged at a small, serene lake, the water reflecting the towering mountain they'd reached. He turned to the others. "Here we are with the mountain, and water for the animals. Let's set up camp here for the night."

"Oh, thank Elohim," Jairus rejoiced, lowering himself onto a nearby rock. "I'm too old for this much walking. A rest will do me good."

"Rest here," Johanan replied, grinning as he and Tobiya guided the animals to the lake. "We'll set up the tents and get a fire going."

The children scattered, gathering firewood from the nearby trees, while the women rummaged through their supplies. Sarah pulled out a pot. "We have some cheese and bread left. How about a lentil soup to go with it?"

With the fire crackling, Sarah heated water, dropping in lentils as Tabitha handed over asparagus, and Martha added chopped cabbage. "We'll have a feast tonight," Hadassah said, eyes bright with anticipation.

Johanan and Tobiya returned, moving quietly but with purpose as they neared the fire. "Jairus is keeping watch over the animals for now," Johanan breathed in deeply as the scent of simmering lentil soup filled the air. "We'll take turns through the night. That stew smells wonderful."

"Let's get these tents set up while the food cooks," Tobiya agreed, nodding toward the travois. They began unloading, carrying the tent poles to each site. The goatskin was supple and light, while the sheepskin added a cozy, familiar weight. The cowhides were thick and heavy, nearly dragging the ground as they set up Tobiya's tent.

Johanan paused, shaking his head. "These cowhides are much heavier, Tobiya. We won't be finding cows out here to replace them. Deer hides might make for a lighter tent. I noticed some deer as we traveled."

Finally, as they stood back to survey their work, Sarah called from the fire, her voice warm with welcome. "The food is ready! Come eat while it's hot."

The boys were the first to arrive, eyes bright with hunger. "We're starving!" they chorused.

Shana grinned, picking up a ladle. "Here are the bowls. I'll serve you. Bathshua, could you get them some bread and cheese?"

The boys stood by the fire as Shana and Bathshua handed them their food. Sarah gestured to a cozy spot near the flames. "Lemuel, Eldad, sit close to the warmth. Hadassah, you too."

Johanan and Tobiya filled their own bowls, steam curling up from the fragrant soup. "Shana, take a bowl to your grandfather." Johanan nodded toward the edge of the camp. "Bring it before the light fades."

The last light sank behind the ridge, bathing the mountains in deep hues of pink and violet—a quiet, majestic farewell to the day.

Martha gazed at the colors with a quiet smile. "Tomorrow, we'll head toward the mountain like the sunset is beckoning us onward."

As the group huddled close, the evening air grew colder, sharpening the warmth of the fire. Each bite of the hearty soup felt like a balm after the long day's journey, and the sight of the fading sunset filled them with peace and a quiet readiness for what lay ahead.

Chapter 15

WITH EACH STEP

In the predawn, crisp air clung to Johanan as he crouched over the kindling, coaxing the fire to life. Its warm glow flickered across his hands, casting a circle of light that held the chill at bay. A pot of water steamed softly nearby. Across the camp, Tobiya stood watch, eyes sharp even in the dimness.

Sarah approached, her breath fogging in the cold. "Good morning. I'll get some water heating," she murmured, pulling her shawl tighter. "Johanan, how will we manage to climb the mountain?"

He glanced at the dark silhouette looming against the barely brightening sky. "We'll look for a valley, some low place to cross. If not, we'll take it slow. No need to reach the peak; we can follow the side. By the end of this, we'll be experts," he added with a grin. "There'll be more mountains, I think."

Sarah nodded, firelight flickering in her eyes. "Yes… and we'll have to trust Yahweh to guide us. Maybe each and every step."

Tabitha joined them, her face still soft with sleep. Sarah held out a small cup. "Chamomile. Would you like to try some?"

"I'm not familiar with it, but I'd like to."

Sarah mixed cups for each of them, the crushed leaves releasing a deep, earthy scent. They sipped the warm tea in silence, its floral flavor grounding them in the quiet dawn.

Jairus and Martha soon emerged and joined the circle.

"Would you like something warm to drink?" Sarah asked with a soft smile. "We'll have cheese and bread before we set out."

As sunlight crept over the horizon, Johanan stirred. "Let's get moving. The sun's rising. Bring the children over here so we can take down the tents."

Shana and Eldad stumbled out, rubbing sleep from their eyes. Sarah handed them folded hides. "Take these to the fire before you settle in."

Jairus stretched. "Our tent's ready. Johanan, help me take it down before I relieve Tobiya with the animals?"

The two men worked in a practiced rhythm, folding hides and securing gear onto the travois.

"Tabitha, is your tent ready?"

"Yes—we're ready for another day," she replied.

The fire had settled into glowing embers. Tabitha poured hot water into a cup for Tobiya, who remained at watch. Johanan scanned the camp one last time. "Let's see how many animals or birds we meet today."

Shana perked up. "Do you think we'll see any new ones?" She sounded half hopeful, half wary.

"It's very likely," Sarah said. "Your father and the others have weapons to keep us safe. They'll hunt if needed, but we won't eat any animals in our care. We'll forage along the way for what else we need."

Eldad leaned forward, eyes shining. "Father, can I learn to use weapons too?"

Johanan chuckled. "Learning to make knives and tools is a good start. We'll have to find some flint to begin with."

As they continued, the mountain seemed to grow, its craggy slopes looming closer with each step. The air was sharp with the scents of damp earth and pine, each breath carrying the freshness of morning.

"Father, look over there," Shana whispered, eyes wide with wonder. A graceful creature with long legs and a patterned neck stretched upward, nibbling leaves from the tallest branches. By her side, a smaller, wobbling version nudged her, eager to nurse.

Johanan's eyes softened. "That's a giraffe," he remarked softly, gesturing for them to keep their voices low. The animal seemed unconcerned with their presence, its serene gaze sweeping over them before returning to her young.

They emerged from the trees as the mountain's ascent loomed sharply ahead. Johanan paused, taking in the rugged terrain as he called out to the group. "We'll rest here for a short time. Tobiya and I will scout to see if there's a valley or if it's an endless range. Meanwhile, get some lunch ready."

The midday sun was climbing as Johanan and Tobiya set out, the silhouettes of trees dappling their path. Jairus took up the watch, his posture alert. "Best to be prepared, Sarah," he suggested. "I'll keep a weapon ready if any trouble comes our way. And we've seen others heading toward the mountain; maybe we could travel together if need be." Those remaining had a light meal of cheese and flatbread from the morning.

The sun was midway down by the time Johanan and Tobiya returned, their faces flushed and windswept. "We'll need to fill every waterskin," Tobiya urged. "There's no knowing when we'll find another stream, and we'll travel until dusk so we can set up camp just below the mountain."

Tabitha passed dried meat around, and they set off in rhythmic steps, the crunch of their footfalls mingling with the quiet murmur of voices. As they drew closer, more travelers converged on the path, their faces bearing the same anxious yet determined expressions.

As twilight fell, they stopped to set up camp. Fires began to show across the slope, casting warm orange glows that illuminated the mountain face in scattered patches. The rich aroma of wood smoke and cooking meat filled the air, mingling with the sounds of hushed conversations and quiet laughter. The mountain loomed, vast and mysterious, but in that shared warmth, the wilderness felt a little less vast, and for a moment, even the mountain seemed to welcome them.

MEANWHILE

Beyond the mountain and far from the familiar fires, other feet pressed to the sunset. They followed no shared trail, spoke no shared tongue, and yet something stirred in them, too—a restlessness, a hunger, a pull. On the other side of the sea, another story was unfolding. Different voices, different faces, yet the same longing burned: to find the place where Elohim would lead them.

Chapter 16

FAR SIDE OF THE SEA: THE HUNT

The salty tang of sea air mingled with the earthy aroma of pine lining the rugged coastline. Seabirds cried in the distance, their voices blending with the rhythmic crash of waves—a serene yet lively nature's song greeting the morning. The cool breeze carried whispers of ancient stories, as if the waters themselves guarded secrets from centuries past. However, had people ever been this way?

Mikael kicked the rock in the trail. He was sick of trekking. They followed the sea, always on their left, as they journeyed to the sunset. When would they stop? Hadn't they gone far enough? How much bigger could the earth be? Maybe something would happen today to liven things up?

"Father, how much further today? Can we stop so we can hunt for a while?"

"Let's cross this meadow; it should take an hour or less. Then we can set up camp and hunt. There have been signs of wildlife, maybe some deer." Jared continued to watch for animal signs: tracks and bare spots that had been grazed.

The boys were herding the goats with Mikael in charge. The three boys were growing quickly: Mikael was thirteen, Mikah was eleven, and Malaki was seven.

Their mother, Elizabeth, watched the three with her chestnut-brown eyes as they guided the goats along. Other than their height, they were mirror images with black hair and blue eyes, all like their father, Jared. Their hair was all getting long. If they rested for a day, she could trim their hair and Jared's. Her hair was also black but had soft waves that tried to escape when they were supposed to be contained in a bun on the back of her head.

"While you are hunting, I will make some flatbread to go along with whatever you catch, or you can eat some flatbread while you wait for it to roast. I think the yogurt should be about ready, too."

The meadow they approached was lush and enclosed with a variety of trees. Some trees bore fruit, and bushes with vibrant red berries dotted the area. The fragrance of wildflowers carried on the breeze, mingling with the earthy scent of grass and soil. The meadow was alive with movement. The birds flitted between trees, some pecking at fallen fruit while others warbled sweetly from the branches.

Elizabeth headed toward the fruit with her basket. "I will gather some of these and see if you like them." She examined the berries. They were red, about the size of a thumbnail, with tiny globes connected together. She popped one into her mouth and smiled as its sweetness burst on her tongue. The fruit on the trees was red and about the size of her fist. It was firm. As she took a small bite, sweet juice filled her mouth, and the white flesh of the fruit was just as delightful.

"Oh, Mikael and Jared, come help me. Bring a bag, I want to dry some of this fruit so we can enjoy it for a while."

They joined her and began picking the fruit, tasting as they worked.

"This is good! Great idea to bring some with us. We'd better fill this bag and keep moving so we will have time to hunt soon," Jared said.

Mikael grinned, "Well, this livened things up. Finally, something different to eat."

Elizabeth looked up from picking and gave a small gasp, "Mikael, you can reach higher than I can! Have you been growing unnoticed as we have been traveling?"

Jared laughed, "Haven't you noticed that he is taller than you now?"

"So, Mikael, are you going to get as tall as your dad?"

Mikael shrugged his shoulders, "Probably."

Nearby, birds pecked at berries and fallen fruit as the family gathered their things and headed back toward the younger boys and the goats to continue across the meadow. The landscape was breathtaking with a canvas of flowers in every color and shape imaginable. A light breeze teased their senses with the floral fragrance, mingling with the ever-present hint of salt from the sea.

The family trudged on, their footsteps indenting the damp grass until they reached a small, bubbling stream on the far side of the meadow. The late afternoon sunlight glinted off the water's rippling surface, casting fleeting patterns onto the smooth stones beneath.

Jared scanned the area, his eyes narrowing thoughtfully. "This will be a good campsite. We can go into the woods to see if we find any game. Malaki, can you stay here and protect your mom? Mikael and Mikah, let's spread out and scout out this grove of trees."

The boys nodded, slinging their bows over their shoulders with quiet determination. The leather straps creaked softly as they adjusted their quivers. They entered the tree line, the soft crunch of dried leaves underfoot quickly swallowed by the dense, shadowed grove. The air within the trees was cooler, tinged with the earthy scent of moss and fallen pine needles. Jared raised his hand, signaling the boys to slow their pace. "Mikael, you take the ridge trail. Move quietly and watch for movement. Mikah, stay with me."

Mikael nodded and veered off, moving uphill where the trees thinned just enough to see farther. Each step was deliberate. The forest breathed around him with bird calls, leaves rustling, the occasional snap of a twig underfoot. His eyes swept over the brush, his fingers poised near his quiver.

Then there was movement.

He stilled. Ahead, half-shielded by shrubs, a young ibex nosed through fallen leaves. Its curved horns bobbed as it grazed, unaware. Mikael ducked lower, choosing his angle. He eased an arrow into place, drew back the bowstring slowly, exhaled, and released.

The arrow struck with a sharp thud. The ibex jolted and crashed into the underbrush, fleeing blindly. Mikael took off after it.

Branches clawed at his tunic. The forest became a blur of brown and green, the trail marked with broken leaves and small blood spatters. At last, he spotted it just ahead, struggling near a dry creek bed.

He approached cautiously, heart still pounding. The ibex kicked once, then stilled. He whispered a quick thanks before finishing the job with his knife. The creature was about the size of a deer, its shaggy coat matted with dirt and leaves. Its large, curved horns gleamed faintly in the twilight, their ridged surfaces catching the last rays of sunlight. As he stood over the animal, breath fogging in the cool air, pride flickered across his face. He had done this. Not for fun, but for survival.

A voice called behind him.

"Mikael!" Jared and Mikah pushed through the brush.

"You found it," Jared approved, eyeing the animal. "That's a good shot."

Mikael wiped his blade on a patch of moss. "It didn't run far."

Jared crouched beside the ibex, running a hand over its flank. "You tracked it cleanly. Quick shot. Clean finish. That matters."

Mikael met his father's eyes for a moment, unsure what to say. Jared didn't often speak praise aloud.

Jared added, softer now, "You're becoming a man out here."

A small flush rose on Mikael's neck, but he only nodded, expression steady. "Too heavy to carry."

"Right." Jared cleared his throat, gesturing to the limbs. "We'll drag it. Mikah, help me clear a path. Mikael, take those front legs. We'll tie a lead and pull it out."

Mikael moved into place, hands already at work. The ibex was heavy, its fur still warm. Working in rhythm with his father, he helped secure a line of braided cord around the legs and shoulders. Together, grunting with effort, they began to drag the animal back toward the meadow, the forest floor scraping and rustling beneath its weight.

It wasn't an awkward silence. It was the kind where something had already been said and fully heard. The kind that marked a turning point, even if neither said it aloud.

Back at the campsite, Elizabeth brushed a strand of loose hair from her face and turned to her younger son. "Malaki, help me get some wood for a fire so I can start that flatbread we talked about. We can have some of this fruit we found, too."

Malaki darted toward the edge of the trees, eagerly snapping dead branches and twigs. Soon, a campfire blazed at the center of their makeshift home, its orange and yellow flames crackling as they leapt into the air. The scent of burning wood mingled with the sharp freshness of the meadow breeze, which tugged the smoke into soft spirals that drifted upward before vanishing into the deepening blue of the sky.

Malaki returned with a long, sturdy stick he'd found and held it as if it were a spear. He stood guard while Elizabeth arranged smooth stones around the fire. She placed the largest ones closest to the flames, letting their surfaces heat for baking. "You can sit by the fire and still be on guard." She smiled at him. "We've been on our feet all day long."

As the rocks warmed, Elizabeth mixed the dough in a bowl with practiced hands, the sticky flour and water coming together into a pliable mass. She kneaded it carefully, then patted out the bread into flat, round discs, the dough cool and soft against her fingers.

A sudden whisper broke through the gentle crackling of the fire. "Mama, look, what is it?" Malaki's voice was tight with curiosity as he prodded at something on the ground with his stick.

Elizabeth leaned closer, peering at the wriggling creature. Its smooth skin shimmered black and green in the fading light, its body about the length of Malaki's forearm.

"I believe that's some kind of salamander," she considered, her voice tinged with nostalgia. "We had those back home when I was in the fields by the water. Be careful, and you can play with it until it decides to move on."

The sound of snapping twigs announced the hunters' return as Elizabeth watched the three of them. Jared was leading, Mikah was chattering excitedly, and Mikael was steady and quiet at the rear. The ibex dragged between them, its horns catching the firelight in brief flashes.

She set her dough aside, wiping her hands on her tunic. Something in the way Mikael walked made her pause. His gait had changed not in body, but in bearing. He wasn't bouncing with boyish excitement like Mikah. He looked older somehow. He didn't glance around for approval. He just did the work.

As they approached, Jared passed her a cut of meat. "Here's a roast. It should be good if you cook it like venison."

She took it, nodding, but her eyes lingered on Mikael. His sleeves were torn at the wrists, and his face was streaked with dirt, but he stood tall. She saw a flicker of something in him—confidence, maybe even gravity.

"You all right?" she asked gently, handing him a cloth for his hands.

He nodded, wiping the blood from his fingers. "It didn't suffer long."

She caught her breath at that. How simply and solemnly he'd said it. No bravado, no flippant humor. Just awareness and responsibility.

Jared was already preparing strips of meat for drying, giving directions to the boys. Elizabeth turned back to the fire, laying the roast into her pot with care, but her thoughts were elsewhere. When had he grown so tall? When had he begun to speak like that?

Behind her, Mikael bent to gather kindling without being asked.

She pressed her palm lightly to her chest, her heart stirring with something between pride and ache. He's changing, she thought. And it's happening out here, not in a village, not surrounded by elders. Out here, in the wild, with his father and brothers and fire and wind—and whatever this journey is shaping him into.

She sprinkled the cinnamon onto the bread, watching the sugar-browned crust bubble. "He'll need more food soon," she murmured to herself with a smile. "All that growing takes fuel."

The boys quickly gathered more wood, their arms piled high with branches. Jared staked thin strips of meat near the fire, arranging them so that the smoke could fully reach them for drying. The fire's warmth spread outward, a beacon against the encroaching dark. Jared pitched their tent some distance from the flames, shielding them from the thick, pungent smoke.

The last light sank behind the trees as night fell swiftly. The stars emerged one by one, each one a whisper of light against the deepening sky. A cool breeze swept in from the sea, carrying with it the faint, briny tang of saltwater. The moon rose high, its silvery light casting an evening veil across the meadow.

The family settled by the fire, the bread's golden crust crackling softly as they broke it apart. Cinnamon tea steamed gently in their cups, its warm, spicy aroma mingling with the woodsmoke. They sipped in silence, their faces lit by the fire's glow. The ibex roast was tender—and soon gone.

Around them, the night was alive with subtle sounds: the distant hoot of an owl, the gentle rustling of leaves in the breeze, and the faint whisper of the stream flowing endlessly onward. Jared stirred the fire with a stick and said, "I don't fully understand this Elohim, the One they say caused the language to be confused, but I believe He's the One guiding us forward."

Together, they stared into the flames, their thoughts drifting toward the unknown path ahead.

Chapter 17

THE WISDOM WE CARRY

The sun lingered behind the mountain, slowly rising, as if gathering strength for its ascent. A soft, pale light crept over the rocky peaks, and slanted beams streaked the landscape in lavender and gray. As the first slivers of light touched the valley, Johanan and his group stirred, ready to begin their trek. He had found a faint animal trail winding up the mountainside, marked by the scuffed prints of hooves and paws.

The morning was unusually quiet, as if even the birds were hesitant to break the silence. Only the crunch of footsteps on pebbles and the soft swish of wool brushing brambles filled the air. Another day of traveling west and always toward the sunset. Shana wondered how long they would go before they'd pause, settle, or prepare for winter in an unknown place.

"Father, can we let the dogs loose now? They'll stay with us, I'm sure!" Shana's fingers itched to unclasp Affie's leash.

Eldad chimed in. "Yes, Kubal would love to run, even just for a bit."

Johanan paused, considering. "All right, but remember, they may not do as we expect. Still, give it a try."

Gently, Shana and Eldad unclasped the leashes. Affie yawned and stayed close, while Kubal darted forward, nose to the ground, sniffing eagerly up the trail.

As they moved on, Shana fell into step with Bathshua. The earthy smell of damp leaves and pine rose from the underbrush, mingling with the faint musk of animals who had passed before.

"Everything has changed so fast," Shana spoke slowly, "We don't even know where we're going…" Shana hesitated. "Are you afraid?"

Bathshua looked thoughtful. "Yes and no. I'm just glad I have you. It was terrifying when we couldn't find people who understood us anymore. My friend Nola… the words just stopped."

Shana nodded, a pang in her chest. "I know. We thought the tower was wonderful. But Elohim saw things differently. Maybe one day we'll learn each other's languages again and be friends."

"Yes!" Bathshua's face lit up. "It could be like teaching babies, pointing to our eyes, our nose, until we understand."

Shana smiled. "I loved the stories of our beginning. After hearing them and meeting Noah, Elohim feels closer. I believe that He'll protect and guide us."

By midday, the sun climbed high, spilling warmth as they began their descent.

"Let's stop here for a meal," Johanan suggested.

The animals spread out to graze, their chewing and the rustle of grass lulling the group into calm. Hadassah curled up nearby, while Affie and Kubal nestled beside her.

Martha chuckled, stretching out on a hide Sarah offered her. "I'll join them. My legs have their limits!"

Johanan smiled and handed her food. "Here, Mother. A rest will do you good."

"Grandma, even our legs are tired," Shana leaned back beside Bathshua. The boys exchanged glances and grinned.

"We're not tired," they blurted, "but we are hungry!"

Sarah laughed, offering a bowl of yogurt drizzled with honey. "Come on over. Try this."

"Yogurt?" Tabitha echoed.

"Yes, we'll *yogurmak* the sheep's milk again tonight," Sarah said, her eyes brightening. "It's my grandmother's word. She taught me how to stir warm milk with a bit from the last batch, wrap it in wool, and by morning it will thicken."

"Like it remembers how to become itself," Tabitha murmured.

A smile spread across Sarah's face. "Exactly."

But her smile faded a little as she looked toward the west, where the hills rolled on into heat-hazed distance. How many more nights like this? she wondered, pressing her hands together.

Suddenly, the sound of bleating broke the quiet.

"The goats, one's climbing that rock!" Eldad called, already scrambling after it.

"Careful!" Johanan stood quickly, eyes narrowing at the terrain. The goat danced along a ledge, hooves slipping, then regaining their grip. Eldad circled from below and managed to guide it back down. Laughter followed him as he rejoined the group, flushed and triumphant.

"Let's keep our animals close," Johanan said, his voice still light, but firmer now. "This land isn't all gentle."

After their rest, they continued down. The trail, now dustier and drier, led through sunlit stones and scrubby bushes. Heat gathered around them, a welcome contrast to the mountain chill.

At the base, Johanan noted, "It's warmer down here. Maybe tonight we won't need the tents. Let's look for a place to secure the animals and check for water nearby."

Tobiya pointed ahead. "Look, the trail goes to a small stream."

They led the animals to drink, the clear water gurgling over smooth stones. A tang of earth and wet leaves lingered in the air. With brush and rope, they set up a makeshift corral.

"Fill the waterskins," Johanan said. "Make use of this while we have it."

The men splashed in the stream, laughing, while Sarah built a small fire. "A warm drink would be lovely." She added chamomile leaves to the pot, the steam rising with a sweet, grassy scent.

Johanan returned, hair wet and glistening. "Now, Sarah, you and the girls should freshen up before it gets dark. We'll tend the fire and watch the meat."

Sarah smiled, but her eyes lingered briefly on the trail behind them. "Come, girls. Bring a change of clothes. Shana, grab the olive and rose oil with wood ash. It's good for our skin."

At the stream, cold water bit at their toes before becoming tolerable. The girls splashed and laughed, while the women washed clothes and shared stories, their voices mingling with the burble of the current. From the shore, Jairus stood watch, spear in hand, his gaze fixed on the tree line where the birds had fallen strangely silent.

As evening fell, the group gathered by the fire. The scent of roasted venison mixed with fresh vegetables they had collected along the way rose in the air.

"The food is ready!" someone called.

They came together and prayed. They were sharing bites, laughter, and moments of quiet reflection, though the silence sometimes stretched long, like thoughts too deep for words. Beside the fire, Shana leaned her head on Sarah's shoulder, the warmth of the flames and the hush of the stars drawing them inward.

The sky turned a velvety blue, streaked with violet as the light withdrew into the west. Stars blinked into view, the sky a tapestry of shimmering light. The moon rose full and glowing, casting silver light over the sleeping earth. There was a silent witness to their steps, marking another day westward on the long journey to the sunset.

Chapter 18

PATHS OF ICE AND GRACE

A distant snap echoed through the morning mist.

Tobiya froze, hand gripping his spear, eyes scanning the underbrush near the stream. Beside him, Johanan crouched low, tracking the trail with practiced calm. They had risen before first light, hoping to catch a deer before the camp stirred. The air held its breath.

Then came only the rustle of leaves and the quiet babble of the stream.

Farther back near the fire, Sarah stirred the flames to life, coaxing warmth from the coals as the pot began to steam. Tabitha approached, arms cradling a bundle of dried stalks.

"Let me share some linden flower stalks for tea this morning," she offered.

"Oh, I don't think I've tried linden flowers," Sarah said, the delicate scent mingling with smoke and damp earth.

Martha joined them, inhaling deeply. "Oh, the wonderful smell of linden. I haven't smelled that for a long time."

Sarah handed her a cup, its warmth seeping into Martha's hands as she cradled it close. Jairus arrived to warm his hands, accepting a cup with quiet gratitude. Children began to stir, and soon Shana, Eldad, and the others emerged, rubbing sleep from their eyes.

"Just a quick bite, then collect wood to keep this fire going," Sarah instructed.

Jairus beckoned Eldad. "We may need to help the goat deliver her kid. We'll stay close."

The girls gathered sticks, their laughter breaking the morning quiet. The sun climbed above the mountain, its golden light softening the long morning shadows.

Johanan and Tobiya emerged from the treeline, dragging a deer between them.

"See, we did it!" Johanan called out, his face bright with triumph.

"We knew you'd come through!" Sarah laughed, handing them food. Soon, they were washing up and eating with satisfaction.

"Shana, can you find some flat stones for the fire? And let's grind some grain," Sarah spoke.

Later, as the dough sizzled on the stones and the meat smoked, Sarah handed Shana a basket. "See if you girls can gather those cherries we saw yesterday."

Shana nodded, calling for Bathshua. As they walked, a sharp cry broke the stillness. Near a sagging tent, a woman and a man looked distressed. A donkey brayed. A small boy sobbed nearby.

Shana brightened. "I can help! They speak like we do!"

She dashed forward. "Do you need help with your animal?" she called.

The donkey flinched and bolted, the tether post snapping. The woman shouted and ran after it.

Shana stood frozen, rope still in hand. The boy's sobs and the woman's glare burned into her skin. "I—I was only trying to help," she murmured.

On the way back, neither girl spoke. Sarah met them at camp.

"What happened?"

"I thought I was helping… but I just made it worse."

Sarah drew her close. "Sometimes help means listening. Let your generous heart grow roots before it leaps."

That night, venison and vegetables simmered in a clay pot. Tents were pitched, the fire stoked, and the dogs curled beside the dozing children. Music floated from Sarah's harp and Tabitha's lyre, blending with laughter and the scent of stew.

The music usually brought calm, but Shana's heart remained unsettled. The woman's silence lingered in her mind.

***

Shana awoke to the scent of smoke and dew and the sound of her father's low voice blending with the morning hush. Another day, each one pulling them farther from what had been, closer to something unknown.

She knew she had to try again. Wrapping warm bread in cloth, she and Bathshua slipped through the mist. The little boy spotted them first with his eyes wide.

"We brought something for your breakfast," Shana trembled, offering the bundle.

The woman emerged, face wary. She looked at the bread, then at Shana.

Shana dipped her head. "I'm sorry."

A long pause.

Then the woman nodded slowly. "Thank you."

Back at camp, Shana told Sarah, who nodded. "That was brave, Shana."

As the group packed and moved out, the air filled with the earthy scent of dew-drenched grass and pine. Birds called from above, and squirrels darted through branches. Kubal and Affie trotted ahead. Higher up, they saw a herd of shaggy animals grazing.

"What are those?" Shana asked.

"Llamas," Jairus explained. "Mountain dwellers. Their wool looks very soft."

They moved closer, but the herd spooked and vanished.

Johanan watched them disappear. "We may have to follow their trail."

The climb was steep. Eventually, they reached the edge of the glacier. Sunlight reflected off the ice.

"Impossible to cross," Johanan said. "We'll find another way."

They skirted the glacier, wrapped in furs as the air turned frigid. At last, they descended toward warmth.

"Why are there glaciers?" Shana asked.

"Noah says they store the water from the flood," Johanan answered.

"And the rainbow?" she asked.

"A promise," he declared.

Jairus added, "Today is the solstice. This is the longest day of the year. By watching the sun and moon, we track time: new moon, crescent, half, full… Each season marks life's rhythm."

"Teach me," Shana requested.

"We all will learn," Jairus replied. "We walk into lands no man has known."

By late day, they reached a pond surrounded by juniper. Johanan declared, "This will do."

Animals were secured, while stew simmered, and children gathered firewood. Women baked flatbread. Martha spun wool, her fingers deft and calm.

"Teach me to spin," Shana said.

Sarah smiled. "And then to weave."

The girls gathered, watching Martha work. As the sun set in vivid streaks, they sat together, sharing food and stories.

Another chapter closed on their journey to the sunset.

Chapter 19

FAR SIDE OF THE SEA: THE CAVE

On the far side of the sea, Mikael and his family continued their trek. Their breath curled in pale wisps, the cold deepening with every step. The wind carried the scent of damp earth and distant pine, threading through the branches, tugging softly as if beckoning them onward. The bite of winter was already nipping at their heels.

"We need to find a more sheltered place to wait out the winter," Jared stated, his voice firm, though lined with the weariness of their long journey.

Mikael adjusted the fur over his shoulders, nodding. "I'll help look as we go. Do you think a cave would be best?" Mikael's eyes flicked to his mother, who was slower and quieter. There wasn't enough time to search forever.

"Yes, that would be best. Boys, spread out a little, but stay within sight," Jared instructed.

They fanned out, their hide-wrapped feet crunching over frost-kissed grass. The air smelled of damp bark and hinted at a nearby stream. Mikah and Malaki zigzagged across one another's paths, their playful rivalry undimmed even in the face of necessity.

Mikah grinned and punched Malaki's arm as they passed. "You stay in the middle so you don't get lost."

"I'm not going to get lost!" Malaki shot back, sticking out his tongue. "I'm going to find the cave before you do."

Mikael allowed himself a brief smile. Even in hardship, some things never changed.

As the morning sun climbed higher, its pale golden rays did little to warm them. At midday, they stopped to eat and rest, seated on rocks dusted with frost. Elizabeth pulled her shawl closer around her shoulders.

"While you search for a cave, keep an eye out for anything edible. We'll need to gather food now that we won't be moving as much. Nuts, berries, roots—anything."

Jared nodded. "And if we see signs of game, we may need to pause and hunt. Keep your bows ready." He glanced at Malaki. "This winter, I'll make a bow for you, son."

Malaki's eyes brightened, but Mikael caught the uncertainty in Jared's tone. The winter ahead would be hard. Any advantage in the hunt would be necessary for survival.

The afternoon passed in slow progress; their search was meticulous yet fruitless. Evening light slanted through the trees, golden and fading, when Mikael's voice rang out.

"Father! Come and see."

Jared and the others hurried to where Mikael stood at the mouth of a cave, its entrance dark like the gaping maw of some ancient beast. The air smelled of damp stone and something musky with an animal scent.

Jared crouched by the entrance, running a hand over the disturbed earth. "Bears have used this for hibernation," he observed. "We'll need a fire to keep them from returning. But this will do."

Relief settled in Mikael's chest. Finally, a place to stop. A place to rest.

They worked quickly, gathering wood for a fire. Elizabeth brought pine boughs to sweep out the cave. Jared fashioned a torch, wrapping fiber around a beech log and sealing it with tree sap. When lit, the torch flared, casting shifting light against the cave walls as they stepped inside. The space was cool and earthy, with a scattering of old leaves and tufts of animal fur.

" We have the fire outside. Should we set up the tent, too?" Mikael asked.

"Yes, we'll need it for the daylight hours," Jared said. "Mikah, fetch water from the stream while Mikael helps me with the tent."

Elizabeth moved toward the fire, rubbing her hands together. "I'll get some water heating for mountain tea and soup. A hot meal will do us good."

***

That evening, Jared took Mikael and his brothers to scout. They moved cautiously through the forest, the cool air thick with the scent of damp earth and decaying leaves. A squirrel darted up a tree, its tiny claws scratching bark. Birds fluttered above, their calls sharp in the crisp evening air.

"Let's spread out a little," Jared directed.

Mikael moved to one side, scanning the ground for tracks. Then— there. His pulse quickened.

"Father," he signaled, pointing to the fresh deer tracks in the damp soil.

Jared and the others moved in. They tracked the signs carefully, quietly moving as one. Then, on a ridge ahead, a majestic buck stood silhouetted against the evening light. Mikael's heart pounded as he raised his bow, his fingers tightening around the arrow's fletching. He drew in a slow breath and then released.

The arrow flew true, striking behind the shoulder. Jared and Mikah loosed their arrows almost simultaneously. The buck staggered, then collapsed.

A solemn hush fell over them. Mikael swallowed hard, staring at the fallen creature. He felt a deep respect for the life they had just taken, gratitude mingling with the sadness of necessity.

Malaki approached, counting the antler points with wide eyes. "Ten points… he must be old."

"Yes," Jared offered quietly, placing a hand on Mikael's shoulder. "And he will feed us well. Thank you…to this Elohim."

They worked quickly, draining and gutting the deer as the sky deepened into twilight. Jared sent Malaki ahead with the heart, wrapped in hide, to tell their mother of their success. The rest of them worked efficiently, knowing the light was fading fast.

By the time they returned to camp, dragging the deer between them, the scent of cooking meat filled the air. Elizabeth had the fire burning strong, and the heart was already sizzling, infused with the last of their garlic and leeks. The warmth of the fire felt like a barrier against the encroaching cold. There was a promise of comfort in the face of winter's approach.

They washed up and settled by the fire, stretching their legs and sipping the mountain tea Elizabeth had prepared. The sunset tinted the sky in vivid streaks of red, orange, and pink, casting a soft glow over their newfound home.

Mikael let out a slow breath, the tension of the day easing.

Shelter, food, and each other, for now, it was enough.

Chapter 20

ONE STEP FURTHER

Day after day, the sunrise was blending into the sunset. The world was shifting hues with every passing hour. They continued their long trek. Another phase of the moon vanished into memory, leaving the nights darker, quieter. The sun blazed relentlessly above, washing the sky an almost unbearable shade of blue. Heat shimmered off the earth, while to the north, the distant sea glinted like liquid silver, vast and unknowable.

The children had stopped asking how much longer. Even Shana no longer counted the days by how often they ate certain meals. Every rhythm had become dust and wind and movement.

Ahead, Eldad walked briskly with Kubal, whose sudden barking broke through the tranquil hum of insects. The boy stopped abruptly, his face twisting in worry as the dog bristled.

"Daddy!" Eldad cried, his voice sharp with alarm. Johanan jogged up the trail without hesitation. "He's afraid of something," Eldad continued, holding onto Kubal's collar with both hands. "He won't let me move."

"Kubal," Johanan knelt, speaking in a steady voice. "What's wrong, boy?" The dog quieted but stood stiffly, nose stretched forward, sniffing at the breeze. His ears twitched.

Tobiya, sensing the tension, hurried to their side. "What are you thinking, Johanan?"

He rose slowly, scanning the trail ahead. "Let's look around. Something's nearby. Eldad, go back to the others," Johanan instructed. "Tell them to build a campfire. Keep everyone and the animals close to it. Tobiya, you're with me."

Eldad hesitated, but Johanan's firm gaze sent him hurrying back. As Tobiya adjusted his bow, slung across his back, Johanan crouched to whisper to Kubal. "Go see," he urged. The dog darted forward, nose to the ground.

The two followed in silence, eyes darting to every darkness beneath the trees. The air here seemed denser, filled with the musk of wild animals and the low hum of unseen life. Suddenly, Kubal froze, his body taut as a bowstring. Johanan's eyes followed the dog's gaze, and there it was.

A pile of scat, unusual in its composition, marked the trail ahead. "I don't recognize this," Johanan murmured, kneeling to inspect it. Tobiya bent down beside him, his brow furrowing. "It might be a bear," he gulped. "We've no idea what kind of wildlife this land holds."

Kubal's low whine grew urgent as the wind shifted. They stepped cautiously around a bend in the trail, where the trees grew thicker, shadows crisscrossing the ground like jagged nets. There, framed by a grove of tall oaks, stood a brown, shaggy bear. She rose, a tower of fur and muscle, breath steaming in the air. Above her, three cubs clung to the branches of a tree, their mewling calls sharp against her guttural roar.

Johanan grabbed Kubal's collar, holding him back as the dog snarled. "We can't shoot her, not with the cubs there. We'll back away, slowly. Don't turn your back," he whispered to Tobiya.

"I agree," Tobiya stated. They backed up slowly, keeping their eyes on the bear. Step by step, they retreated, the bear watching their every move.

But just then, another sound broke through the trees, a low, guttural growl that didn't come from the mother. A second bear, larger and darker, stepped from the underbrush—the male.

Johanan's stomach dropped. "This is why she had them in the tree," he whispered.

The male bared his teeth, pacing. Tobiya raised his bow, but Johanan shook his head. "Not yet. Move slowly. If he charges, we shoot."

The male lunged forward a step, testing. Kubal barked again, furious. The cubs shrieked in the tree, and the mother bear turned protectively. The male advanced.

"Now!" Johanan shouted.

Two arrows flew. Tobiya's arrow struck the bear in the shoulder; Johanan's landed deeper in the chest. The bear roared, staggering forward. Kubal darted sideways, drawing its eye just long enough for Johanan to notch another arrow and release.

This one struck deep, true and final.

The male collapsed with a final growl that shook the trees. Silence fell, broken only by the rustle of leaves and the sharp panting of Kubal.

The mother bear grunted, calling her cubs down. She gave the fallen male one wary look before guiding her young into the shade.

Johanan and Tobiya stood still for a long moment.

"We couldn't have avoided that," Tobiya said at last. "It was him or us."

"We need the meat," Johanan replied grimly. "Let's bring him back."

Johanan and Tobiya returned to the camp carrying the first cuts of bear meat, their clothing streaked with dirt and sweat. Kubal trotted beside them, ears alert but no longer bristling.

The camp had quieted, but unease still clung to the air like smoke. A campfire crackled in the center. They all sat together, and every rustle in the woods turned heads.

Eldad ran to his father, his small face streaked with ash from tending the flames. "What happened, Daddy?" he asked, clutching at Johanan's tunic.

Kubal bounded over, licking the boy's face before settling beside Affie, his tension dissipating.

"It was a bear," Johanan explained, setting a reassuring hand on Eldad's shoulder. "She had cubs, so we didn't want to do anything with her." Johanan knelt beside him. "But then another bigger bear appeared, a male. We had no choice. He would have attacked. But from now on, you stay close. Understood?"

Eldad nodded solemnly. They had taken one step further—into danger, and into the wilderness that would not yield easily.

Sarah moved swiftly, practical as always. "Bring the rest of the meat. We'll dress it up quickly before the sun is too high. We'll have to smoke most of it before it spoils."

"We may as well have a quick bite while we wait," she added. Shana, eager to help, handed her mother a bundle of dried sage leaves and cups.

"What else can I bring, Mama?" Shana asked, her hands fidgeting.

"Flatbread from last night," Sarah replied. "And maybe some dried venison."

"I've some dried blackberries," Tabitha chimed in, her voice wistful. "Perhaps we could add them to the tea instead of honey. Oh, how I miss honey."

"Yes," Sarah agreed with a chuckle. "If we find a hive, Johanan will have to fetch some for us."

Martha's warm laughter joined in. "Oh, Johanan's good at that. Jairus taught him well."

Jairus piped up, "We will have to watch for that honey. Where there is bear, there is honey."

The tea was ready, its aroma earthy and faintly sweet from the blackberries. As cups were passed around, the clan gathered close to the campfire. Eldad and Lemuel played with sticks, pretending they were knives, while the dogs curled up by Hadassah. Her small face was peaceful in the soft light.

"I like the blackberries in the tea," Sarah noted, taking a long sip. "Maybe by tonight, some of the goat cheese will be ready."

Johanan grinned. "You've been scheming about cheese, haven't you?"

"Goat cheese," Sarah confirmed, her voice teasing. "Your mother's watching over it like a hawk."

Time passed in a tranquil lull as they listened to the soft rustle of leaves, the chirping of birds, and the occasional crackle of the campfire. When the campfire was put out, they resumed their journey, moving onto a meadow that unfurled before them like a vibrant carpet. Wildflowers of every hue swayed in the breeze, and the tall grasses brushed together as the animals grazed.

The girls wove flower chains as they walked, their laughter blending with the symphony of nature.

The boys, ever energetic, dashed ahead with their makeshift weapons. Kubal and Affie scouted the trail, their tails wagging as they sniffed at the meadow's earthy scents.

Jairus broke the silence. "Do any of you feel... an inkling, perhaps, of when this journey might end?"

"No," Johanan replied, his gaze fixed ahead. "We'll keep going until Yahweh Elohim tells us to stop or until winter makes the decision for us. But I'll admit, I'm weary of walking."

"I feel that Yahweh Elohim will bring us to a place to begin new people through our clan. Somehow, we will know," Tobiya stated.

Martha responded, "I hope that Jairus and I will be able to continue with you until that place is found. It seems I may have grown stronger with all the walking, but I am worn out."

"I hope we can stay together," Sarah added. "This huge world will be difficult to live in without other people."

Tabitha agreed. "As it is, we will have to pray for our children to find mates. He wants us to multiply, so Yahweh Elohim will bring others when the time is right."

"Mama, but if we can't understand those people, what will we do?" Shana questioned.

"If Yahweh Elohim wants us to associate with those people, he will help us learn the language. It may take some time, but I think it would be possible, like when we teach little ones to talk."

"That makes sense!"

The group fell into a thoughtful silence, their steps slow but steady, as if their shared prayers pressed gently behind each step.

Chapter 21

THE LANGUAGE OF BELONGING

Shana cried out as she tossed and turned in her sleep, her body slick with cold sweat. Her muffled sobs pierced the quiet of the tent, broken by whispered pleas that dissolved into choked murmurs. The air inside felt heavy, as if the remnants of some unspoken dread clung to the walls.

Hearing the soft cries, Sarah moved quickly to her daughter's side. She laid a cool hand across Shana's damp forehead, and Shana's eyes flew open, wild and wet with fear.

"Oh, Mama, no one understands me!" she cried, her voice trembling, raw. The words spilled out like a wound reopened, her anguish deeper than the dream itself. "Even when people say they do, it doesn't feel like it. Everything changed. Everyone changed."

Sarah's heart twisted. She pulled Shana into her arms, cradling her tightly. "Shana," she whispered, steady despite the sting in her throat, "Yahweh divided the languages by clans so that we would spread out across the earth. It feels painful now, but it isn't punishment. It's for a purpose. And you are not alone. We understand you. I'll pray for peace to settle over your heart like morning mist."

Shana's shudders eased little by little, her mother's words and warmth folding over her like a covering. The scent of worn leather and woodsmoke drifted between them. Sarah gently lay her back down, brushing a curl from her daughter's forehead.

Outside, the first blush of dawn stretched across the horizon. Johanan stirred and rose, stepping into the chilled air. He moved through the quiet with practiced hands, gathering kindling. The soft stir of animals waking, the snap of twigs beneath his feet, and the distant bleat of a goat ushered in the new day.

Sarah joined him at the fire pit, her arms folded tightly across her chest against the cold. "Shana had a rough night." She lowered her voice. "That dream brought it all back. I think she feels like she lost more than words that day."

Johanan nodded slowly. "I understand. We all did. When the languages were confused, I kept thinking it was temporary and that it would clear. But then people we'd known for years became strangers overnight."

"We never really talked about it," Sarah interjected. "Not deeply. We kept moving. Kept surviving. But the fear, what if we never find stability? What if we can't rebuild what we had?"

Johanan poked at the coals, and the flames answered with a low flare. "Let's bring it up today. Not just the logistics, but the heart of it."

She gave a small nod, eyes thoughtful. "Let's go wash up before the others stir."

The river glinted in the early light, its surface dappled with reflections of rose and gold. As they approached, deer at the far bank startled and bounded into the trees. Sarah and Johanan stepped into the shallows with sharp gasps, the icy water stealing their breath.

"The water is freezing!" Sarah laughed, hurrying out. The cold clung to their skin as they wrapped their cloaks tighter and returned to the fire's glow.

Tabitha, already warming water, offered Sarah a steaming cup. "This will help."

Sarah took it gratefully. "Thank you. We'll need to find shelter soon. Something that won't collapse under snow."

Tabitha nodded. "Somewhere quiet. Somewhere safe. Do you think Elohim will move us again once the thaw comes?"

Sarah glanced at the rim of the sky. "I hope we stay. Or if we do move, that we move together. Even if we spread out a little, I want to know you're still near."

Johanan spoke up, his voice gathering the group's attention. "It's time to prepare to move again. We'll need to find a place with better protection for the winter—something stronger than tents."

Jairus agreed. "We don't know where this road ends, but we can't risk being caught in the mountains when the snow begins."

Martha, shouldering her bag, smiled. "I'm stronger than I was. If Yahweh brought us this far, He'll lead us forward. He knows."

Before they broke camp, Johanan lifted his voice again. "Before we go, I'd like us to speak—really speak. Shana's dream about the confusion of languages reminded me that we've carried our fears without naming them. If anyone would share, I think it would help."

There was a long pause, then Tobiya stepped forward. "I was at the market when it happened. One moment I was buying salt—then a man started shouting at me. I thought he'd gone mad. Then I realized I was the one who couldn't understand." His voice cracked. "I couldn't even call for help."

Tabitha nodded. "I remember people screaming, not from pain, but confusion. I tried to calm my neighbor, but she didn't know me anymore. We were like strangers standing in the same room."

Sarah's hands trembled slightly. "I remember shouting for the children. I was afraid they wouldn't understand my voice. That they'd be lost and I couldn't reach them."

Once by one, others added fragments of their experience. There were tears and silences between words. But in the telling, the sharp edges dulled. In the sharing, something shifted.

Shana, her eyes concerned while listening, finally spoke. "Thank you for talking about it. I thought I was the only one who still felt scared." She reached for Affie and rubbed her smooth fur. "Affie and I can understand each other. If Elohim brings us to others, maybe they'll teach us their words—and we'll teach them ours."

Sarah reached over and squeezed her daughter's hand. "You're right. There will always be differences in a community, but they aren't always meant to divide us. They can teach us how to love more."

A thoughtful stillness settled on the group. The fire crackled, casting golden light across tired, thoughtful faces. They did not have answers, but under the sky of a new day, they belonged to one another.

Chapter 22

HAZELNUTS AND FUR

More mountains came into view as they trekked along the rugged path, jagged peaks piercing the azure sky. The early morning air was crisp, with a faint tang of pine and damp earth lingering from the night's dew. Sunlight spilled across the terrain, turning the frost into shards of crystal. Yet the beauty felt distant, like a dream just beyond reach, their weary limbs burdened by every step.

Johanan spoke with Jairus and Tobiya as they trudged forward, their breath misting in the cold. His tone was steady but thoughtful. "It looks like there are ways to move through the mountains without climbing." He glanced at the ridges. "But maybe it's worth climbing one. Let's see if Elohim shows us anything."

Tobiya paused, his leather-wrapped feet crunching the frosted leaves. "That may be wise." Concern crept into his voice. "We'll need to settle soon, before another moon phase passes. It's growing colder, and we're all running low."

"I agree," Jairus added. "We need to stop long enough to hunt and gather food. We'll need serious provisions for a winter we can't predict."

Sarah stepped from the trees behind them, her cheeks flushed with cold. "We've been talking, too," she stated. "We're ready to stop when you are. But one day of rest, just one, would help."

They moved on, the silence between them heavy as the landscape. The forest thickened, and ancient oaks gave way to fir and beech. Tracks wove through the soft ground, squirrels, deer, birds and others. Tobiya paused to pluck a clump of coarse, dark fur from a low branch.

He turned it in the light. "Fresh."

Johanan frowned. "Bear?"

Tobiya nodded. "Close."

Jairus's voice dropped. "Then maybe we won't stop here."

"We'll post a watch," Johanan replied. "There's cover here. Warmth. That's more than we've had in days."

Tobiya exhaled. "The cold's not the only danger; we're fraying at the edges. We'll take the risk."

The sun dipped behind the peaks. In a ring of tall trees, they found a natural hollow where the ground leveled out just enough for tents. It was sheltered, quiet. Johanan struck a spark, and a fire kindled in the heart of camp, sending curls of warmth into the dusk.

Sarah knelt nearby, sorting through the small cache of hazelnuts she'd found earlier. She arranged them on the rock, their shells cracking faintly as they roasted. Tabitha sliced cheese beside her, while Sarah patted out rounds of dough with practiced rhythm.

"I've got a little dried linden left." Tabitha lifted a pouch with a small smile. "Something special for tonight."

"That would be lovely." Martha's voice was soft. "The nuts will be a treat, too."

Shana and Bathshua, along with Hadassah, settled near the fire's edge, its amber light casting warm tones across their faces. Affie curled up beside them, ears twitching. Eldad and Lemuel lay nearby, heads resting on their arms, their wooden staffs at their sides, with Kubal nestled protectively between them.

Once the tents were pitched and the animals secured, the men returned to the warmth of the fire. Bread and cheese passed between hands as the group slowly unwound.

Sarah set a wooden bowl out for the nuts. "Try to save a few after you taste one," she teased.

"We'll try," Johanan said with a faint grin. "Tomorrow we'll climb and see what Elohim shows us. Then, we rest."

He paused. "Let's pray. We need His voice."

Jairus bowed his head. "Yahweh Elohim, guide us. Show us where to stop. Confirm Your will. Amen."

A quiet "Amen" followed.

Later, as the meal wound down, Shana sat still beside her mother, staring into the glowing coals.

"Why do we have to climb tomorrow?" she asked, her gaze fixed on the fire.

Sarah turned. "Your father wants to see what's ahead."

"We've been climbing every day," Shana muttered. "Just not mountains. I just want to stop."

Sarah placed a gentle hand on her shoulder. "So do I. We're just not there yet."

Shana leaned into her slightly, silent.

Above them, the sky deepened into twilight, lavender, rose, then indigo, studded with stars. Around the fire, the group grew quiet, holding onto the warmth.

The bear fur, the weariness, the quiet fear, it hadn't left them. But neither had the hope.

The air, the food, the hush of the mountains, it all wove into a tapestry of faith. Another day had ended, its moments strung like pearls. They were still walking west, still chasing the light of the setting sun, still listening for the Voice that would tell them when to stop.

What would tomorrow bring?

Chapter 23

THE SONG WE CARRY

The morning broke cold and sharp, the horizon streaked with faint orange and pink. The group stirred early, hearts lifted with the hope of reaching the mountains by nightfall. The biting air gnawed at exposed skin, breath curling like smoke as movement stirred the frosted world. A fire crackled to life, its warmth battling the morning chill. The children gathered close, shivering, hands outstretched toward the flames. Tea steamed in their hands, offering brief comfort, and breakfast was spare, dried meat and a bit of cheese, but enough to move them forward.

The women moved with practiced rhythm, packing belongings, organizing bundles. The men folded tents, their breath visible in the crisp air. Finally, to Johanan's relief, the travois was strapped to the ox; his shoulders still remembered the ache of dragging it himself. Tobiya led the ox forward as the caravan resumed its trek. Boys trailed beside them with sticks, keeping the smaller animals in motion.

"At least we can see where we're heading today," Johanan remarked, eyes on the distant mountains, their peaks faintly cloaked in mist.

"Let's hope they get bigger soon," Jairus replied with a wry grin. "Could still be quite a long way off."

The sun climbed slowly behind them, casting golden light through the dense forest. The trail was quiet except for the steady crunch of feet on dry leaves and the occasional bleat or low from the animals. Squirrels darted between trees. A woodpecker's rhythm echoed through the canopy. The tang of damp leaves and the earthy perfume of autumn filled their lungs.

As they walked, the conversation faded and a hush settled, not of silence but of intention. Their steps fell into rhythm, and with that rhythm came a kind of music—steps on earth, birds in the trees, wind weaving through branches like a flautist's breath.

It was Martha who finally broke the stillness. "When we stop tonight, could we hear some music?"

Shana looked up. Her feet dragged slightly as she walked beside her grandmother. Music. The word struck her like sunlight through clouds. A memory rose unbidden—her mother's fingers on the harp, each note lifting into the air like a prayer. Her own smaller hands were trying to follow, guided gently by Sarah's warm touch. The vibration of strings had once felt like something sacred, a bridge between the seen and the unseen.

She nodded slowly. "That would be nice," she said, her voice faint. It wasn't untrue. But there was weariness, too—an ache not just in her legs but deep in her chest. Joy felt farther away now, muffled beneath layers of dust and distance. Did her mother see it? How much she missed the music—and how much she missed feeling near to her?

Bathshua's voice carried gently. "Me too. But I'd like to hear my mother play more than myself."

Sarah smiled at the girls, her eyes thoughtful. "I've missed it too. Maybe tomorrow we can find a moment to practice. When the men return from scouting, we'll gather and play. We must remember the songs of our ancestors and the music of our traditions. Perhaps we'll start with the Creation Hymn."

The mention of that hymn stirred something in Shana. She could still hear the memory of their voices, rising, harmonizing, echoing in the gathering space at Naxuana. The hymn had sounded like the first light of dawn breaking over the world. It made her feel as though Yahweh Elohim was near, closer than breath.

Music had always done that, opened a space inside her where the world made sense, where sorrow softened, where faith became more than words. In the song, she could remember the garden, the ark, the promises. In the song, she was never alone.

Tabitha added, "The men have been carving spindles with such skill—perhaps they could make more instruments for the girls."

"That would be wonderful!" Shana's face brightened. A spark lit in her, sudden and clear, pushing aside the fatigue. "We could all play together. Let's think of the instruments we know: the harp, the lyre, the flute, the shofar, and drums. Let's try to remember them all, maybe there are more we can rediscover."

As she spoke, her mind wandered ahead, past the climb, past the hunger, to a circle of firelight, where the wind carried music instead of silence. She imagined their small band of travelers transformed into something more than wanderers. They were a people with a voice, a song that carried not just memory, but hope.

Martha leaned closer, her voice warm. "I've seen flutes made from hollowed bones in several places. Drums can be stretched hide over bowls, or hollowed logs. But sometimes, Shana, music comes from whatever you have in your hands."

Eldad piped in eagerly, "Lemuel and I can find things to use for a drum!"

The conversation drifted into ideas and laughter as the mountains loomed larger, their snowy peaks bright against the gold and crimson forest below. The air thinned and sharpened as they climbed.

"We'll keep moving until sunset," Johanan called over his shoulder. "Then fire first, animals second, tents last."

Sarah nodded. "Tonight we'll cook something hearty. We all feel hungry. And children, we'll need your help gathering grass. The animals need to eat, too."

***

With the day drawing to a close, the animals grew restless. The ox stumbled, the goats bleated.

"They must smell water," Johanan murmured, moving ahead. Soon his call rang out: "There's water here and space for a camp!"

Relief swept through them. They quickened their pace toward the stream. Its bubbling voice greeted them like an old friend. Firewood was gathered quickly; soon a blaze threw wavering light across the clearing. The women cooked, roasting meat and baking flatbread on hot stones. The savory smells filled the air.

Jairus patted his knees and turned to Johanan. "As much as I'd like to climb with you tomorrow, I'd best stay behind because I'd slow you down."

Shana saw him rub his knees and glanced toward Martha, who nodded quietly. It was hard, growing old on a journey like this.

Later, as they sat by the fire, Hadassah edged closer to Martha. "Grandma Martha, can you be our grandma too?"

Martha's eyes softened. She pulled the child close. "That would be a good idea, Hadassah. For all three of you. I'd be honored."

Lemuel added, "Then Jairus can be our grandpa!"

Jairus laughed gently. "I'd like that very much."

***

After the meal, the women brought out their instruments, deciding it was a good time to practice. Sarah gently unwrapped the harp and passed it to Shana, her fingers brushing her daughter's with quiet encouragement. Shana settled it in her lap, her hands tingling as they found the strings. Beside them, Tabitha tuned her lyre with practiced ease while Bathshua, her daughter, mimicked each motion with careful attention. The first notes were uncertain, hesitant. But the second was stronger. Then a chord. A melody. The firelight gleamed on the strings as the music began to take shape, old songs carried forward by new hands.

They began the Creation Hymn, soft at first, like dawn itself. Then fuller. The harmonies wrapped around them. Eldad tapped a rhythm on a hollow gourd. Lemuel joined in. Sarah's voice lifted in quiet harmony. It wasn't perfect, but it was theirs.

And it was enough.

Jairus leaned forward, eyes reflecting firelight. "Elohim has a special place for us." His voice was low. "We only need to arrive. Let's pray for tomorrow's climb."

His prayer was steady, calm, and trusting.

Later, the fire was banked and the tents sealed tight against the cold. The forest shifted softly, the stream ran steady beneath it, and above them, the stars watched in timeless silence.

And somewhere beneath it all, Shana still heard the echo of the music, the invisible thread tying her… to her people.

To her faith.

To the beginning.

To home.

Chapter 24

THE LAND BEYOND

"If I pass sage and return empty-handed, Sarah will not be pleased," Johanan said with a faint smile. "We might use some for seeds or drying. I'll let her decide."

Tobiya chuckled. "We've all come to value the little things on this journey, haven't we?"

They stood at the foot of the mountain, a jagged blade of stone cutting into the sky. The dawn light spilled golden over the forest they had left behind, carving lines across the trail. The sharp scent of sage filled the air, earthy and strong, mingling with the crisp bite of the wind. Johanan stooped to pluck a few sprigs, brushing them clean before tucking them into a pouch.

Soon, the trail turned rugged. Loose gravel and jagged stones slid beneath their feet. With each step, the incline pressed harder against their thighs. The mountain loomed above them, snow-tipped and silent, a sentinel of stone and sky.

They spoke little. The climb pulled at more than muscle; it reached into memory. For Johanan, the quiet weight of leadership bore down like the bundle on his shoulders. Every decision, every path, had consequences. For Tobiya, each step was a silent prayer for protection, for meaning, and for the people they carried with them.

The wind picked up. Higher up, it moaned through narrow crevices, a hollow, mournful sound that made the mountain feel alive and watching. The air thinned, each breath colder and more precious. The terrain grew treacherous, and their progress slowed. Even the silence around them shifted. There were no birds, no insects. Just wind and crunching snow underfoot.

Johanan glanced sideways. "Do you think the snow will grow deeper the higher we climb?"

"Perhaps," Tobiya replied, his breath escaping in brief clouds. "But we'll climb as far as we can."

Below, life at the camp bustled. Martha worked steadily at her lap loom, fingers threading bright strands into neat rows. Sarah and Tabitha pounded grain and washed clothes in rhythm with the morning sun. The children laughed as they helped gather firewood or chased the dogs. The dogs barked as they helped the boys move the animals. It was a day like any other, yet something felt close, like the edge of a story turning.

Above, nearing the glacier, Johanan and Tobiya paused to wrap their feet in furs and pull heavier coverings over their shoulders. The path they made gleamed in the sunlight, untouched and crystalline, but the snow masked patches of slick ice. One misstep could mean injury—or worse.

Their breathing turned shallow as they neared the top. Then, finally, a plateau revealed itself. They climbed the final rise and stepped onto a small, level clearing just below the summit. The world unfolded around them like a scroll.

The sun hung high, painting the snowy ridge with silver light. The horizon was endless. To the right and left, vast bodies of water shimmered, their mirrored surfaces catching the sun's blaze. Ahead, the land unrolled like a promise, wide, waiting, and unbroken.

Johanan stood still. "What do you see?"

Tobiya turned slowly, eyes wide. "It is a land bridge. To the right, the sea glitters. To the left, another. But forward lies open land, as far as we can see."

Johanan exhaled, his face taut with wonder. "Then that is where we will go. The land beyond calls to us. A promise of something more."

They lingered for only a moment. The cold stung their skin, and the descent would be slower to be safe. As they began their careful return, Johanan's eyes caught motion across a distant ridge. There was a herd of mountain goats picking their way across the cliff with impossible balance.

"See those goats?" he whispered, hand resting on his bow. "We could hunt one… but carrying it back?" He shook his head. "That's for another day."

Tobiya nodded. "Today is not for hunting. It's for finding the path ahead."

Back at camp, the scent of stew welcomed them as the sun lowered behind the trees, casting the forest in warm hues of amber and rust. The golden glow touched every face. Sarah handed them each a cup of chamomile tea. "Rest first." Her voice was gentle, like the tea in their hands.

"Then tell us what you saw," Jairus added, already drawing the others near.

As the fire blazed, everyone settled in. Shana sat close to Sarah, plucking softly at her mother's harp, the notes light as drifting leaves. Despite the weariness in her limbs, her spirit felt lifted. The music moved through her like breath, a warmth she didn't need to explain.

Johanan told the story of the climb, of the ice and snow, of the stillness at the summit. Tobiya followed, describing the view—the seas, the shining land bridge, and the unbroken horizon ahead.

Silence fell. The fire popped, sending up a soft shower of sparks. The path ahead was clear, but heavy with the unknown.

Shana's heart beat faster. Could this be the end of their journey? Was this where they would stop and build a home? Or was it only another step? She wasn't sure whether it was hope or fear she felt swelling inside her. She glanced at Sarah, whose steady presence gave her calm, and at Eldad, whose twitching legs mirrored her own unrest.

"I think Yahweh will show us where to stop," Jairus said, voice quiet but firm. "We will pray and listen."

Shana nodded emphatically. "I think we're ready to stop. We're ready for a home!"

As the group bowed their heads in prayer, the stars emerged, one by one, above the treeline. Shana squeezed her eyes shut, giving her own plea to Yahweh.

Later that night, long after the fire had burned down and the camp had gone still, Shana stirred from her bedding. The moon hung low and luminous. Pulling her cloak tighter, she stepped away from the tents and sat with the harp in her lap, its familiar weight grounding her.

She began to play.

Soft, searching notes fell into the silence. The melody was one her mother had taught her, something gentle, like a lullaby, but tinged with longing. As her fingers moved, tears welled in her eyes. Not of sadness, but of fullness. The music said everything she could not: her weariness, her hope, her fear of not understanding, her fear of the journey's end, and her faith that Yahweh still heard.

She finished with the final chord trembling in the air.

No one stirred. No one clapped.

But the stillness felt different now—like someone had listened.

Chapter 25

THE RIVER AHEAD

The storm had passed. The air was crisp, tinged with the briny scent of the nearby sea, and the camp stirred with quiet urgency. Tents, now dry from the night breeze, were swiftly folded and secured. A fire crackled back to life, sending thin ribbons of smoke into the sky. Tea steamed in carved cups, offering brief comfort against the morning chill.

Shana paused, gazing eastward where the sea met the sky. A hush settled over her chest as she remembered the sunset, a blaze of red, gold, and indigo streaking the clouds like a masterpiece from Yahweh's own hand. A faint rainbow had shimmered in the last light. I want to remember this forever, she thought. I wish there were a way to keep it, so I'll never forget. She crouched down, thoughtful, and drew the shape of the rainbow in the dirt with her finger.

Sarah's voice broke through her thoughts. "We'll enjoy these pumpkins through the winter, but we must keep watch for more food as we go. Somehow, we need enough to last the season."

"We'll hunt when we settle," Johanan assured her. "Once the weather turns colder, we should be able to preserve the meat."

Tabitha added, brushing hair from her face, "Our grain is nearly gone—barely enough to grind."

Martha, listening quietly, murmured with conviction, "Yahweh will provide, just as He has guided us this far."

They resumed their journey. The mountains loomed to the left, sharp and snow-dusted, while to the right, the sea stretched endlessly. The rhythmic sounds of hooves, footsteps, and the creak of the travois mingled with the steady sigh of the wind.

Shana, weary of silence, turned to her grandfather. "Grandpa, tell us a story."

Jairus smiled. "Let me think… Ah! When I was a boy, my brother and I found enormous bones. We imagined we'd slain a mighty beast in battle."

Eldad's eyes widened. "What did you think it was?"

"A mastodon, perhaps. We weren't sure."

"Tell us one about Father!" Shana prompted.

Johanan groaned playfully. "Must we?"

Jairus chuckled. "There was once a little boy who tried to befriend a turtle. He lay beside it so long that he fell asleep. When he woke, the turtle was already in the pond. He gave it a nudge—and it swam away fast as anything."

"You're always helping things, Father," Shana giggled.

They pressed on until Sarah called a halt near a clear stream. "Let's rest. The animals can drink, and we'll refill our waterskins."

As the fire kindled, Tabitha stirred a pot of stew, the scent of leeks and simmering meat thick in the air. Shana sat beside Martha, offering her a warm drink.

"Grandma, I'm afraid for you."

Martha smiled faintly. "Let me rest, dear one. When I need you, I'll tell you. Yahweh is with me."

Nearby, Jairus crouched, concern etched in his face. "Tell me what you need, Martha."

"I will," she said softly. "We're nearly there. I just want to see it with all of you."

Sarah and Tabitha took the girls foraging. They found beans nestled under heavy vines. When the foraging group returned with full baskets, Johanan glanced at the sky. "We'll keep moving until sundown."

As they descended into a valley, the mountains receded behind them. The path narrowed. Shana suggested, "Let's sing, it makes walking easier."

The children lifted their voices:

We have come a long way on this journey to the sunset.
We love adventure, day by day.
We have become family on the way.

Then Sarah led them in the promise song:

As long as the earth endures,
Seedtime and harvest,
Cold and heat,
Summer and winter,
Day and night
Will never cease.

They sang it again and again, voices strong and sweet. Then, cresting a hill, they stopped short. A mighty river stretched below them, catching the last light like liquid gold. Johanan, Tobiya, and Jairus stood at the edge in silence, the air thick with awe.

Johanan finally spoke. "We'll descend and camp by the river tonight."

As they settled near the bank, Tabitha asked softly, "Is this the place we stay?"

Sarah placed a steady hand on her shoulder. "We'll pray. Yahweh will guide us."

Later, the men returned from scouting. Johanan stood beside the fire, eyes on the river. "We must continue. We must cross. If Noah could build an ark, surely we can build something to carry us across this water."

Shana lay back on her mat, staring up at the vast sky. The full moon bathed the world in silver, and the river lapped gently beside the quiet crackle of flames. How did Yahweh make everything so beautiful? she wondered. And how will He bring us across this river? She closed her eyes, listening to the night's quiet chorus, the murmurs of the fire, the lap of water, the steady pulse of the journey still to come.

Chapter 26

THE RIVER'S EDGE

The campfire warmed the early morning chill as steam rose from carved cups and the scent of sage tea mingled with woodsmoke. The forest stood hushed and tall around them, and beyond its edge, the wide, glinting river waited. Though winter had not fully claimed the land, its breath lingered in the frost-bitten air.

Sarah moved quietly, gathering ingredients with practiced hands. She reached for the grain they had ground the day before, feeling its coarse texture. Tabitha joined her, pouring fresh milk, still warm from the cow, into the bowl. The mixture steamed as it met the meal. A few drops of oil added richness, and together they formed rough rounds of dough, setting them to sizzle on flat stones.

The camp stirred slowly. Children remained curled in their furs, unmoving in sleep. The hush of morning was broken only by soft voices near the fire. Martha, still weak, remained inside her tent. Sarah silently prayed that this brief pause might restore her strength.

When the bread was ready, Sarah and Tabitha brought warm tea and food to the men. Johanan looked up, face resolute. "We've talked and prayed. We'll stay here for now, but we need more shelter. We'll search for something better, a cave or a thicket, anything to protect us from storms."

Tobiya exhaled into his hands. "We also need to watch the river. If it freezes solid, we may be able to cross safely."

Sarah hesitated. "Have you walked on ice like that before?"

Tobiya nodded. "Yes, but this river is wide. It must freeze completely."

They fell silent, gazing at the water's dark surface. There was no ice yet, only the warning of it.

Sarah folded her arms. "Then we prepare."

Shana emerged, rubbing her eyes. "What's happening?"

"We're staying here for a while," Sarah replied. "And everyone must help."

Eldad stumbled out next, yawning. "If the sun's up and we're not walking, something's gone terribly right."

His comment brought chuckles, breaking the tension. Bathshua and her siblings followed, wrapping furs tightly. Affie and Kubal sniffed the air before curling near the fire. Even Martha emerged, steadier than before.

Johanan stood. "Tobiya and Jairus, let's each scout in a different direction for shelter. Whistle if you find anything."

Tobiya nodded. "Lemuel and Eldad, tend to the animals."

Sarah pulled her cloak tight. "We'll take the girls and look for food nearby."

They split off in quiet pairs. The forest was cold and watchful. Sarah stopped beside a spruce. "We can grind this bark into flour." She cut thin strips, and Shana packed them into a skin. The scent was sharp and earthy.

Tabitha crouched near a plant. "This is good for soup. Bathshua, help pack it."

Back at camp, they put together a rich herb-scented broth. Shana warmed her hands at the fire. Then, a sharp whistle. Johanan.

Footsteps charged through the brush. Johanan brushed twigs from his tunic. "It's a cave, dry and solid."

Tobiya added, "Signs of animals, but if we keep fires going, it should be safe."

Jairus exhaled. "Then Yahweh has guided us again."

Sarah passed bowls of soup. As warmth spread through her body, Shana's heart softened.

"We'll each carry supplies," Johanan said. "Let's move quickly."

The group moved with practiced rhythm. Bundles hoisted. Tents collapsed. Travois loaded.

The cave waited. Dark, wide, and still. They swept the floor, secured the animals, and set a fire near the entrance. As dusk fell, its light cast golden reflections on the stone.

Later, gathered by the fire, Shana looked around at her people, weary faces, bright eyes, calloused hands, and shared fire.

The river shimmered, slow and unknowable.

"Tonight is special," she announced. "Can we sing the Creation Hymn?"

A pause.

"Yes," came the answer.

The harp and lyre were tuned. The women began to play. Voices joined. And though the words were familiar, they rose like a fresh prayer, fragile, strong, ancient, new.

Shana closed her eyes and listened. Not because of comfort. Not because of certainty. But because they had stopped moving. Because they had light and warmth and one another. Because they remembered.

And because Yahweh had brought them here.

Chapter 27

THE STORM AND THE EAGLE

As the journey had stretched on, the passage of time became an enigma. The days blurred together, one bleeding into the next, until no one could say for certain how long they had traveled. They longed for structure, for a way to mark their progress, and most importantly, to restore the sacred rhythm of rest.

After much discussion, they resolved to count the days more carefully. To measure longer spans, they turned to the moon, watching its steady cycle of waxing and waning. Its phases, predictable and unwavering, became their guide.

They knew that, from the beginning, Elohim had established a pattern of seven days. But how could they hold to it when every sunrise and sunset felt indistinguishable from the last?

Jairus took it upon himself to mark each day on a strip of leather, rolling it up carefully to preserve their record. He studied the arc of the sun, the shifting shadows, and the quiet pulse of the seasons. Over time, he began to notice the subtle rhythms around them—the way the wind changed, the way the stars reappeared in different places

Most nights, the sky was so clear the stars felt close enough to touch. Around the fire, he gathered the children and taught them to trace patterns in the sky. They pointed out a great bull, a dipper, and a mighty hunter who watched from above. Their voices, hushed in reverence, named each formation, not for worship, but for knowledge and awe. The heavens had been placed above them for signs and seasons, after all.

***

Shana sat cross-legged beside her grandmother, watching Martha's fingers move with slow precision as she wove. The wooden loom creaked gently with each pass of the shuttle, its rhythm a quiet song in the stillness.

Nearby, Sarah, her cheeks smudged with faint streaks of dye, sorted through bundles of plant fibers. "This root should give a deeper red if we soak it longer." Sarah ran her fingers across the stained strands, mostly speaking to herself.

The men were busy, too. Tobiya, knife in hand, whittled a bow for Lemuel, testing its flex. Jairus hunched over a contraption he had been tinkering with for weeks. "If I can keep the travois from dragging so much—" he muttered, his voice trailing off as the others chuckled.

On a flat rock, Johanan worked on a harp for Shana. The scent of freshly carved cedar filled the air, mingling with the fire's warmth. He ran his hand along its frame, smoothing the wood. "It'll sound mellow," he said. "Warm and full."

Life in the cave had almost become routine. Almost safe.

But they all knew better.

***

That afternoon, the air grew heavier. The breeze shifted, colder and erratic. Clouds gathered low in the sky like a herd of restless animals.

As they finished their evening meal, the first drops began to fall, sharp and sudden. The wind picked up, snatching at the tent coverings.

Shana turned her face skyward. "It's coming fast."

"Get the furs inside!" Johanan shouted. "Cover the fire!"

The storm descended like a wave. Thunder cracked overhead. Rain lashed the rock face and flooded toward the cave's mouth. One of the goats bleated wildly as the wind knocked over a woven basket of dried roots. Eldad rushed to grab it, slipping in the mud.

Inside the cave, the fire hissed and smoked, struggling to stay alive. Water pooled near the entrance.

Shana sat frozen, her hands gripping her cloak. Her heart pounded like hooves in her chest. What if the cave floods? What if the animals scatter? What if the wind doesn't stop?

Sarah knelt beside her, wrapping an arm around her shoulders. "We're safe, Shana. Yahweh is with us."

Minutes passed. Then the thunder moved farther off. The rain softened, becoming a gentle rhythm against the rocks. Slowly, the air began to clear.

Shana stepped out with Bathshua. The wind had stilled. Moonlight spilled through the thinning clouds.

Then came the cry—a long, clear call from above. They looked up. An eagle soared overhead, its wings stretched wide, gliding silently across the silver-lit sky.

Bathshua whispered, "Do you think it's going right over the river?"

Shana drew in a quick breath. "Maybe... Maybe it is."

The fear inside her eased. Something about the eagle, the way it flew, the way it found its place above the storm, felt like a sign.

***

Back at the fire, Jairus stirred the embers and spoke softly. "This is why we count the days. So we remember who holds them."

They said little as they prepared for sleep. The storm had passed, but it left a silence behind, a silence that wasn't empty, but full.

Shana lay down with the unfinished harp beside her, her hand resting lightly on the cedar frame. The stars returned. The wind quieted. And she let herself believe, just a little more, that Yahweh was still leading them—through the days they carefully counted, and even the ones that slipped past unmarked.

Chapter 28

CROSSING THE FROZEN RIVER

Johanan burst into the cave, his breath misting in the cold air, eyes wide with urgency. "The river is frozen! I saw a herd of elk cross it. We can go!"

His words cracked open the stillness like thunder. In an instant, the camp stirred to life.

Tobiya stood and tightened his cloak. "Then we move now, while the ice holds. No waiting."

Sarah hesitated, her hands pausing in the warmth of the fire. Outside, the wind moaned through the trees, carrying the scent of pine and snow. "And once we're across? There's no shelter waiting for us."

Johanan knelt beside her, his voice low but certain. "We'll find it. There will be another cave. There always is." He reached for her hand, rough and cold. "Sarah, you've been so resilient. Let's pray before we begin. Jairus?"

Jairus bowed his head. "Yahweh Elohim, guide and direct us. It is hard to leave, but we trust You. Strengthen us. Provide a haven on the other side. Amen."

Martha, wrapped in her thickest cloak, nodded by the fire. "The walk will be short but necessary. Yahweh will help us."

Shana swallowed the lump in her throat. The cave's steady fire, the scent of cedar smoke, even the hard ground, had all become familiar. Safe. But deep down, she knew this was never meant to last.

The cave burst into motion. Sarah and Tabitha prepared food with swift, practiced hands. The pot hissed as stew was stirred. Wooden bowls were passed. Baskets filled with dried meats, nuts, and tubers were sealed and packed tight.

In the corner, Martha gestured to the looms. "Can we bring these?"

"We should," Tabitha replied. "Let's wrap them with tanned leather."

Sarah nodded. "Good thinking. Keep the cloth inside from rubbing."

Outside, the boys herded animals toward the clearing. Eldad shouted commands to the goats, his breath coming in white puffs. Kabul barked in rhythm with the wind.

"If everyone carries a basket with their bag, we'll manage," Johanan said. "It should take half the day, if we move steadily."

By midday, they sat shoulder to shoulder around the fire, steam rising from their cups of sage tea, bowls empty save for the final scraps of stew. Fat snowflakes began to fall, drifting lazily. Shana caught one on her glove, marveling at its fleeting beauty. So much detail in something so small.

Night fell slowly. The firelight etched the cave walls in amber waves. The dogs curled up near the children, their breath soft and steady. Sarah nudged Shana and Eldad toward their bedding. Before lying down, Shana dipped a finger into the small bowl of dye her mother had made from crushed berries and traced a simple arc on the cave wall—a rainbow to remember the one she'd seen.

"Tomorrow's long," Sarah said. "Rest well."

Before dawn, Johanan and Tobiya were already outside, herding animals and strapping down supplies. The snow from the night before blanketed the ground in soft white.

Shana slipped outside, rubbing her hands together. She watched as her father secured the final rope and nodded to Tobiya.

"Time," he said.

The fire burned low inside. Sarah stirred the last pot of tea, passing out warm bread to the children.

"Eat quickly. Then wrap up tight," she instructed.

The boys, despite the moment, couldn't resist lobbing snowballs. Sarah's scolding was swift and stern.

They gathered near the edge of the river. The sun had climbed just enough to throw light across the frozen water. It gleamed—hard and slick as ice could be, hiding whatever waited beneath its silent, sealed surface. Shana's steps crunched over snow. A low groan echoed beneath them.

She reached for Eldad's arm. "What if the ice cracks?"

He gave her a crooked smile, though his voice wavered. "Then we run really fast."

"Step by step," Sarah called, eyes scanning every movement. "Watch your footing."

The crossing dragged on. Each step felt heavy, deliberate. The wind bit at their faces, tugged at their cloaks. The dogs whined, hooves slid, breath came in short puffs.

Then, Johanan stepped onto the far bank. "We made it!"

A collective breath escaped the group. Smiles bloomed across tired faces.

The bull snorted and tossed his head, sending snowflakes flying.

Tobiya patted its side. "He was holding his breath, too."

Johanan wrapped Sarah in his arms. "Let's set up camp. Shelter won't find us."

Shana looked back at the river. It stretched behind them, silent and unmoving. A bridge of ice. What lay ahead remained a mystery.

They built a fire in the snow and huddled close. Sarah and Tabitha prepared hot drinks. The men took bows and dogs and spread out in search of shelter. The boys led the animals to graze.

Shana crouched by the fire. "There isn't much we can do now, is there?"

"No," Sarah said, rubbing her hands. "Sometimes waiting is harder than walking."

"Patience is part of the journey," Martha added. "And sometimes, it is the hardest part."

"We'll do what we can," Sarah said. "Let's keep the fire strong."

The girls gathered wood, piling it carefully.

As the sun began to set, its last light stained the snow in streaks of crimson and gold. Then, figures appeared through the trees.

"We found a cave!" Johanan called, breathless. "Do we move now? We have torches."

"Yes!" came the cry.

Animals were readied. Supplies were gathered. They moved as one through the snow, torchlight guiding the way.

The cave was dark and wide. Johanan circled with the torch, revealing high walls and space enough for all. They stepped further inside, leather-wrapped feet scuffing rock.

Blankets. Food. Quiet laughter.

A fire rose in the center.

Jairus bowed his head. "Thank You, Yahweh Elohim. For safe crossing. For shelter."

Shana curled beneath her blanket, the harp tucked close beside her. Outside, the wind tore through the trees. Inside, the cave held warmth and safety.

They had crossed the river.

They had found shelter.

But the journey was far from over.

TO THE SUNSET

When the dust of travel settles, what remains is not the place, but the people. The sun dips low,

not to the end of the day, but to light the way forward—into promise, into peace, into the unseen.

Chapter 29

FAR SIDE OF THE SEA: THE PROMISE

Mikael furrowed his brow, staring into the distance where the horizon swallowed the fading light. He exhaled sharply and ran a hand through his thick hair. What should he do? What *could* he do?

Five winters had passed since Mikael and his family had taken shelter near the sea. What began as a refuge had slowly become home—stone walls, thatched roof, and familiar routines carved from hardship and silence. Life had shaped him in those years, and still, something within him remained unsettled.

Something inside him twisted. There was a restlessness that would not fade. This Elohim, mysterious yet undeniably powerful, seemed to be calling him to journey toward the sunset. To leave his family behind hollowed his chest, but the pull of the unknown gnawed relentlessly at his soul.

He could hear the faint bleating of their goats from the pen and the chatter of his younger brothers by the fire when he glanced at them while they all continued to work with their father. His mother, Elizabeth, sang softly as she worked, her voice weaving peace into the camp's rhythm. But Mikael watched his mother closely as she worked. Her movements were slower than before, her shoulders slumped with exhaustion. Concern knotted in his chest.

"Mother… you've seemed tired lately. Are you feeling well?"

She offered him a small, tired smile. "I'll be fine, Mikael. I just need some rest."

Although Mikael wasn't convinced, he held his tongue.

To leave all this—his family, his home, and the security they had built. It felt impossible to go without any certainty of what lay ahead. Worse still, Elohim's command seemed to contradict everything practical. Shouldn't he be going in the other direction, where other families were known to have settled? There, he might find a wife, someone to build a life with. Elohim had declared that people must disperse and multiply, but if he stayed, would he ever find her? If he left, would he ever see his family again?

His chest tightened, and he swiped his palm against his tunic, his hands clammy with uncertainty.

When the evening meal began, his family's quiet conversation wrapped around him like a familiar blanket, but tonight, it offered no comfort. He knew he had to speak.

"Father, Mother," Mikael began, his voice low but steady, "these are my thoughts…" All eyes turned toward him. Jared, his father, set down his knife and looked directly at him. Elizabeth, his mother, folded her hands in her lap, a crease of concern forming on her brow. Mikah and Malaki, his younger brothers, leaned in, curiosity showing in their faces.

The words tumbled from Mikael, the prompting of Elohim, his fear of the unknown, and the unshakable feeling that he must obey. He confessed his struggle, how his heart ached to stay but burned to go.

A heavy silence fell over the group. The fire snapped and popped, sending sparks into the evening air.

Mikah scoffed, his voice sharp. "What are you thinking? You don't even know if there are people out there! You'll wander for nothing." His eyes narrowed, disbelief written all over his face.

Mikael's throat tightened. Did he sound foolish? Was this just a wild thought born of restlessness?

Jared lifted a hand, steady and calm. "Wait. Mikael's been thinking about this for a while—you can tell. Besides, other travelers have come and gone. They say people have settled far off. If Elohim is calling him, then Mikael must obey. I don't understand this Elohim either, but..." he paused, his gaze glanced to the fire, "...He's powerful. We saw it with the confusion of languages. I wouldn't stand in His way."

Elizabeth pressed her hand to her mouth to stifle a sob. Her voice trembled. "Oh, my heart breaks at the thought of you leaving, Mikael. To never see you again... never know if you are safe or well..." Her breath caught, and she shook her head. "But this is what we had to do with our families. If this is what Elohim is asking of you, then my blessing will go with you. Just... give us a few days to adjust, and we'll help you prepare."

Mikael let out a slow breath, his chest loosening. Tears burned behind his eyes. "Thank you, Mother. That... that makes it easier." His gaze swept the faces of those he loved most. Firelight danced across their features, warmth and sorrow in their expressions. "You're settled here now, safe in this home we've built together. Mikah and Malaki will be here to help. But before I leave, could we go on one last hunt together? I'll need meat for the journey."

The fire crackled as they sat quietly, each lost in their own thoughts. Jared finally broke the silence. "We're due for a hunt anyway. The warm weather has nearly passed, and it's starting to cool. Mikael, you'll need to find shelter before the winter sets in."

Mikael nodded. "I know. I've been thinking... if I head below the sea, the climate may be milder."

"We've already gathered in the grain, so we can leave for the hunt tomorrow," Jared said.

Malaki, grinning eagerly, leaned forward. "Can I say something? I want to go with Mikael! I love trekking. It is always a new adventure. Things get so boring here sometimes, the same thing over and over."

Mikael laughed, ruffling Malaki's hair. "You still need to grow up a little more! Father still needs your help!"

"But it's not fair! You get to go on a grand adventure."

Jared chuckled, "You don't remember the boring days, step by step, that brought us here."

Silence fell once more, save for the crackling of the fire. The tension in the air felt heavy, but resignation settled over them like nightfall without stars.

Elizabeth reached out and grasped Mikael's hand, her grip firm despite her trembling fingers. Her face was pale, streaked with tears. "Promise me something," she whispered.

Mikael turned toward her, his heart pounding. "Yes, Mother?"

Her voice cracked as she spoke. If you find a wife, bring her back to us someday so we know that you are alive and we get to meet her."

A lump formed in Mikaels's throat. "I promise I will try, Mother."

The home warmed with their shared smiles, but the reality of separation weighed heavily. Mikael stared into the fire, the flame's restless flicker echoing the ache within him. Tomorrow would bring another step closer to the unknown—to whatever lay waiting at the sunset's edge.

Elohim had a plan in place. Was there a young woman waiting for him to journey to her?

Chapter 30

OF THREADS
AND WILD THINGS

Shana surveyed the area, taking in the familiar sight of mud-brick homes bathed in the warm glow of the setting sun. The scent of earth and livestock mingled with the faint aroma of cooking fires, and the distant bleating of goats mixed with the laughter of children. A gentle breeze carried the sound of grain fields swaying beyond the village. The rhythmic pounding of grain being ground into flour reached her ears, blending into the steady rhythm of life that had settled in this place.

She smiled, crossing her arms over her chest. "This is my home—Mother and Father's home, Grandfather and Grandmother's... along with a home for Tobiya and Tabitha's family." Her voice carried a quiet pride. More families had joined them over the years, and their settlement had grown, not just in numbers but in strength. The flock of sheep had multiplied, the goats roamed in greater numbers, and even their herd of cattle had expanded. Their fields provided a variety of foods, some new discoveries, others treasured staples from their journey.

Jairus's wooden contraption, what he called a wheel, had proven invaluable. Johanan used a similar idea in shaping pottery. The wheel had found other uses, also. Attached to a travois, it made moving supplies easier, and they even used it in their machine for preparing the ground for planting. Shana ran a hand along the smooth wood of one such contraption, marveling at how much had changed. Had it really been five years since they wandered the vast, untamed lands with no idea where they would settle? She still remembered the aching uncertainty of those days, the way each sunrise held questions instead of answers. Now, here they stood, rooted in the land and thriving.

She was nearly sixteen now, a grown woman by the standards of her people, and skilled in the many tasks of running a home. Cooking had become second nature, as had working beside her mother to cultivate their crops. Grandma Martha's lessons in spinning and weaving had shaped her nimble hands, and now she wove not just with wool but also with flax—a fabric far cooler for the sweltering heat of summer. The soft strands slipped through her fingers as she thought of how their village had adapted to the land.

Shana met her grandfather along a familiar path and walked with him until something made her pause. She shaded her eyes. Movement on the ridge. She leaned forward, her breath hitching. A group of creatures surged over the hilltop, their manes streaming like dark rivers against the sky. They moved as one, a fluid, pulsing wave of power and grace. At the head, a magnificent black figure led them, its muscles rippling beneath a sleek coat, nostrils flaring as it tossed its head. Shana gasped, pressing a hand to her chest as her heart pounded in awe.

"Grandpa, what are those?"

He followed her gaze. Across the clearing, shapes emerged through thinning mist—tall, fluid, grazing near the edge of the trees. Coats shimmered in the morning light: russet, gray, black. The black lifted its head, definitely in charge.

"Horses," Jairus stated. His face softened with memory. "Oh yes, those are horses. I saw them long ago. Some people hunt them, but... Elohim must have something greater in mind for a creature that moves like that, like wind turned alive."

Shana's breath caught. "They're beautiful."

She watched the black stallion toss its head, nostrils flaring. Already her heart was galloping.

Shana called for Eldad. "Come with me, just for a little while. There are horses on the hills—I want to see them up close."

"Alright, for a little while. But I've got to help Father tonight," he said.

They climbed to the hills, crouched near a rise, and crept forward, hidden behind brush. The herd grazed peacefully, foals shifting beside their mothers. The black leader stood watch. Shana lowered her chin to her arm. Every flick of the horses' ears etched itself in her mind.

When Eldad nudged her, she didn't want to leave.

But as they backed away, the black stallion gave a sharp call, and the herd surged forward, hooves thundering.

That night, her hands worked the vegetables, but her thoughts still ran with the herd.

***

Another morning rose, the sky scrolled out in soft hues of lavender and gold as the sun crested on the horizon. A crisp breeze carried the scent of damp earth and the lingering fragrance of last night's fire. Shana stirred the embers in the hearth, coaxing them back to life as she set a pot of water to boil for tea. The faint hiss of bubbling water filled the air, blending with the distant chatter of birds greeting the new day.

"Mother, I'm going to Grandma's to work on the weaving. Need anything first?"

Sarah, busy kneading a mound of dough, wiped her flour-dusted hands on her apron. She smiled warmly. "No, go on. It's good to finish that piece!"

"It's been fun working with Grandma. She's told me some stories from when she was little—not Noah-old, but still old!" Shana laughed. "Did you know she's fifty? And Grandpa's sixty?"

She poured the tea into two clay cups, inhaling its earthy aroma. "We're using lots of the colors you all figured out from the plants we found."

"What's the project you are working on and what is it for?" Shana asked.

Sarah laughed, the sound rich and warm like the scent of baking bread. "That's a secret—for now. But you'll see soon enough."

Shana raised an eyebrow but grinned. "All right. I'll be back later."

Sarah watched her daughter disappear down the well-trodden path, her heart swelling with love. She chuckled softly. "Perfect timing. I can finally work on my project." She set to work on preparing a pot of stew. As she diced vegetables, her mind wandered to the fine flax veil she was weaving in secret. She wiped her hands, then smoothed a hand over the delicate fabric, her fingers tracing its intricate patterns. "Someday, Shana will see this," she whispered. "Yahweh, please... bring him here."

***

Martha gathered Shana in her arms the moment she entered, the scent of wool and dried herbs clinging to her robes. "Will you be able to weave today?"

Shana nodded. "Yes, Grandma. I know I've been behind, but I'll catch up. Where should I work?"

"Let's use that new blue today." Martha led her to the loom, where bundles of dyed yarn lay neatly arranged.

As Shana ran her fingers over the soft fibers, she glanced toward the open doorway, where the meadow stretched out beyond. The horses, their coats gleaming in the sunlight, moved with effortless grace out on the hills. Her gaze lingered on them, admiration shining in her eyes.

"Grandma, I really love watching the horses. They're amazing."

Martha chuckled. "Your grandpa says you're spellbound by them!"

Shana sighed. "I wish I could move like that. I've heard some people ride animals. Have you ever seen that? Maybe someday..."

Martha's eyes twinkled. "I've heard stories from travelers. Some say people ride horses as if they're part of them. Imagine!"

They settled in front of the loom; the room filled with the wooden frame. Martha pulled out the skein of deep blue yarn Sarah had helped her dye, the color rich and bold. "Let's put the blue into the warp every third row."

Shana nodded, pulling out her shuttle, a smooth wooden tool her grandfather had lovingly crafted for her. "This blue's from woad, right? What about the red?"

"Your mother used madder root," Martha explained. "She figured it out from the dyes she used on leather. Then we tried it on wool, and it worked beautifully. This one'll have red, blue, and the natural wool color."

Shana smiled as she guided the shuttle through the threads, enjoying the texture beneath her fingertips. "It's beautiful, Grandma."

Martha hesitated, then spoke softly. "Shana, your mother and I have been praying for someone, for you and Eldad. The younger ones will have matches here... but you're the one without anyone close to your age."

Shana's hands stilled for a moment before she nodded. "I've been praying, too. Thank you for praying with me."

They continued talking as they wove, the cloth slowly growing beneath their hands. The afternoon light cast a golden glow over the room, illuminating the vibrant threads as they intertwined, each row a testament to love and hope.

Martha reached out, smoothing the fabric. "Shana, I'd like this weaving to be for you when you find someone to share your life with. It would make a fine piece for your bedding."

Shana looked up, her chest tightening with emotion. "Oh, Grandma... that would be so special. I haven't thought much about preparing things for that time. I'll have to start on bowls and cups, too. Father makes good ones."

"Talk to your mother," Martha encouraged. "She'll want to help."

Shana nodded, her fingers still working the shuttle as a soft smile played on her lips. For now, she wove not just a fabric, but a future, stitch by stitch, and prayer by prayer.

The sun was setting in beautiful reds and oranges as Shana moved to return to her home. She looked longingly at the meadow as the black stallion rounded up his herd to move them to a more protected area for the night.

"Mother, did you make progress on your project? We got a lot done on ours."

"Of course I did."

"Grandma got me thinking. I should start preparing things in case someone comes. Someone who... might want to share life with me."

"That's true. We'll work on it."

***

Johanan and Eldad arrived from the fields and the animals. "Long day! We've been drying grasses for winter feed," Johanan sighed.

Jairus and Martha entered as well, joining them for the evening meal. Sarah had prepared lamb meatballs along with some garlic and onions, alongside some tubers roasted to perfection. An earthenware container of mountain tea, fragrant with the sweet and earthy flavors, steamed beside her. They still settled around the fire to keep warm, though the homes provided more shelter than in their early days.

***

In the morning, when Shana and Bathshua returned with water, Johanan met them with a concerned expression. "Girls, next time take one of the boys with you. We've seen some large tracks. Best to stay in the village for now."

Shana's brow furrowed. "What do you think it is?"

"We're not sure yet. We're watching the herds closely," Johanan replied. He glanced toward the fading light of the horizon, his jaw tight. Johanan, Tobiya, and Jairus, along with Eldad and Lemuel, all regularly carried their bows, but they also now carried spears.

When some of the men from the other families had arrived, they brought knowledge of spear-making, which they shared with Johanan and the others. In turn, Johanan and the others had taught them how to make bows and arrows. These people, also from the tribe of Javan, and each of the clans all spoke a slightly different language, but over time, they had begun to understand each other. The men had set up a rotation for watching the herds and flocks, as well as guarding the village. Safety was important to everyone.

Inside the house, Johanan addressed them all. "Some of us are going to try to track the animal tomorrow to see what it is and if we can eliminate it."

Sarah's eyes widened. "Be careful. You said it might be very big."

"Five of us will go track it. The rest will guard the herds, and the children, and the village," Johanan emphasized.

As the men spoke of their tracking plans for the morning, Johanan stretched. "I'd better turn in; we'll leave quite early."

Jairus turned to Martha with a tired smile. "We'd better get home. Long days now with the sun staying up late."

Shana lingered a moment longer by the doorway, staring out into the night. The wind stirred the trees, and she felt it again, that pull, gentle but certain. Something was coming.

Chapter 31

BEAST OF ANOTHER TIME

The first light of dawn had barely kissed the horizon when Johanan and Tobiya joined the other men, their breath clouding in the crisp morning air. The weight of their mission sat heavily upon them. They were tracking a beast of unknown ferocity, one that had already left destruction in its wake.

Johanan had considered bringing the dogs, but caution held him back. They knew too little about this predator. Instead, they relied on their own eyes and instincts. The first signs were clear in the soft mud. They were massive paw prints, larger than any they had seen before, pressed deep into the earth. The sheer size of them made Johanan's stomach tighten. This was no ordinary beast.

They followed the tracks through the underbrush, past trees scored with deep, vicious claw marks where the creature had marked its territory. A few feet ahead, a sickly-sweet stench filled the air, the unmistakable scent of decay. Johanan's heart pounded as they discovered a half-eaten carcass, the bones splintered as if snapped by powerful jaws. Flies buzzed angrily over the remains, feasting on the spoils of a hunt that had ended in the dead of night. The men exchanged glances. If the beast had fed recently, it might still be nearby.

As they neared the lake, a blur of movement caught their eyes. The creature was there—just a shadow among the trees at first, then a streak of power and muscle as it bolted deeper into the forest. The men instinctively crouched, their grips tightening on their spears. Johanan gestured quickly, signaling for them to fan out, encircling the predator.

The forest held its breath. Every step forward was slow, deliberate, their ears straining for any sound beyond the rustling leaves. A sudden gust stirred the trees, and a hush followed. Then, a sound tore through the silence like a blood-curdling scream, high-pitched and piercing, like a woman in agony. Johanan felt his skin prickle. It was a sound not meant for this world.

A branch cracked. Tobiya froze mid-step, his eyes locking on something through the foliage.

A saber-tooth tiger.

It stood poised at the base of a great tree, its massive shoulders heaving, its dagger-like fangs gleaming with the remnants of its last kill. Its golden eyes burned with untamed fury, locking onto the men who dared to challenge it. The muscles in its legs tensed. The beast snarled.

Johanan exhaled slowly, steadying his nerves.

"Now," he whispered.

In one swift motion, the men hurled their spears. The weapons cut through the air and struck true. The saber-tooth shrieked, a wail of pain and defiance that sent birds scattering from the treetops. It staggered, blood darkening its thick fur, but it didn't fall.

With a roar, it charged.

Panic surged. The men scrambled to ready their second weapons. Tobiya threw another spear. Johanan raised his own, aiming directly for the beast's throat. The saber-tooth lunged toward them, jaws gaping until Johanan's spear found its mark. The beast collapsed mid-leap, skidding across the forest floor, its limbs twitching.

Silence returned, broken only by ragged breathing.

Still, the men hesitated. Even in death, the beast was a monstrous sight. One of the men, voice rough with awe, muttered, "It's a saber-tooth tiger. I've hunted them before… but never one like this."

Johanan finally stepped forward, pulling his spear free. The others followed suit. The reality of what they had faced settled over them. They had taken down a creature thought to belong to another time, a beast of legend.

With respect, they removed its massive claws and formidable teeth, trophies of their hunt. The pelt was carefully stripped, a prize to remind them of the danger that lurked in these lands. The carcass was buried, lest it draw even worse predators from the depths of the wilderness. Unlike their usual hunts, none of them could stomach the thought of eating this creature. It was not prey. It was an adversary.

As they returned to the village, the weight of their discovery pressed upon them. The gathered people gasped as they beheld the enormous teeth and claws. Fear whispered through the crowd.

"The creature was a saber-tooth tiger!" Johanan announced, holding up the gleaming fangs. "We don't know if they travel alone or in packs, so we must remain vigilant."

Fear rippled through the villagers. Some of the women clutched their children tighter, and others whispered prayers. Tears welled in the eyes of a few, terror sinking deep into their hearts.

Eldad stepped forward, his youthful curiosity shining through his fear. "How big was it, really? A saber-tooth tiger? I thought they were creatures from before the ark."

Johanan gave a grim smile. "I thought so, too. But it seems Noah must have squeezed a pair in next to the lions."

Sarah rushed to Johanan, gripping his arm tightly. "Is everyone all right?" she asked, her voice barely above a whisper.

He wrapped an arm around her reassuringly. "Yes, Sarah. We're all safe. It was a united effort—without it, the outcome might have been different."

Jairus, having been relieved from his watch over the flocks, arrived in time to hear the tale. He crossed his arms and nodded solemnly. "We've grown too comfortable. After everything we've been through, we must not become complacent. We must be prepared for whatever else this land hides."

Shana appeared from the crowd, her eyes wide. "Father… were the screams we heard from the animal?"

Johanan nodded; his expression dark. "Yes. And I have never heard anything like it."

The village stood together in uneasy silence, the weight of the encounter settling over them like a heavy shroud. The beast was dead. But what else might be lurking in the unseen, just beyond their knowing?

Jairus could feel the heaviness in the gathering. "May I pray to thank Yahweh Elohim for His protection?"

"I don't bother with Elohim very often, but this seems like an appropriate time," one of the men admitted. There were nods of agreement.

"Yahweh Elohim, we do thank You for Your guidance and protection in this hunt. We faced a monster of the past, yet You allowed our spears to fly true. Continue to protect and guide us. Amen."

The heaviness lifted slightly as the prayer brought comfort, though mothers still held their children close as they returned home.

Martha called to Jairus and Johanan, "Eat here tonight. Sarah has been worried the whole time you were gone."

"Thank you, Martha, let me get what I have," Sarah responded.

"Mother, I will get it. You rest," Shana offered. She felt the reassuring weight of her knife at her belt as she walked, though she knew it would do little against such a beast. Still, it helped her feel safer. She quickly collected the bread they had prepared and returned.

As they ate, Johanan revealed, "The men have allowed me to keep one of the teeth for leading the hunt. Each of us received two claws. Tobiya was asked to tan the pelt—he is the best at it. The village may keep it as a symbol of our unity."

The warm stew Martha had made filled their bellies, the firelight painting soft patterns around them. Sarah had calmed. "We must begin preserving food soon. The root vegetables will be stored in the cave, and the legumes will be dried. Johanan and Eldad will hunt for winter meat."

Shana smiled. "I'm just glad we don't have to struggle as much for food anymore."

A voice called from the door. Tobiya and his family had arrived.

Martha beamed. "Come in, sit by the fire like old times."

Shana pulled Bathshua beside her. "So much has been happening! My grandma tells me she is praying for someone for me and for him to come to our village. Then, as if reminding me that Yahweh Elohim has told us to be fruitful and multiply," Shana mused. "Yahweh will have to provide the men who will become our partners. He led us here, so He can lead others too."

Bathshua laughed, brushing stray curls from her face. "I hope these men are ready to settle when they get here! No more trekking for me."

Shana chuckled, but a wistful sigh escaped her lips as she turned her gaze toward the sunset. A familiar longing stirred within her chest, one that had never fully faded.

"Sometimes when I see the beautiful sunsets," she murmured, "I still wonder, what lies beyond?"

As the sun set in streaks of pink and purple, the group that had traveled so far together found peace in each other's company, the day's terror melting into the comfort of familiarity.

Chapter 32

SOMETHING IN THE WIND

Dawn light bathed the village in soft gold as the fire was rekindled and morning scents filled the air—bread, smoke, and the promise of rest. It was the seventh day, a day to be still.

Sarah had the yogurmak ready, its tangy scent filling the air as warm bread rested beside it. When Tobiya and Tabitha arrived with their family, they brought fresh curds, and Jairus and Martha added baked fish to the meal. The simple feast was humble yet rich, a gift from Yahweh Elohim. As they bowed their heads, Jairus prayed, his voice deep and reverent. "Thank You, Yahweh Elohim, for providing food for us. Bless those who have prepared it. Help us to be refreshed as we partake in this day of rest. Amen."

For a time, there was only the soft murmur of satisfaction as they ate. After a while, Jairus spoke again. "Let us remember why we rest today. Elohim finished the work of creation by the seventh day; so, on the seventh day, He rested from all His work. Elohim blessed the seventh day and made it holy."

Martha stretched her arms, smiling. "Do you think we could have some music this morning?"

Sarah nodded. "I believe our instruments are ready."

Shana retrieved the harps from the shelf, their polished wood cool beneath her fingertips. Tabitha and Bathshua reached for their own instruments, their lyres. They strummed softly as they warmed up. The familiar melodies, first the solemn Creation hymn, filled the air, blending with the morning breeze, followed by other songs that spoke of Yahweh's glory. The music lifted their spirits, carrying them to a place of quiet reflection. The flames of the fire caused the light to dance on the faces of the gathered family. Afterward, a peaceful hush settled over them with unspoken prayers and gratitude, broken only by the occasional sip of tea and quiet conversation.

The moment was broken as Eldad and Lemuel rose to tend the animals, the dogs, Kabul and Affie, padding after them. By the fire, Hadassah sat with a puppy curled up beside her, its small body radiating warmth against the morning chill.

Shana and Bathshua chatted about their weavings. Shana ran her fingers over the intricate patterns of a half-finished textile, its colors woven with precision and care.

"Bathshua," Shana confided hesitantly, "Grandma told me that the beautiful weaving we've been working on is for me… for some day when I have someone to share my life with. She said I should start preparing other things as well. We talked about Yahweh Elohim sending someone. Are you praying for someone to come? Has your mother talked to you about it?"

Bathshua smiled. "I can wait a little while longer, but yes… There isn't anyone in the village for us. We'll have to encourage each other and trust that someone will come."

Shana embraced her. "Yes, we can pray and encourage each other."

After a moment of contemplation, Shana turned to her father. "Father, may I go to the hills for a little while? I'll take my spear."

Johanan studied her before nodding. "All right, but remember, stay in sight. We'll be outside soon, keeping an eye on the hills. I presume you want to see the horses?"

She grinned. "Yes, but I'll be careful. Bathshua, do you want to come?"

"Not today, but thanks for asking."

Shana quickly gathered her spear, a small waterskin, coverings for her feet, and some dried meat. "I'll return when the sun is midway down. Mother, Father."

Sarah gave her a measured look. "Be careful. You never know what you might find!"

The thrill of freedom surged in Shana's chest as she left the village behind. The crisp autumn air tingled against her skin as she climbed toward the hills, the scent of drying leaves and damp earth filling her lungs. Cresting the ridge, she dropped to her stomach, her chin resting on her arms as she peered into the valley below. The sight of the horses stole her breath.

The black stallion stood tall, muscles rippling beneath his sleek coat as he watched over his herd. The mares grazed peacefully, tails flicking, their bodies thickening in preparation for winter. But something was wrong. The stallion's ears pricked forward, his nostrils flaring. A moment later, he whinnied sharply, herding his family into motion. The horses streamed into the hills in a fluid, breathtaking display of power and grace.

Shana's heart pounded. Wouldn't it be incredible to move like that? But how could such freedom ever be possible?

A sudden sound, footsteps, quick and sure, made her stiffen.

From the shadow of the mountain, a voice rang out. A voice she did not recognize.

"There… the black stallion with his herd."

Mikael slowed his steps, the breath catching in his throat. The sight struck him with unexpected familiarity, the fluid motion of dark manes, the stallion's commanding presence.

"I've seen them before," he murmured aloud, eyes following their silhouettes across the slope. "So, I've found you again."

He stood motionless for a heartbeat, memory rising unbidden—a glimpse across a misted ridge weeks ago, just before he left the highlands near the sea. The horses had appeared like shadows from the edge of a dream, cresting on top of a far hill. He had paused in wonder then, watching them disappear into the haze. Something about them had stayed with him—their strength, their freedom, their impossible beauty. He had taken it as a sign. And now, here they were again.

This was no accident.

He stepped closer.

A figure stood among the grass. A woman. Young, poised, and utterly unexpected.

Mikael blinked. Was he imagining her? The herd was vanishing over the ridge, but she remained, unmoving, watching them.

"A beautiful woman…" he whispered, awe laced in his tone. "Where could she have come from?"

Shana spun, her breath catching. A stranger! A young man stood a short distance away, his black hair falling in untamed waves, his form strong and lean. Her pulse thundered in her ears as she instinctively raised her spear into a throwing position. His clothing, the way he held himself, it all spoke of a journey long and difficult. His sky blue eyes met hers, filled with wonder.

He halted and slowly raised his hands, palms out in a gesture of peace as he looked into eyes the color of dark dates. He spoke, his voice calm, but the language was foreign to her ears, its cadence unlike anything she had ever heard. He gestured toward the horses, his gaze questioning, and spoke again.

Shana hesitated, searching his face, tension thrumming in her limbs, but something about his presence didn't feel threatening. Her grip on the spear loosened slightly. She pointed toward the horses and called, "Horse."

A smile broke across his face, and he repeated, "Horse." Then, placing a hand on his chest, he called back, "Mikael."

Shana hesitated, watching him. Then, slowly, she lowered her spear and placed her hand on her chest to match his. "Shana."

The sun stood midway to sunset. Realization struck. She needed to return before her father worried. Glancing back at Mikael, she gestured for him to follow. His expression shifted, curiosity deepening as he gathered his belongings. He followed, and she stole glances at him over her shoulder to ensure he was there.

As they neared the village, Shana spotted her parents resting in the sunlight. Her heart pounded with excitement. She bounded forward. "Father, Mother, this is Mikael!"

Johanan and Sarah rose, eyes fixed on the stranger.

"Mikael?" Johanan echoed, his voice calm but wary.

Mikael nodded, placing a hand on his chest. "Mikael."

Johanan pointed to himself. "Johanan." He turned to his wife. "Sarah."

Shana turned on her heel, "Father, I'll get Grandpa. Maybe he will understand."

She sprinted toward Jairus's house, breathless as she entered. "Grandpa! Grandma! Please come! Grandma, how much have you been praying? Come see Mikael!"

Jairus and Martha exchanged looks before following her outside, their curiosity evident. As they approached, Mikael straightened, his blue eyes wary yet hopeful. When Jairus saw Mikael, his eyes flickered with understanding.

"Hello, Mikael. Where are you from?" he asked in the original language, the one Noah and the elders still spoke.

Mikael's face brightened. "I have come from the other side of the sea. My family is of the tribe of Gomer, the clan of Riphath."

Sarah's hand flew to her mouth. "Jairus, invite him inside. He has traveled far. Shana, didn't I tell you that you never know what you will find! Heat some water."

Jairus nodded, "Mikael, come inside, you have traveled far."

Shana's heart raced as she led him inside and pointed to a fur by the fire. Mikael settled onto the fur. His gaze roamed the warm interior, the firelight playing against the clay walls. He exhaled slowly, murmuring, "I have not been around this many people in a long time."

The villagers gathered outside, eager to see a new person, maybe hear some news. Jairus waved them back. "Give him some time. We will introduce him tomorrow."

Shana knelt beside him, offering a cup of mountain tea. As he took it, his fingers brushed hers. A thrilling tremor coursed through her, unexpected and electric. Her heart pounded as she busied herself filling other cups.

Mikael took a sip and sighed with a smile, "This tastes like home." Jairus continued to translate as Mikael spoke.

Johanan affirmed, "Mikael, it is good to have you here. May we thank Elohim for bringing you safely to us?"

Jairus translated to Mikael.

"Elohim… I know so little about Him, but He has called me to journey to the sunset."

Jairus prayed, "Thank You, Elohim, for bringing Mikael safely on this journey to the sunset as we have traveled. Continue to guide him and direct him."

Shana's breath caught. "You were called to journey to the sunset? We traveled that path until we arrived here. Sometimes, when I watch the sunset, my heart longs to know what lies beyond." She met her mother's gaze, a silent question passing between them. Her mother smiled knowingly.

Later, when Mikael left with the men, Martha chuckled. "Take a breath, Shana."

Shana exhaled, dazed. "Grandma, how can prayers be answered this quickly?"

Sarah laughed. "Not quickly, child. I have prayed for someone for you since the day you were born."

Shana, barely breathing, silently said to herself, "Did you pray for a man this handsome to walk into my life?"

Chapter 33

NEW WORDS, OLD SONGS

Tabitha came by, her eyes wide with curiosity. "What is happening there? Some man appears from the hills?"

Shana laughed, the sound light but laced with excitement. "Yes, and are you praying for someone for Bathshua that is extremely handsome? I will have to ask this man to somehow tell his brothers to come!"

Tabitha smirked. "Oh, and we have to wait until tomorrow to see this man?"

"Well, Lemuel is with the men. Did Tobiya join them? They will probably come to the house with them. Maybe you and the girls could slip in and join us for the evening meal," Sarah whispered. "I have a venison roast baking and will add some vegetables soon."

Tabitha inhaled deeply, savoring the rich aroma wafting from the fire. "Mmm, I think we can find something to bring." She peeked out cautiously before quickly crossing back to her home.

Shana shifted uneasily, stirring the pot with more force than necessary. "It will be good for them to come, but Mother, I don't want Bathshua getting any ideas. She wants to wait a while."

Martha chuckled, eyes twinkling. "Maybe you should wait and see what Mikael thinks about the women suddenly appearing before him."

The men returned. Shana busied herself with the food, yet her gaze kept drifting toward Mikael. There was something about him, an air of mystery, of resilience hardened by time and solitude. Her father approached for a drink and, catching her gaze, nodded subtly. A warmth bloomed in her chest, though she quickly turned back to her task, cheeks burning.

Tabitha and the girls soon arrived, slipping into the gathering with bright eyes and knowing smiles. Bathshua nudged Shana playfully. "Can I help with anything?" she asked, taking the cups from Shana's hands to pass around.

Shana straightened, shaking herself slightly. "Here, take these bowls too." She busied herself, willing her heart to steady.

Jairus spoke, his voice carrying easily over the quiet hum of conversation. "We have learned some basic words from Mikael in his language, and he has learned some of ours. We have a few more people who have joined us. Mikael, these are Tobiya's family: his wife, Tabitha, and his daughters, Bathshua and Hadassah."

Hadassah, her small frame barely reaching Mikael's chest, giggled. "Your hair is the blackest black!"

Mikael tilted his head, his sky blue eyes flicking toward Jairus. "Tell her she is the smallest woman I ever remember seeing."

Hadassah's eyes widened before she quickly hid behind her mother, peeking out with shy amusement.

The scent of roasted venison and seasoned vegetables filled the space, mingling with the crisp night air. The women brought out the food, placing it before the gathered company. Jairus lifted his hands. "Let me pray over the food. Dear Yahweh Elohim, thank You for this meal, for the hands that prepared it, and for the nourishment it will bring. We also thank You for bringing Mikael to us. Amen."

Mikael, brow furrowed slightly, turned to Jairus. "Jairus, what does it mean when you say Yahweh Elohim? I know a little of Elohim as God, but I have never heard of Yahweh Elohim."

Jairus's expression softened. "Yahweh is personal. He desires to know you and have a personal relationship. The stories we heard from Noah at the time of confusion of the languages tell of this relationship. We will share the stories with you, if you would like."

Mikael nodded thoughtfully. Shana interjected, her voice eager. "Grandpa, that would be wonderful. We haven't heard the stories in a long time."

Jairus stroked his beard. "Let me think and pray on this. Perhaps it is time to share the stories with the villagers as well. When we introduce Mikael tomorrow, we will see how they feel about it."

Johanan, leaning back, nodded. "That sounds good to me, but for tonight, to end our day of rest, let us have some more music and worship Yahweh Elohim."

Tabitha and Bathshua had brought their instruments, as was their custom, and Shana retrieved their harps, settling where she could watch Mikael without being too obvious. Her fingers trembled slightly as she plucked the strings, fine-tuning the notes.

Jairus turned to Mikael. "Do you know any songs to Elohim? Especially the Creation Hymn?"

Mikael shook his head. "No, I haven't heard music for a long time, except for the birds singing and the animals making their noises. I suppose my mother hums sometimes when she works."

Johanan smiled. "We sang the Creation Hymn this morning, but I think we would all like to sing it again."

Martha leaned forward. "Jairus, why don't you tell Mikael the meaning of the words before we sing? Then he will be able to listen and take in the flow of the song."

Jairus agreed, translating as the instruments played softly. Then, voices lifted in harmony.

They continued singing for some time. As the final notes faded, Shana set down her harp and rose, moving fluidly to fetch more tea for everyone. The fire flamed, casting golden light across their faces. A cool breeze slipped in, sending shivers through the group. Johanan stood, moving to shut the door.

"Winter will soon be upon us," he expressed. He turned to Mikael. "What is your plan? Do you intend to continue your journey, or would you stay and winter in our village?"

Jairus translated, a knowing smile tugging at his lips. "It has been an eventful day. Would you like to think over Johanan's question at least overnight?"

Mikael laughed, the sound warm and rich. "Those are big questions. I will try to have answers by morning."

Shana sipped her tea, heart pounding. I could help you answer those questions! she thought.

Chapter 34

THREAD BY THREAD

Johanan chuckled as he settled onto a low log. "We have had other travelers come and go, but I think this one might stay for a while. My thought is to take Mikael with Eldad and me as we work this morning. Then, after the midday meal, we'll introduce him to the village. I will see what Father is thinking."

As they ate, the warm aroma of sage tea filled the room. Shana cupped her hand around her clay vessel, letting the steam rise to her face. The earthy, slightly peppery scent intertwined with the sharp freshness of morning air seeping through the open door. She sipped, the warmth spreading through her, calming her swirling thoughts.

"Mother, what do you need me to help you with today? I would like to weave with Grandma at some point."

Sarah's hands worked deftly, kneading dough for the midday meal. "We can talk about the basic things one would like to have when setting up a home."

Shana tilted her head, considering. "Oh, that would be good, I hardly remember back to when we were trekking and had only a few of the basics."

By now, Johanan and Eldad had left, their figures visible in the distance, walking with Mikael toward the fields. Shana watched them go, a strange mixture of nervousness and curiosity tightening her chest.

Sarah spoke again; her tone practical. "When you are traveling, you only want enough dishes for the two of you—two cups and two bowls, along with a pot for food and another for water. You are used to spices, so you will want something compact to keep them in. It is good to have a change of clothes in case you get wet. Your father will want you to take your spear, bow, and keep your knife in your belt."

Shana turned slightly, glancing through the doorway toward the fields. In the distance, three figures moved steadily: her father, Eldad, and Mikael. The breeze lifted the edge of his cloak, and though she couldn't see his face, something in his posture, alert and steady, made her heart skip. She quickly turned back to her mother, hoping her thoughts weren't too obvious.

Shana traced the rim of her cup, her mind drifting between past memories and uncertain futures. "Grandma wants me to take the beautiful weaving we are working on. Will I have room?"

Sarah wiped her hands on a cloth. "That remains to be seen. What kind of traveling will you do? Now, these are all good things to think about and prepare, but you need to be patient to see what will happen. We'd better get the midday meal going."

They stoked the fire, the rich scent of burning wood filling the air as a lamb roast was set to cook. Shana watched the flames flicker; her thoughts wandering. Soon, they would add vegetables, the natural sweetness mingling with the savory aroma of the meat.

Sarah glanced at her daughter. "Let's look at the cloth I have finished weaving to see if we can make another tunic for you. You haven't sewn much, so I need to work with you to make one for yourself—and a man's tunic if we have time. Why don't you go to your grandmother's for a little while this morning? Your grandparents should come back with you for the meal, and then the villagers may start arriving."

Shana let out a small breath, trying to steady her emotions. "A lot is happening. I will be back in time to help you." She pulled her shawl tighter around her shoulders and stepped out into the morning light, making her way toward her grandparents' home.

She knocked on the wooden door, and after a moment, Martha opened it, her wise eyes warm with welcome.

"Are you in a hurry?" her grandmother observed, gesturing for her to enter. Inside, the familiar scent of wool and drying herbs filled the room.

Shana offered a sheepish smile. "We can't finish today, but we will keep working on it."

Martha chuckled softly and nodded toward the loom. "Your mother and I spoke of preparations. There's much a young woman might begin gathering."

Shana shifted beside her, her fingers brushing the edge of the woven cloth. "She mentioned a few things—things I might want someday. What do you think I should begin with?"

Martha gave a thoughtful hum. "Linen for clothing for summer and wool for winter; the same for bedding. And perhaps some smaller cloths... for little ones, should that day come."

Shana flushed, glancing toward the doorway. "Grandma!"

Martha's eyes twinkled. "Child, I've seen many seasons come and go. Sometimes, those seasons arrive sooner than we expect."

Shana gave a quiet laugh, her voice tinged with something between shyness and hope. "Maybe... but we don't even know if this man will stay or if he sees me at all."

Martha reached over, resting a warm hand atop Shana's. "Let that unfold in its time. But there is no harm in weaving with the future in mind."

Their conversation continued as they worked on the weaving. The blue thread was nearly finished, its deep hue reminiscent of the sky just before nightfall. Shana let her fingers glide over the fabric, feeling its fine texture.

"You, of course, will both come for a midday meal. Then Grandpa can be ready for the villagers. I'd better head back now to help Mother."

Martha nodded. "Go on, then. There's much ahead for you, I think."

Shana stepped out into the daylight, her heart lighter but her thoughts no less filled with wonder.

Chapter 35

THE SOUND OF HER NAME

The men returned from the fields, their foot coverings caked with mud, and the chill of the late autumn air clung to their fur coverings. The scent of stew, rich and savory, filled the air, mingling with the warm aroma of fresh bread. Inside the dwelling, the hearth crackled, casting a warm glow on the earthen walls and offering a comforting reprieve from the encroaching cold. Shana ladled steaming portions of stew into wooden bowls, the fragrant broth releasing hints of garlic and herbs, and then she poured the linden tea, its floral scent delicate and soothing.

Jairus and Martha had joined them for the meal, and the small space buzzed with quiet conversation and the occasional scrape of spoon against bowl. Shana moved gracefully among them, handing out bread, her fingers brushing Mikael's as she passed him a piece. He murmured what sounded like words of thanks, his deep voice laced with a soft foreign lilt. Then he turned his gaze to Jairus, his expression serious yet hopeful.

"Jairus, " he hesitated, pausing as if to gather his thoughts. "I would like to ask if it will be all right if I stay with you through the winter. I would like to know all of you, and learn more about Yahweh Elohim."

Jairus translated, his eyes brightening. "Sounds wonderful to me. What about the rest of you?"

Johanan grinned as he tore off a piece of bread. "It can get boring during the winter without much fieldwork. We still have to tend the flocks, but it would help to hear someone else's stories."

Eldad leaned forward eagerly. "It would be good to have someone closer to my age. Grandpa, will you help us understand each other?"

Jairus chuckled. "What about you women? Will it be all right to cook for another man who may eat more than his share?"

Shana looked down, her cheeks burning with sudden warmth. She fidgeted with the edge of her sleeve and murmured, "All right."

Sarah exchanged a knowing smile with Martha. "It is all right with us."

Jairus clapped his hands together. "Well, that's settled then! The villagers will be here soon. Mikael, we won't expect you to know everyone's name today."

Mikael smiled, his gaze sweeping over the gathered faces. "I will practice. Let's see—Shana, the first one I met, as I recall. I called her a beautiful woman…" He glanced at her, and she turned red again, busying herself with the dishes. "Then Jairus, my translator, Johanan and Sarah, and of course, Eldad, who apparently wants some man-to-man talks."

His accent wrapped each word in an unfamiliar rhythm. Shana found herself replaying the way he had said her name—*Shana*—softened by his voice, reshaped by a different tongue. It was the same name, yet it had sounded entirely new.

Jairus nodded. "Yes, you have everyone."

Mikael glanced down, noticing the two dogs curled at their feet. "Ah, and Kubal and Affie," he added, scratching behind Kubal's ears. The dog sighed contentedly. Affie, meanwhile, rested her head on Shana's leg, her tail wagging lazily.

Sarah looked toward the entrance. "The villagers are arriving. We'd better go outside, I don't think there is room for everybody in here. The sun is out today, so I think it will be warm enough."

Everyone scrambled to their feet. As Shana rose, the dogs moved at the same time, tangling around her legs. She stumbled, her arms flailing, and before she could catch herself, Mikael reached out. His hands found her waist, steadying her with firm, gentle pressure. She inhaled sharply, her pulse quickening at the unexpected closeness. Her eyes met his, deep and unreadable in the dim firelight.

"You didn't need to do that," she blurted out, flustered, "but thank you!"

He smiled, his hand lingering for a brief moment on her shoulder, as if ensuring she was truly steady before letting go.

Outside, the villagers gathered beneath the sprawling branches of the old tree whose leaves were blazing red. Sunlight filtered through the leaves, scattering dappled patterns across the ground. Jairus raised his hands for silence.

"This is Mikael, from the far side of the sea. He traveled for two moons to reach us. He has decided to stay the winter with us, so you will all have time to get to know him."

Approval rippled through the crowd, and then, a warm round of claps.

Jairus turned to Mikael. "Let me introduce families so you have an idea of who belongs to whom." One by one, the families were introduced, the children peeking shyly from behind their mothers' skirts. Then Jairus asked, "What questions do you have for Mikael?"

Tobiya spoke up first. "What kind of hunting do you do? It is time for us to hunt for the winter."

Jairus translated, and Mikael nodded thoughtfully before replying. "We mainly hunt deer, but there are also gazelles and ibex. A bear, when we are fortunate, is a great help for winter provisions. We also trap rabbits and other small animals for food and fur.

One of the older women asked, "What about your mother? What does she do? Does she weave?"

Mikael's face softened. "My mother does what women do. She makes our home warm and filled with love. She cooks, she cleans, and yes, she weaves the flax and wool. She puts up with all of us men."

Jairus translated, and the women clapped appreciatively, nodding in approval.

Then, someone asked, "Where are you going?"

Mikael's expression grew solemn. "Elohim is directing me on a journey to the sunset. But a rest here may help me learn more about Him."

Jairus took a deep breath. "Mikael would like to hear the stories of the beginnings. Some of you may have heard the stories before, but others haven't. As winter progresses, I thought I could share them with you, as we have done in the past. We can also hear some of Mikael's stories. Would you be interested?"

A cheer rose from the crowd, and the clapping started again. It was decided, then. Stories would fill the long winter nights, and Mikael, a traveler from the far side of the sea, would become part of their village, at least for a season.

Chapter 36

TRUSTING THE WILD

Mikael awoke to the crisp morning air, the scent of damp earth mingling with lingering smoke from the hearth. Before his eyes even opened, a plan had already settled in his mind.

I have to check on the horses today. And I need... help.

He stretched beneath the woven blanket, which slipped from his shoulders. Outside, the village sprang to life, footsteps over packed earth, the distant lowing of cattle, the rhythmic thud of a wooden pestle grinding grain.

Inside, Jairus and Martha were already stirring. Martha's hands, dusted in flour, moved steadily over a flat stone as she shaped morning bread. Jairus hovered near the fire, squinting at a cloth marked with symbols. He exhaled slowly.

"In a moon phase, it will be time to start a new year," he muttered to himself. "We should offer a sacrifice then. Maybe if we tell the stories of the beginning, the ones that speak of sacrifice, the villagers will understand."

Mikael stepped inside, rubbing sleep from his eyes. "I think I understood your words about the sacrifice. I want to hear those stories, too."

Jairus looked up, surprise softening into approval. "Then we'll plan to hear one soon. Perhaps tonight."

Before Mikael could respond, the door flap lifted. Cool air rushed in with Johanan and Eldad, their garments still streaked with soil.

"We're finishing up the fields today," Johanan announced. "We want to be done before the next cold snap."

Mikael straightened. "If we finish today, may I check on the horses tomorrow? They're still in the hills. I'd like to try to guide one. I've seen travelers ride horses before, and I want to see if it's possible. I'd like to bring someone with me."

Johanan raised an eyebrow. "That's the longest speech I've heard from you, and I think I understood most of it." He clapped Mikael on the back. "You're learning our language faster than we're learning yours! Do you want Shana's help?"

Mikael nodded, a little hesitant.

Eldad smirked. "Then I suppose I should go too. Wouldn't want the villagers spinning stories about my sister."

Mikael smiled faintly, then grew serious. "I'll ask her at midday meal."

***

Shana's fingers moved rhythmically through the threads of the loom, the blue and red pattern slowly unfolding under her touch. Across from her, Sarah continued with the pattern. Nearby, Martha leaned forward with a knowing glint in her eye.

"Shana," she whispered, "Mikael's going to ask you to go with him to check on the horses. He wants to try to guide one. He'll ask at the midday meal. Act surprised."

A thrill shot through Shana. Her hands faltered, then resumed weaving.

"I am getting close to the horses now," she murmured. "It would be wonderful to touch one."

Martha nodded slightly, then leaned back, her tone turning casual. "How are your supplies coming along?"

Sarah added with a playful note, "Johanan's even made her some wooden bowls and cups."

Shana paused in her weaving. "He seems to like Mikael," she mused, quieter now. "It will be hard to leave. But I suppose you both did the same."

Sarah exchanged a glance with Martha, then leaned closer. "He seems to care about you, too."

Heat crept up Shana's neck.

"Patience," Sarah reassured with a smile. "That time will come."

"Like this weaving," Martha added. "You can't rush it or it falls apart."

Shana sighed, her fingers brushing the pattern once more. "I get nervous."

"Then let's make sure you're at the midday meal," Martha emphasized. "We'll help you with his words."

They rolled up the finished weaving together, wrapping it in soft skins. A quiet peace settled over the room, unspoken but understood.

***

The meal filled the home with warmth and scent. Stew bubbled gently, its savory aroma mingling with the crisp scent of bread heating on the hearth stones. The men returned from the fields, faces streaked with dust, hands coarse from labor.

Shana passed steaming bowls around, Sarah followed with cups of mountain tea, and Martha tore flatbread into pieces to share.

Jairus took a sip of his tea and set it down with a thoughtful nod. "Tonight, we'll tell the story of the beginning. We will continue to tell the rest of the stories. The new cycle is near, and we must prepare for the sacrifice. It's getting colder. We'll need to gather indoors."

"Eldad," Johanan directed, "get Lemuel to help you spread the word after we eat."

Jairus turned to Mikael. "There may be weather coming tomorrow. Maybe see if your idea works this afternoon instead."

Mikael blinked. Afternoon. So soon. He cleared his throat, heart pounding. "Shana," he said, forcing himself forward, "I was wondering, would you come with me? To the hills? The horses seem to trust you more than me. I want to try to... guide one. Back home, travelers rode them. Maybe we can try."

Shana's heart leapt, but she steadied her voice. "That would be wonderful. I haven't been up there in a few days."

Johanan gave a pointed look. "Eldad will go with you."

"Of course," Shana responded, glancing at Martha, who was hiding a smile.

"Father," Shana continued, gathering the bowls, "can we take some grain? Maybe it will be a treat."

"A little," Johanan replied. "They mostly graze, but it may help."

***

As the others cleared the meal, Shana stepped aside, gathering her wrap and securing a pouch of grain. Her hands worked steadily, but her mind drifted.

He asked me. And he said my name.

She repeated the sound of it silently. His accent wrapped each syllable in an unfamiliar rhythm. It made her name feel different, weightier, more real.

When Eldad returned from his errand, the three of them set out. The afternoon air was cool and golden, brushing their faces with wind from the hills. Shana walked beside Mikael, a quiet flutter in her chest, the sound of her name still echoing in her thoughts.

Chapter 37

SOFT AS BREATH

The horses were unafraid as Shana, Mikael, and Eldad approached the herd grazing the golden autumn hills. A gentle breeze carried the scent of trampled grass and the distant rippling of a stream winding through the valley below. The villagers had not needed to hunt them for food, as the land had been generous with other game.

They crouched low, inching forward until they reached the concealment of a thicket. From here, they could observe the herd without disturbing it. The horses' coats gleamed in the slanting light of the setting sun, thickening in preparation for the coming winter.

Mikael's voice was barely a whisper. "I would love to capture the black stallion, but I don't want to take him from his herd. There's a younger stallion—glossy brown, strong, but he hasn't challenged the black yet. What about you, Shana? Which one have you been thinking about?"

Shana's eyes followed the horses, taking in their movements, their quiet power. She had watched them for days now, trying to decide. Finally, she answered, "I like the chestnut one with the blaze on her face."

Mikael nodded. "Eldad, you're here to help us. Are you interested in having one?"

Eldad considered. "It is an interesting idea. But we'll have to help Father build an enclosure. How high do you think it would need to be to keep them from jumping out?"

Mikael exhaled thoughtfully. "Good point. We'd also need a contained space to train them. I haven't seen them jump much, but a fence about the height of a man should be enough."

Silence settled over them as they continued watching the herd. The horses moved with a natural grace, tails flicking, nostrils flaring as they tested the crisp air.

The black stallion lifted his head and stared in their direction. His dark eyes gleamed with intelligence as he tossed his head, a warning. Shana held her breath. The stallion's presence was commanding, a ruler among his own kind.

Slowly, Shana reached into the pouch at her side and scattered a handful of grain in the grass ahead. The faint rustling of kernels falling was lost in the breath of the wind.

Mikael stated, "If we could build an enclosure at the base of the hills, we might be able to drive the horses into it. Then, once we secure the ones we want, we can release the rest. But we don't know if they'll winter here. Something moved them here in the first place. I first saw them after I had traveled for a few days, then I would see them once in a while."

Eldad turned to Shana. "They seem to be comfortable with you. Why don't you try approaching them? Have some of the grain ready."

Mikael tensed beside her. "I don't know if it's safe. Maybe I should do it."

Shana hesitated. Her heartbeat quickened as she considered the risk, but also the opportunity. "How about I go first, and you stay right behind me?"

Mikael met her gaze, concern in his eyes. After a pause, he nodded. "All right. Just be careful."

Shana rose slowly from her crouched position, stepping out from the cover of the brush. Mikael shadowed her, his presence steadying. The stallion's ears flicked forward, muscles coiled, ready to react. Shana stretched out a hand and let a clicking sound escape her lips, an instinctive call. A young foal took a hesitant step forward, nostrils quivering. Then another. It reached her outstretched hand and nibbled at the grain resting in her palm.

Shana's breath caught at the warm, soft touch of the foal's nose. Before she could fully savor the moment, the stallion snorted and whirled, driving the herd into motion. Hooves pounded against the earth as they galloped to the far side of the hills, their presence nothing more than a fleeting whisper of dust in the fading light.

Shana stood frozen; her palm still open as if cradling the ghost of the foal's touch.

Mikael stepped to her side, his hand finding her arm. "Are you all right? Did he nip you?"

Shana turned to him, eyes wide with wonder. "No. His nose was the softest thing I've ever felt. I've dreamed of touching them."

Mikael's fingers slid down her arm before he pulled away. The warmth of his touch lingered, sending a strange thrill through her. She swallowed hard, uncertain of the feeling that had blossomed inside her. Their eyes met in the dimming light, his sky blue and hers like ripened dates, and for a moment, the world around them faded.

Eldad's voice broke the silence. "We made progress. If we keep coming every day, we might actually be able to do this! Did you hear me?"

Shana blinked, her mind snapping back to the present. "Yes, I heard you, and you're probably right!" She glanced at the horizon. The sun folded itself into the earth like a weary traveler beneath a woven blanket, and the sky bloomed with the quiet fire of amber and violet. "We'd better get back. Mother will need help with the evening meal. And Father, too, with getting everything ready for the village gathering."

Mikael chuckled as he fell into step beside them. "So, brothers and sisters bicker no matter where they're from."

Shana smirked. "Eldad isn't as irritating as he used to be."

Eldad laughed. "And now that she calls herself a woman, she thinks she can boss me around!"

Mikael raised an amused eyebrow. "That does seem to be a pattern."

***

As the sun slipped behind the hills, they returned home, dusty and windblown.

"Mother, is there anything I can still do?" Shana asked.

Sarah turned from the pot, hands on her hips. "You can all wash up first. You look as if you've been rolling in the mud. Mikael, that includes you. Jairus and Martha will be joining us also."

They hurried outside to clean up. Shana returned first, her eyes alight with excitement. "Oh, Mother, one of the horses touched my hand! His nose was so soft."

Johanan strode in, his presence grounding the room. "Everyone all right?"

Shana beamed. "Yes! It was incredible. The foal ate grain from my hand."

Mikael followed, shaking his head with a smile. "I was right there to keep her safe, but there was no danger."

"Come, let's eat," Sarah said warmly, just as the first stars began to pierce the sky.

The villagers arrived. Johanan guided them to their places. Jairus raised his hands to quiet the chattering.

"This gathering reminds me of when our journey first began. Many of the tribe of Javan stopped at Noah's village to hear the stories of our beginnings. If we meet a couple of times in each seven-day cycle, I can finish the stories as this moon phase ends and a new one begins. I will explain why, as the stories unfold."

He paused and bowed his head. "Before I begin the story, I will pray. Elohim, please honor this story of the beginning and help the villagers to understand the truth of it. Amen."

He began the story of Elohim and the seven days of creation, his voice weaving through the quiet night. When he finished, the harps and lyres joined in the Creation Hymn. Those who knew it sang, and the villagers added their voices as the melody became familiar. When the hymn ended, a thoughtful silence settled. Slowly, the villagers began to disperse.

Jairus, Martha, and Mikael lingered near the fire. Mikael exhaled; his gaze distant. "It's wonderful. I always believed there was Someone in charge. But I never knew how."

***

The next morning, Mikael and Jairus came to fetch Johanan and Eldad to walk the edge of the hills and talk about building the enclosure.

"There are about fifteen horses," Mikael explained. "We won't try to keep them all—but if we don't build big enough, we might lose the ones we want."

Johanan ran a hand through his beard. "We'd better fell trees near the site to save hauling. It will take help."

"Tobiya and Lemuel have oxen," Eldad added. "I'll go ask them."

They walked the land together, pacing the length and width of the proposed corral. Johanan raised an eyebrow as Mikael marked a corner with his heel.

"We'll need both strength and strategy," Johanan muttered, but Mikael just grinned.

"Once we have the trees," Jairus said, "we'll need every spare hand to help drive the horses in."

Mikael glanced toward the hills. "Let's hope they stay long enough for that."

THE QUIET BETWEEN

The hills were still as Shana, Mikael, and Eldad returned the next afternoon. The air was cooler, tinged with the earthy scent of turning leaves. The herd grazed quietly, their movements unhurried, unafraid.

Shana crouched low and scattered grain in the grass. The foal was the first to notice. Ears flicking, he nudged his mother again. This time, the mare stepped forward without hesitation, her breath visible in the cool air.

She reached Shana's hand and gently licked the grain from her palm. The foal followed, brushing its soft nose against her wrist.

A beat of silence passed.

Then the black stallion huffed sharply and trotted forward—not aggressively, but enough to stir the herd. The mare turned and ran, the foal close behind.

Shana exhaled, her heart pounding.

"She came again," she whispered.

"She trusts you," Mikael said, crouching beside her. His gaze lingered on her profile before he added quietly, "And so does the foal."

Shana turned to him, searching his face. She didn't reply. But she didn't look away either.

***

That evening, as coals dimmed to glowing embers and the others drifted to sleep, Mikael remained by the fire, staring into its soft light. Johanan joined him, dropping onto the log beside him with a grunt.

Mikael offered a half-smile. "You sit quietly, but I know you see everything."

Johanan chuckled. "I try."

They sat in silence for a while before Mikael spoke again. "When did you know Sarah was meant for you?"

Johanan stirred the coals with a stick. "Long before I admitted it. We were young. She sang a song over her little brother once when he was sick. I watched the way her voice quieted the room. Not just the child, but the whole house. I thought, 'That's someone who could bring peace to the storms in me.'"

Mikael nodded slowly. "I think... I'm beginning to understand that."

"You've traveled far," Johanan said. "Sometimes the heart follows the journey before the words do."

Mikael gave a short laugh. "I worry I say too little."

Johanan looked at him, eyes steady. "Shana hears more than you think."

***

Later, Shana sat just outside the home, the village quiet around her. She cradled her harp in her lap, fingers idly tracing the carved wood but not playing. The stars above twinkled faintly, and the cool night brushed against her cheeks.

Her thoughts weren't tangled, just... full.

The mare had come. Mikael had stood beside her. And something between them had shifted, gentle, like breath.

194

She smiled softly to herself.

Then, without fully realizing, she began to play a simple melody from childhood, soft enough not to wake anyone, and steady enough to still her heart.

Chapter 39

FROST AND FLAME

As the first light of dawn crept across the frosted fields, streaking the pale sky with lavender and gold, the men rose from their beds with a sense of purpose. A crisp hush lingered. It was the kind that foretold winter, when the breath of the earth began to still beneath the soil.

Mikael stepped into the morning with resolve in his stride. The air bit at his skin as he gripped the rope harness tethered to a log. "We'll need a gate that swings closed quickly," he said. "Once they enter, we can't hesitate. Rawhide might work to brace it."

The thud of axes soon echoed through the timbered valley. Tobiya and Mikael worked side by side, breaking the earth for fence posts. The ground resisted. The subtle crunch of frost had not yet hardened, but was close. Steam rose from their shoulders as they dug, sweat mingling with the morning chill.

Johanan surveyed the timbers. "We should be able to fell all the trees we need by nightfall."

Jairus wiped his brow. "Then we focus all our strength on building the enclosure. It's good work, honest and needed."

Johanan glanced toward Jairus, "Father, maybe you should head to the site and supervise. Let us manage the trees. Eldad and Lemuel can help guide them as they fall."

Jairus nodded, easing against a nearby rock. "I'll rest here a while. Don't let the trees fall the wrong way."

***

Inside the house, the scent of salty air clung to the fish Shana and Sarah were preparing for the midday meal. Shana bent over the stone slab, carefully slicing into the flesh with a sharp flint blade.

"Mother, what else should I know?" she asked. "I've cooked venison, but never this. Can ibex or gazelle be cooked the same way?"

Sarah smiled as she scaled another fish. "Most, yes. You'll learn by trying. Some meats stew well, others roast better, and some are best left for Mikael to pretend to enjoy."

Shana laughed. "Mother!"

A soft knock at the door interrupted them. Martha entered, cheeks flushed from the cold, holding a small loom wrapped in linen.

"I brought the hand loom," she said, placing it on the table. "Good for soft cloth—the finer flax works well when layered."

"I'll come watch in a little bit," Shana said. "Mother's still teaching me how to prepare a fish properly."

Sarah chuckled. "Vegetables stew nicely with fish, or else stir them quickly over hot coals. Herbs help, if you've found the right ones."

Martha held her hands near the hearth. "It's the same everywhere. "We cook with what we find. Roots, leaves, nuts when the trees are kind. Soon we'll dry what we can, and freeze once the frost sets in."

Sarah glanced toward Shana. "You're doing well. You do the best you can with what you have."

***

Shana brushed aside the leather curtain. Sunlight poured across the hills where the wild horses grazed.

"They've returned," she exclaimed.

"Come and sit," Martha said. "Have you worked with flax much?"

Shana settled beside her. "Only a little. I helped Mother weave and stitch my robe."

"It's the same as the wool," Martha assured her. "Just finer. Slower."

Shana reached for the loom. "There's no pattern or color. That helps. I still have the loom Father made. I can take it, and keep weaving if I have thread."

Sarah stood. "Nearly midday. Let's fry the fish. The men will come back hungry."

***

The aroma of crisp fish filled the home, mingling with the warmth of the hearth.

When the men returned, clothes dusted with sawdust and sweat, Mikael brushed bark from his sleeves then stepped toward Shana.

"We marked out the space for the gate," he told her. "Tomorrow, we will start fitting the posts."

"Mikael," she said with a smile, "I think I understood everything you said. I still need to learn more of your language. Can we go to the horses after the meal?"

He chuckled. "Yes. We need to know if we're building for something real. The horses will let Eldad and me approach following you." He gently patted her shoulder.

As they settled around the hearth, Sarah poured tea into carved wooden cups. Shana passed the crisp fish and browned vegetables. The clatter of spoons and quiet murmurs filled the house with life.

Shana tied her hair back with a leather strap, even though wisps always escaped. As she fastened her foot coverings, her heart quickened— not just for the horses, but for the quiet certainty of Mikael's presence beside her. He said little, but she remembered the way he watched, the steadiness in his hand when hers trembled.

***

The sun hung just past its peak as the trio climbed the slope. Their steps brushed through the tall, sun-dried grass.

Mikael paused, hand out. "There," he whispered. "Top of the hill."

They dropped low. Wind stirred Shana's hair as her eyes found the colt and mare.

She cupped her hands and released a clicking sound. The colt lifted his head, ears flicking. The stallion stood watch, unmoving. But some of the others shifted and now trusted.

Shana held out her palm, grain spilling through her fingers. A colt came first, muzzling her hand—young, curious, and not hers to keep. Another followed, then turned away. The herd moved around her in a rhythm of nibbling and retreating. Then the chestnut mare with the white blaze stepped near. She had no foal—too young still, not yet in her third summer. But Shana's gaze lingered on her.

They backed away slowly, not disturbing the fragile peace.

Mikael turned to her. "Will you be all right going back on your own? We'll check the enclosure and let the others know what we saw."

"I'll be fine. You'll watch until I reach the village."

***

The aroma of roasted venison met Shana as she stepped inside.

"More horses came close today," she said.

"That is good?" Martha asked, knowingly.

"I've saved flax," she added, setting the bundle on the table. "Tomorrow we'll make cloth."

"I'd like that," Shana said. "But the horses, they're so exciting right now."

Sarah raised a brow. "Maybe someone else is, too."

Shana laughed. "Maybe. For so long, nothing changed. Moon after moon. Now everything's happening at once."

"That's the way it often is," Sarah said gently.

Martha looked around the room. "Time to make room. We'll need space for another story tonight."

***

By twilight, the hearth glowed and voices filled the room. Lemuel's family had joined them. A place was deliberately left open beside Shana.

She poured tea just as Mikael entered and sat beside her.

Eldad spoke up. "The horses came to Shana. Mikael and I rose slowly—just in case."

Mikael added, "She was so brave. We just wanted to support her."

His hand rested on her arm. She didn't pull away.

***

As the room filled, Johanan opened the door wide. "Find a seat. We'll make room."

Once all had settled, Johanan stood. "You've seen what we're building. It's an enclosure—for the wild horses. Shana has been watching them since spring. Mikael came from a land where people ride them. Today, they ate from their hands. We'll need help to secure the horses. They will choose certain ones and release the rest. If any of you are interested in one, let Mikael know. Think about it."

He stepped back, and Jairus rose. "Let me pray. Elohim, this is a hard story. Help the people hear Your promise in it. Amen."

"This story isn't lovely, like last night's. This is the fall—how we came to know right from wrong." His words wove through the room like wind through dry grass, telling of Eve, of the serpent, disobedience, and sorrow, and of the great breaking between man and Elohim.

When he finished, the silence was deep. The soft, mournful strains of harp and lyre filled the space with lament.

201

The villagers left in silence, carrying the story with them into the deepening night.

Chapter 40

THREADS OF BECOMING

The fire in the hearth softened the early morning chill. The women gathered indoors, where the scent of drying herbs mingled with wool and woodsmoke. Sarah's loom stood near the hearth, its frame catching the firelight. Threads of warm brown, cream, and glints of dyed blue stretched taut across it.

Sarah wove at the top, her hands confident and practiced. Martha worked steadily in the center, slower but sure. Shana, seated near the bottom, moved with careful energy, her fingers guiding the weft—the threads that wove side to side—through the warp, the upright strands held firm like the bones of the fabric. They began adding the treasured blue threads—dyed from the woad Sarah had cultivated and saved.

The loom clicked rhythmically beneath their hands.

"Mother," Shana said, brushing a curl from her cheek, "I'll grind the grain for the bread so it can rise in time for tonight. I'll make enough flatbread for midday, too."

Sarah nodded. "Let me know when you need a rest."

"I'll need a good mortar," Shana added, glancing toward the shelves. "Did Father shape yours?"

Sarah looked up, eyes thoughtful. "When you return to the hills, keep an eye out for a heavy stone with the right shape… He can help you form it if needed."

Later, with the mortar in hand, Shana began to grind the grain. The soft crunch of stone against grain joined the sounds of weaving. A warm, nutty scent rose as the flour broke down beneath her hands.

"The grain is ready," she said, wiping her palms. "Should I mix the dough?"

"Go ahead," Sarah replied.

Martha chuckled. "Then we can tell everyone, including Mikael, that you made it."

Shana laughed, then caught herself as she mixed the dough. "What if it's terrible?"

"We'll take a little taste in secret," Martha teased.

Shana smiled and leaned over the loom. "Mother, thank you for setting the warp threads. They're perfect." Her hands reached for the blue fibers now, the color deep and hopeful.

Sarah nodded. "You're learning fast."

"We're making good progress," Martha said, stretching her back. "Let's get the flatbread started while the dough rises."

***

Later, as the others focused on the loom and conversation drifted to recipes and patterns, Shana stepped outside with a cup of warm tea.

The sky was pale, layered with soft gray clouds. Her hands curled around the cup. She sipped slowly, the steam rising like breath. She had thought her life would follow a single path—helping her mother, learning weaving, maybe becoming a midwife like Tabitha someday.

But now…

She looked toward the hills. A rope of blue thread lay coiled in her palm, a piece Sarah had handed her earlier. She wound it around her fingers. This blue brought to mind… Something is unraveling, she thought. But something else is being woven.

She didn't know if it was love yet. But she knew she wanted to walk wherever that thread might lead.

***

Outside, Johanan rubbed his hands briskly. "We'll have frost tonight, maybe snow. When should we move the horses?"

Mikael and Eldad looked to Shana. She stepped forward, voice clear.

"Soon, before the stallion moves the herd to a new place. Tomorrow is a day of rest. But the day after, if we start before sunrise, like a hunting party, we can drive them into the enclosure while the light grows."

Mikael nodded. "It could work. But can the men stay quiet?"

Johanan grinned. "We'll tell them no talking. Just like hunting."

***

After a simple meal of flatbread, cheese, and stew, Mikael rose. "Let's check the herd. They're still near the stream. The sounds haven't scared them off."

By sunset, the rail enclosure stood complete. The last timber was in place. As they returned, the horses grazed in the golden distance, aware, but not alarmed.

***

As they walked back toward the village, Shana and Mikael drifted a little behind the others.

"Do you ever miss your home?" she asked softly.

"Yes," Mikael said after a pause. "But not in the way I used to."

He didn't explain, and she didn't press. The silence between them felt neither awkward nor empty. She glanced over at him, at the dust in his hair and the way his quiet confidence settled into each step.

Not just a stranger anymore, she thought.

***

Morning brought cold light and slower rhythms. Inside, the hearth crackled softly. The scent of roasted grain and steeped herbs filled the home. Shana sat near the fire, rolling thread between her fingers, watching the shadows flicker on the wall.

Some villagers arrived for the day of rest, bringing bundles of preserved fruits, roots, and tea leaves. Tobiya and his family arrived as expected, arms full and spirits warm.

Jairus stood and bowed his head. "Thank you for this day of rest, Yahweh Elohim. Bless this food and those who prepared it. Guide us in our fellowship with You. Amen."

The meal passed quietly. Between bites, villagers asked gentle questions about the stories they'd heard the week before. No one hurried. Peace gathered like a shawl around their shoulders.

After the meal, the instruments emerged—Sarah and Shana's harps, Tabitha and Bathshua's lyres, a bone flute, and a small drum stretched tight. The music rose soft and steady—praises, laments, songs of hope. Shana's fingers were sure now, her voice steady.

Then came silence, and each heart turned inward in prayer.

Jairus closed with a final blessing, and the villagers slowly departed, leaving behind warmth, music, and the hush of sacred things.

Outside, the sky was silvering. Shana gazed at the hills and thought, tomorrow, the wind will rise, the hooves will thunder, and I think I will learn what it means to be brave.

Chapter 41

HE DOES GUIDE

The morning air was sharp with cold, brushing their skin like invisible needles. Darkness still veiled the land, stars slowly fading behind the waning moonlight. Frost clung to the blades of grass underfoot, moving softly with every step. Shadows stretched long as Mikael, Shana, Eldad, and several men from the village moved like phantoms, circling the slumbering herd. Even whispers seemed too loud.

Shana hugged her cloak tighter around her, breath visible in the chill. Mikael leaned close, his voice low and tense.

"Shana, stay by me in case things become dangerous." His hand found her arm, fingers warm through the fabric. "Be careful. They're powerful."

She gave a quiet smile, steady despite the adrenaline building inside. "I will," she said, patting his hand gently.

As the horizon bled from charcoal to pale gold, the first rays of dawn brushed the hills. Shana's sharp click of the tongue was the only sound to break the stillness.

Like ghosts rising from the earth, the men emerged from their positions, moving steadily inward. The herd began to stir, ears twitched, and muscles rippled. The black stallion, majestic and tense, snorted and reared, catching the scent of men. He gathered the herd and began to lead them straight toward the enclosure.

A flurry of motion followed. Men leapt up, shouting, waving arms, making themselves wide. Thunderous hooves pounded the ground, the rhythm like drums. Dust kicked up in clouds as the animals surged forward.

At the last moment, the black stallion veered sharply away, disappearing like smoke into the hills. But the rest of the herd poured into the enclosure. Jairus and Tobiya slammed the gate shut and dropped the rail across it.

For a long breathless moment, the horses churned within the enclosure, tossing their heads, eyes wide and flaring. Then they began to slow. Hay, carefully placed by Mikael and Eldad at the far end, drew them in. A few began to settle, chewing, though tension still rippled through their limbs. A young brown stallion paced the perimeter, not yet ready to calm.

Mikael's eyes locked with Shana's across the fence, wide with wonder. "We have secured them!" he said, breathless.

Before she could answer, he laughed, grabbed her by the waist, and spun her in the air. She gasped as he lifted her, then threw her head back in surprised laughter.

"We have, with all this help!" she called out. "Thank you, everyone!"

Mikael, grounding his feet again, still grinning, added, "I'll stay and watch them. The black stallion may return."

"I'll stay too," Eldad said quickly.

Shana grinned and gave her brother's shoulder a mock punch. "Then I suppose I'll bring food for both of you."

She turned toward home, heart still racing, not from fear, but from exhilaration and something warmer she didn't yet have words for.

***

Back at the house, she arrived just as her father and Jairus stepped in. The scent of burning wood and fresh cheese greeted her. Her mother handed out clay cups of hot spiced tea.

"Sit," Sarah said, already slicing flatbread and laying out the goat cheese Martha had brought over. "Let me get you food."

They gathered near the fire, hands outstretched, warming chilled fingers.

"Mother, I'll take some food and tea to the enclosure," Shana said.

Her mother helped her prepare a small bundle, wrapping the bread in linen and the tea in a skin-lined pouch.

As Shana wrapped herself in a thick shawl, she paused near her father and touched his arm. "Can you believe it?"

He chuckled, pride in his eyes. "We did it. Now let's see what Mikael can do with them."

****

Shana hurried back, mist curling around her ankles, the bundle warm in her arms. She approached quietly.

"How are they doing?" she whispered.

Mikael took the bundle from her, setting it on the ground. His movements were slow and gentle. "Our plan worked," he whispered, still in awe. Then, without thinking, he reached out, pulled her close, and kissed her forehead. His hand lingered a breath longer than necessary.

Shana didn't move. She felt it, not just the warmth of his touch, but the certainty of it. It settled in her chest, steady and sure.

Eldad coughed dramatically and flopped to the ground. "Remember, I'm still here."

Mikael laughed. "Sorry, but your sister was the one who brought them together. I was just showing some appreciation."

Shana knelt beside him, cheeks burning. She brushed his hand as she handed him the food. "I'd better keep watch while you eat."

"We can see fine from here," Mikael replied, but he didn't argue.

"What will you do next?" she asked softly.

"We'll pick which horses to keep and release the rest. That may calm the stallion."

Eldad tore off a piece of bread. "I hadn't thought of keeping one, but now it makes sense. They could carry game or our supplies."

Shana turned to Mikael. "You'll try to ride one?"

Mikael met her eyes, gaze steady. "That was my first thought, the day I saw them. They move like the wind, free and wild. I want to be a part of that."

"I feel the same," she echoed. "Like I could run with them forever."

Mikael's voice softened. "But when I saw them here on the hills, there was a beautiful woman standing among them. I thought she couldn't be real, but she is."

Shana looked away, heart pounding.

Mikael leaned closer, quiet now. "If she would come with me, I'd like to ride into the sunset with her."

Shana smiled, eyes shining. "Please talk to my father."

Mikael nodded. "I will."

She stood quickly and walked away, her steps light, almost dancing.

***

Mikael watched her go, a soft smile lingering.

"Eldad," he said, "would you like a brother?"

Eldad squinted. "You'd be him, wouldn't you? Even if you're leaving. You want to take Shana?"

"If she'll come."

"She didn't say no." Eldad grinned, then added with a shrug, "I'm not looking for a wife. Not yet. If Father comes out, I'll disappear so you can talk to him."

***

Later that morning, Johanan approached the enclosure. His eyes took in the pacing stallion, the grazing herd, the quiet figures nearby.

"How are things?"

"We'll ask if any villagers want to keep one," Mikael said. "Then we'll release the rest."

Johanan nodded, then glanced at Mikael. "Anything else on your mind?"

Eldad raised both hands and backed away, grinning. "All right, I'm out. You two talk."

Mikael cleared his throat. "I don't know your customs," Mikael said quietly, "but I hope to take Shana as my wife…I have no bride price to offer, but I will care for her with everything I have."

Johanan studied him for a long moment, saying nothing. The morning wind stirred the edge of his cloak.

"You've traveled far," he said at last. "You arrived unsure of us. Unsure of Elohim. But you've listened. You've worked. And you've loved her honorably."

Mikael stood still, waiting.

Johanan's voice softened. "We've prayed for a man who would love our daughter and follow Yahweh Elohim. Not one of many gods, but one whose heart is turning toward Him. We see that in you. We trust her to you."

Mikael's breath released slowly, deeply. "Thank you. I was praying, clumsily, maybe, but asking for guidance. Then I found her. Among the horses. Full of strength and wonder."

Johanan smiled. "Elohim guides the willing. Even when they don't know how to ask."

"I want to do this the right way," Mikael said. "I'll wait for your word on how to proceed."

"I'll speak with Sarah. She'll want it done properly."

"Of course," Mikael said. "Whatever I must do."

They stood together a moment longer, watching the young brown stallion finally lower his head to feed. The dust settled, and the sun rose higher.

Two men, different in history, united by hope, stood watch over something wild… and something just beginning.

Chapter 42

A PIECE OF THE FUTURE

Morning arrived veiled in silver mist, curling low around the legs of the enclosure. The ground held the night's chill, damp and fragrant with crushed grass and hay. A lone bird called through the hush, its voice thin and clear, full of beginnings.

Mikael was already at the fence, leaning quietly, watching the herd stir. The horses had calmed somewhat overnight, though the young stallion still paced now and then, breath puffing in soft clouds. The black stallion had not returned, at least, not yet.

Shana approached slowly, cloak pulled close. She carried a bundle of flatbread and a flask of warmed goat milk. Her steps softened near the fence, and Mikael turned at the sound.

"I didn't think you'd be up so early," he said, his voice low, careful not to startle the horses.

"I couldn't sleep," she replied, setting the bundle on a flat stone. "I kept dreaming they escaped."

He chuckled. "That might happen if we don't figure out how to lead them."

Shana stepped beside him, eyes settling on the young stallion, who had stopped his circling and now stood alert, ears forward. His dark coat gleamed like oiled cedar in the rising light. She felt her pulse stir, not in fear, but in awe.

"What do you think we start with?" she asked.

Mikael took a moment. "I think they have to trust us. Not fear us. Maybe just one at a time. Let them choose first."

"That sounds like something someone wise once said," she teased.

"It's something I hope is true." He smiled faintly. "We'll find out."

Eldad arrived then, rubbing sleep from his eyes and chewing on a piece of bread. "If it's trust you're speaking of, save it for later. I need food before wisdom."

Mikael laughed and stepped into the enclosure, shoulders relaxed but alert. The horses flinched at his movement, hooves scraping the soil, but he made no sudden moves. He just stood, calm, hands at his sides.

The young stallion snorted and took a few steps forward.

Shana held her breath.

The stallion's eyes locked on Mikael, mist curling around his legs like smoke. He tossed his head once, not defiant, but attentive. Mikael's heart lifted.

"I think he's chosen you," Shana whispered, resting her chin on the rail.

Without a word, Mikael reached into the satchel at his hip and drew out a handful of dried sweetgrass. He held it out with his palm open. The stallion hesitated. Then, inch by inch, he stepped forward and ate. Shana let out the breath she hadn't realized she'd been holding.

Behind them, Eldad gave a low whistle. "Well. That one's decided."

Shana stood near a blaze-faced chestnut mare, strong, alert, with eyes that met her own without flinching. Shana had coaxed her with apple slices, but it was more than that. The mare had stayed near her from the beginning.

Shana stepped closer to the mare, brushing her fingers lightly along its neck. "I want this one," she said. "I think she was waiting for me."

Mikael nodded. "She kept watching you even when the others turned."

Tobiya, quiet most of the morning, pointed to a muscular, compact bay. "That one will suit me. Strong, but not wild."

Eldad squinted at a mare. It was a lean black horse with long legs and a sharp look. "She seems fast. Maybe she can carry me and a deer."

Mikael grinned. "If she throws you, it won't be for lack of warning."

Later that morning, they opened the enclosure just wide enough to release the rest of the herd. Johanan and Jairus stood at the far end, guiding with quiet gestures. There was a moment of hesitation—then hooves thundered, and the herd broke into motion, galloping into the hills like wind made flesh.

Inside the fence, four horses remained.

The black stallion did not return, but Mikael thought he glimpsed a shape, high on a distant ridge, still as stone.

***

The day unfolded in slow rhythms with learning, presence, and patience. No ropes yet, just being near. Letting the horses grow used to being seen, touched, and known.

When the sun began to slope westward, golden between the trees, Johanan called them together. A taller fire pit had been built; stones stacked high, the ground cleared. Children ran laughing toward it, and smoke curled into the cooling air. Sarah passed around flatbread and honeyed figs. Villagers wrapped in blankets drew near in quiet circles.

Shana sat beside her mother, knees tucked to her chest. Mikael stood with Johanan. Eldad poked the fire with a stick, muttering about "romantic smoke" blowing in his face. Lemuel laughed quietly nearby.

Johanan raised a hand, his voice clear even before darkness fell.

"Tonight, another story, one from before the ark. A choice… and the

One who still walks among us." He turned. "Jairus?"

Jairus rose and began, "This is the story of the sons of Adam and Eve. They gave offerings—one accepted, and one not." He continued, speaking of sacrifice and heart, of Cain and Abel, and the cost of sin.

"We will offer a lamb before the day of rest as a sacrifice. Anyone may join us. Ask for your sins to be covered."

Shana leaned her head on her mother's shoulder. Across the fire, Mikael caught her gaze. He said nothing. But he didn't need to. She felt it. That the day had given her something rare: a piece of the future.

Chapter 43

A PROMISE MADE

Mikael had left with Johanan and Eldad just after first light. They moved in practiced silence, their breath rising in small clouds. The forest around them was familiar. There were older trees with thick trunks, their bark furred with moss, and uneven hills that concealed the path from view. Mikael studied the land with quiet diligence, noting landmarks, a twisted pine, a split boulder, as they spread out to drive the game.

The fresh snow made tracking easier. They fanned out, stepping carefully through the underbrush, cloaks snagging brambles. The hunt began with sudden energy, shouts echoing through the valley to push the deer toward waiting bows. Mikael's pulse quickened not just from the chase, but from the shared purpose of it. His fingers tightened on his spear, waiting for his moment.

****

Back in the village, smoke curled above the roofs in thin spirals as the women began their morning work. The air smelled of pine and frozen earth. Shana stepped from the warmth of the house, a cloak pulled close. A hush fell over her chest as she looked toward the hills. The world beyond seemed vast and untouched, and the snow-like silence poured over the land.

She trudged through the drifts to the enclosure, where the four horses stirred at her approach. They stood tall, winter-thickened coats steaming gently in the early light. Shana reached out, her hand brushing a soft muzzle.

"You're really here," she whispered. "I still can't believe it."

Affie padded up beside her, tail low but wagging. Shana chuckled and scratched her head.

"I'm not sure they'll like you, Affie. But maybe if you're gentle, they'll get used to you." She crouched beside the dog. "If I leave… you'll stay here, won't you? You belong with Kabul." The words lingered in the cold, heavier than she'd expected.

Brushing snow from her tunic, she turned back toward home. The scent of linden tea drifted from the doorway, familiar and warm. Inside, the fire crackled, casting amber light over Sarah, who worked steadily at the loom.

"Thank you for saving some tea," Shana said as she stepped in. "It's quiet without the men."

Sarah nodded, hands never still. "Yes, but we'll finish quite a bit today. Your grandmother should be by soon. I've prepared the coverings for the meat we'll freeze."

A knock at the door was followed by Martha entering, cheeks pink from the cold. "Already working, I see," she said with a smile. "What else is happening on this quiet morning?"

Sarah shared a glance with her daughter, then looked up from the threads. "Well… Johanan told me something. Mikael's spoken with him about taking Shana as his wife."

Shana froze, cup halfway to her lips. "What?"

Sarah's eyes twinkled. "Johanan wanted to ask what customs we should follow. You remember our wedding, Martha. But what about you and Jairus?"

Martha leaned on the table, thoughtful. "There must be a feast.

Jairus would want to speak, or Johanan, or both. It doesn't have to be large, but it should be meaningful."

The loom clacked softly beneath Sarah's hands, the motion steady as their conversation wove around it like thread.

Shana sat for a moment, then murmured, "I've never been to a wedding. Everyone who's come here was already married. There are always babies… but I've never seen how it begins."

The room quieted. Only the pop of the fire and the gentle tug of thread filled the space.

"Then we'll make something beautiful," Sarah said, setting her shuttle aside. "There are no strict rules. We'll create what fits you."

"We could sing," Martha said. "A hymn everyone knows. That way, it belongs to the whole village."

"And flowers," Sarah added, glancing at the bundles of dried herbs and blossoms hanging near the ceiling. "Not many are fresh, but I can still weave a crown."

Shana tilted her head. "What does the woman wear?"

Martha laughed. "Something beautiful."

They chuckled together, and some of Shana's tension loosened.

Sarah leaned closer. "What would feel meaningful to you, Shana? What would help you remember it?"

Shana's gaze drifted to the fire. "I think… I would like to walk to him. Not be given. Just walk, while people sing."

"Then that's what we'll do," Sarah said. "We'll weave your wedding robe with calm hands, prepare food, and tell the village."

Martha nodded. "It's the first wedding *here* since the village began. That makes it special."

Shana blinked fast, her throat tight. She didn't speak again for a while, but something warm had wrapped around her. Not just hope, something like belonging.

***

The quiet day passed in the rhythm of work and reflection. Late sunlight glazed the fields, touching the snow with amber.

Just before dusk, the men returned. Their shoulders were weary but triumphant. Several deer and two gazelles were hauled in, already cleaned and ready for dividing. The snow bore their blood like ink spilled across parchment, dark and red against the white.

The village stirred at once. Women emerged with knives and cloth, laughter and instructions following them. Soon, meat was skinned, cut, and sorted; some was for drying, some for the freezing cave, and some for supper.

Inside, a thick stew bubbled over the fire. The scent of garlic and roasting meat filled the home as the men crowded in, cheeks flushed, stomachs eager.

"Mikael got a big one!" Eldad said proudly. "An eight-point buck!"

Mikael flushed and shrugged. "We all helped. A good doe feeds just as well."

Dinner passed in a blur of laughter, warmth, and clinking wooden bowls. As the meal ended, Mikael leaned toward Shana. "Want to check on the horses again before dark?"

"Yes," she said, a quiet thrill in her voice. "They'll be ready for more hay."

They bundled up once again, with Eldad trailing behind. "I'll check on my horse too," he said with a wink. "Just to keep you from getting lost."

***

While Eldad and Tobiya busied themselves with the animals, Mikael drew Shana to the far side of the enclosure. The snow hushed the world. The horses shifted and nickered softly, their breath misting in the cold.

The sky was turning amber and rose.

Mikael took her hand, his fingers warm. "Shana," he said, steady and sure, "will you be my wife?"

Her breath caught. For a moment, everything stilled, even the wind.

She gripped his hand. "Oh, yes."

A smile broke across his face, and he pulled her into his arms. His kiss was gentle, full of promise.

"I've wanted to do that," he whispered, "since the first time I saw this woman with fire in her eyes."

Shana laughed softly, brushing his cheek. "Well, now you can." She smiled. "Anytime."

Chapter 44

A PROMISE
AND AN OFFERING

The wind whispered through the bare trees, rattling brittle branches like old bones. The air was cold and dry, stinging cheeks and turning breath into clouds. It would soon be the day of rest, but the day before was set aside for something solemn, something sacred. Today, they would bring the sacrifice.

Johanan had chosen the lamb with painstaking care, watching it daily for signs of injury or imperfection. It grazed with the flock under his vigilant eye, never far from his reach. It was as pure and whole as he could find, a fitting offering.

Jairus, ever thoughtful, had suggested they retell the story of Noah and his altar before the sacrifice itself. A reminder, he said, of the meaning behind the fire. They would make the sacrifice just before the evening meal, followed by a celebration. The whole community stirred with anticipation. Women passed baskets and clay jars between tents and homes, exchanging spices, dried fruits, and roasted roots. The scents of roasting meat and fresh herbs mingled in the crisp air. Laughter and light conversation warmed even the coldest corners.

As far as Johanan could tell, none of the villagers were worshiping idols or bowing to carved images. That knowledge filled him with quiet gratitude.

Out near the enclosure, Mikael, Shana, Eldad, and Tobiya worked with the horses, their hands raw from the cold and from braiding thick strands of leather into halters. The horses, still wild, stamped their hooves and tossed their heads, wary but curious.

Tobiya showed them how to coax the halter over the horse's head. "With oxen," he explained, rubbing the nose of his mare, "you first let them grow used to the halter. Then you guide them gently, with steady hands. They learn to trust you."

The others followed suit, speaking in soft tones, offering bits of apple and hay. The animals responded with flicking ears and cautious steps, allowing the halters to be slipped on, one by one.

"That's enough for one day," Tobiya said finally, brushing off his hands. "They need time to grow comfortable. Let's give them water and more hay."

Steam curled up from the waterskins as the horses drank, their sides heaving with the exertion of the day.

Eldad looked toward the distant hill. "I'd better check with Father about the flock. He'll be bringing the lamb soon."

Mikael nodded. "I'll go with you. I can't just play with horses all day." He turned to Shana, brushing a windblown lock of hair from her face. "Go warm up. I'll see you soon." He gave her a warm, brief embrace, his gaze lingering a moment before he turned away.

Shana wrapped her shawl tightly around her shoulders and hurried back to the house, her breath white in the fading afternoon light.

"Mother!" she called as she stepped into the warmth. "Tobiya helped us get the halters on. Maybe soon we'll be able to lead them!"

"That's good news," Sarah replied, brushing flour from her hands. "Here, have some tea to warm up." The home smelled of roasted meat and herbs, of smoke and earth. Her grandmother, Martha, folded a piece of woven cloth.

"We've nearly finished the weaving," Sarah said with a smile. "Soon we can start making your robe."

"I'll help," Shana offered. "Like Mikael said, we can't just play with the horses."

Sarah raised a playful eyebrow. "So… has Mikael said anything else to you?"

Shana looked between her mother and grandmother, a smile blooming on her face. "Didn't I tell you? He asked me a couple of days ago to be his wife! We can start making plans!"

Martha clapped her hands together, her old eyes sparkling. "Praise Yahweh! That is wonderful!"

Sarah beamed. "Today marks the end of this moon's cycle. One full moon phase sounds just right for a time of preparation."

Shana's grin widened. "Should I tell Mikael?"

"Of course," her mother said, then added more softly, "But we'll still have winter. He won't try to leave before the thaw, will he?"

Shana's voice softened. "I'll talk to him. It would be too dangerous to travel before spring."

When the men returned for the midday meal, the house was warm and bustling with activity. Steam curled from bowls of broth. The fire crackled as the family gathered close, rubbing hands together, cheeks flushed from the cold.

Mikael finished his meal and stood as Shana gently pulled him to her side. Her voice was soft in his ear, "One full moon, then we'll marry."

His face lit up with joy, and he pulled her into a quiet hug, resting his forehead against hers for a heartbeat before letting go. Shana brushed his face with her fingertips and laughed as she broke away.

For a moment, they just stood there, the silence between them full and unhurried. The sounds of the others nearby, footsteps, a clatter of kindling, slowly came back into focus.

Johanan's voice carried across the clearing. "Tonight, there will be a gathering of the villagers. Let's move everything back to the walls before they arrive," he said, gesturing toward the fire pit. "They'll come in cold and hungry."

Sarah chimed in, "Maybe we should light a fire outside, too—it'll be crowded in here."

"Good thinking," Johanan agreed. "Eldad and Mikael, get one set up."

***

By dusk, the villagers had gathered, their breath fogging in the air as they made their way toward the stone altar near the riverbank. Children clung to parents, and the quiet was reverent. The women had dropped off their dishes earlier, platters covered with cloth, filled with the scents of home and harvest.

Mikael stood with Johanan and Jairus, eager to learn. He watched every movement, every word.

Jairus lifted his arms and addressed the gathering. "Before the sacrifice, let us remember Noah. When he stepped from the ark, he built an altar to Yahweh and offered burnt offerings. And Yahweh was pleased. This is when the song, 'As Long as the Earth Endures,' was first sung."

Jairus and Johanan stepped forward with the lamb. As the fire was lit, they followed the proper rituals, including the draining of the blood, then placing the lamb on the altar with solemn reverence. Smoke rose into the darkening sky.

Jairus prayed aloud, "Yahweh Elohim, receive this sacrifice. Forgive us. Cleanse us. May we walk in fellowship with You. Amen."

Silence fell. The fire crackled and popped, and the scent of burning wood and sacrifice hung heavy in the air. Shana felt tears prick her eyes, both for the lamb and for the grace it represented. Around her, others stood still, eyes lowered, hearts full.

As they returned to the village, low voices began to stir once more, gentle greetings, shared remarks about the meal, the fire, and the sky.

Eldad had already kindled the outdoor flame, and villagers clustered around it, hands outstretched to its warmth.

"Come in," Johanan called. "Find a warm place. There's food for everyone."

Mikael lingered with Jairus, glancing at the flames, then at the gathered families.

"What if… we don't have lambs?" he asked, voice low. "Are other animals acceptable for the sacrifice?"

Jairus considered the question seriously. "Yes. Sheep, goats, oxen, deer, and gazelle—all are acceptable. Even birds, if they're not birds of prey. These were the animals Noah understood as clean, set apart by Elohim. It isn't only the animal, though, it's the heart behind the offering."

Mikael nodded slowly, absorbing the weight of it.

"I'll have more questions," he said, sincerely. "I want to understand. I don't want to offer something out of tradition. I want it to mean something."

Jairus smiled. "That's the best beginning."

Later, as the crowd settled indoors and the warmth of food and fire seeped back into weary limbs, Shana found Mikael sitting near the hearth. The light played gently across his face, catching in his eyes when he looked up at her.

She sat beside him, searching his expression. "What did you think about the sacrifice?" she asked, her voice soft, almost private.

He leaned forward, elbows resting on his knees. "It felt… weighty. Holy. Not just a ritual, but something sacred. I've never done anything like it. But I want to understand it, truly. Not just the act, but the meaning."

Shana nodded slowly. "It matters to me," she said, her voice thick with honesty. "Not because someone told me it should. Because it's where I've found peace. Fellowship with Yahweh Elohim is what holds everything together. When the world tore apart, it was the one thing we could still choose."

She hesitated, then added, "If I go with you… I need to know we'll still be walking with Yahweh Elohim. Not perfectly. But together."

Mikael didn't answer right away. The silence stretched, but not uncomfortably. Then he leaned closer, his voice quiet and sure.

"You've walked with Him longer than I have. But I feel Him calling. And I want to learn how to lead, not just in the wilderness, or with a spear, but in faith. I can't offer what I don't have yet. But I will seek Him with you. I promise that."

A sharp breath escaped her, not from surprise, but from the deep truth of his words. She reached for his hand, their fingers lacing without effort.

They sat in stillness as the fire crackled, the hum of voices all around them. But for Shana, everything had narrowed to this: Mikael had his hand in hers, and the steady assurance that faith would not be something she carried alone.

Chapter 45

STILL WILD AT HEART

Winter deepened, blanketing the land with snow so thick it muted even the wind. The world outside shimmered with frost, and every breath left clouds in the air. Despite the cold, training the horses had become Mikael's obsession. He felt the call to continue toward the sunset more urgently now, like a silent drumbeat in his bones. The horses were no longer just companions; they were lifelines.

He knew riding would make the journey more bearable, especially for Shana. She had grown strong, but the road ahead was still unknown, and riding might spare her some of the hardship.

Today was the day Mikael would attempt to mount Storm.

They had made progress. Storm and Beauty could now be led confidently and taken to the river to drink without resistance. But riding was another matter. The stallion was proud and wary, not yet ready to trust completely.

Snowflakes clung to Mikael's lashes as he stood at the edge of the enclosure, his breath fogging the air. He rubbed his covered hands together, then stepped toward Storm, who watched him with flicking ears and snorts of white steam. The halter had been modified with a second lead, fashioned after the ox guide Tobiya had once designed.

Eldad and Shana stood just outside the fence, bundled tight against the cold. They had agreed that one person at a time would try.

"I'll be first on Beauty, too," Mikael had told them earlier. "If something goes wrong, it'll be me, not her." He didn't say it aloud, but fear for Shana gnawed at him.

He approached Storm slowly, murmuring in low tones, then leaned his weight across the horse's back. Storm shifted sharply, his muscles taut beneath Mikael's chest, but Mikael held on, whispering steady reassurances. After a tense minute, he slid off, breathing heavily, and ran his hands down Storm's flank and back, reinforcing the bond between them.

Storm's skin twitched under his touch.

Mikael turned and grinned at the others. "Better try again."

He led Storm in slow circles, speaking softly the entire time. Then, in a single breathless motion, he flung his weight up and over, gripping Storm's mane and squeezing tight with his legs. The horse bucked hard, but Mikael held fast, rocking with each jolt. Then, just as suddenly, Storm settled. Stillness could be just as dangerous.

Mikael waited, heart pounding, then eased himself off, landing in the snow. He stroked Storm again, and the stallion gave a soft snort before nudging his chest with his nose.

Cheers broke the silence. Shana and Eldad leapt in excitement, clapping covered hands and laughing in surprise.

"You did it!" Shana called.

Storm stamped a hoof and shook his head—then stepped forward and nuzzled Mikael's shoulder.

"I won't be able to try today," Shana said, breathless and glowing from the moment. "I have to get to work at the house. Tell me everything at midday." She turned and hurried off across the snow. Her steps were light.

Inside the house, warmth wrapped around her like a shawl. The scent of herbs, wood smoke, and simmering stew curled around her as she shut the door behind her and tugged off her snow-crusted cloak.

"Mikael got on Storm," she announced to Martha and Sarah, who were seated near the hearth. "Eldad will try tomorrow, and then me. They're worried I'll get hurt, but I think I can do it if someone lifts me."

"Well, I should think they'd be concerned," Martha said, setting down her stitching. "I am too. It seems risky."

"I agree," Sarah added, brushing wool fibers off her lap. "But I know Mikael. He wouldn't rest easy if you only walked beside your horse. You'll have to find a way to ride."

Shana sighed, then stepped forward as Sarah gestured. "Come here, we need to fit this."

She stripped off her outerwear and let them pull the soft wool tunic over her. It was thick, warm, and newly woven. It fit snug around her shoulders, and she smiled at the feel of it against her skin. The quiet hum of the house, the clink of tools, the warmth of the fire—all of it filled her with a complicated sense of comfort and sadness.

The journey would begin soon. And she would leave this behind.

"We'll start Mikael's next," Sarah said, stepping back. "He's taller than your father, so we'll adjust. Can you prepare the warp threads after the meal?"

A light knock came at the door, and a gust of cold air followed as Bathshua stepped inside, cheeks pink from the wind.

"Mother said I could come help with the yarn," she said brightly.

Shana smiled and reached for her, wrapping her in a quick hug. "Come warm up first."

"I heard about Storm," Bathshua said, eyes wide as she shrugged off her cloak. "My father said he's crazy to try riding a stallion this wild. Are you really going to ride, too?"

"I hope so," Shana replied. "But I think Mikael would rather face a storm on foot than let me ride untested."

Bathshua smirked. "That sounds like him. Careful—you're marrying a storm as much as a man."

Shana flushed, laughing in spite of herself. "Maybe. But I think I was made to ride storms."

The girls joined Sarah and Martha near the loom.

"Let's think practically," Sarah said, shifting gears. "What else will you need? We'll have to separate wants from needs. The horses will help, but space is still limited."

At the loom, Shana counted off her belongings like a list in her heart: the woven blanket she and her grandmother had made, wooden cups and bowls, a pot for water, and another for stew. She also had herbs and dried leaves for tea, dried meat, dried roots, two spears, their bows, her hand loom, and her spindle.

"My harp," she added softly. "Mikael will want to take everything he came with. I just hope we can manage it all."

The silence stretched until Sarah cleared her throat.

"Now," she said slyly, "let's talk about this marriage of yours."

Shana blushed, but grinned.

"Could Mikael use your home to bring Shana to?" Sarah asked Martha. "Then you and Jairus can stay here for the night. We'll have the feast and whatever ceremony the men arrange here."

Martha nodded. "That makes sense. We can find a space."

The door opened, and the men trudged in, cheeks ruddy, fingers stiff, the cold clinging to their outerwear. Shana stepped away from the loom. Her heart was leaping.

"Any more progress?" she asked Mikael.

"I was on longer this time," he said, brushing snow from his sleeves. "Eldad tried next—he stayed on for just a few seconds, but we're getting closer."

She smiled and touched his arm, warm under her fingers even

through the thick leather. He leaned into the touch for just a second before removing his covering.

"Tobiya's coming tomorrow," Eldad said, stamping snow from his covered feet. "We'll help each other."

"You'll have to lift me up," Shana said. "I doubt I'll reach otherwise."

Mikael gave her a long look. "We will. Carefully."

But there was something in his expression, a concern. Shana's heart tightened. He wouldn't say it aloud, but the danger haunted him. The path ahead, the risks, the unknowns. All of it.

They gathered near the hearth, bowls of steaming stew warming their hands. The room filled with the sound of spoons against pottery, the pop of the fire, the clatter of thoughts unspoken.

Outside, the snow kept falling.

Just as they were settling into their bowls and quiet conversation, a sharp whinny pierced the air, cutting through the low murmur of voices.

Shana looked up. "That was Storm."

Mikael was already moving, leather flapping as he burst out into the cold. Shana grabbed her outer garment and followed with Eldad right behind.

Outside, the wind had picked up again, swirling flakes into miniature storms. The sky had darkened, and the snow reflected an eerie gray glow. Storm was bucking wildly at the far end of the enclosure, his hooves striking the frozen ground, eyes wide with panic. Beauty neighed nervously nearby with her ears pinned back, pacing.

One of the gate latches had come undone in the wind.

Storm had his halter twisted in the rope, tangled and half-loose. He kicked at the post, eyes rolling. Mikael moved forward, slow and steady, his arms out.

"Easy… easy," he murmured. "Storm, easy now."

But Storm reared suddenly, jerking the rope taut, and let out a scream that echoed off the frozen trees.

"He's going to break free!" Eldad shouted.

Without thinking, Shana ducked under the fence and darted into the enclosure.

"Shana!" Mikael's voice cracked like thunder.

She didn't stop.

"Get out of here!" he shouted again, fear threading sharply through his tone.

"You need help," she shot back, keeping her eyes on Storm. Her voice was low. Steady. But laced with fire."I know him. I've been part of this, too."

Mikael cursed under his breath, torn between anger and panic as Storm reared again, rope twisting taut.

"Don't argue with me in the pen," he snapped.

"Then don't treat me like I'm helpless," she said. "You weren't alone in training him."

Storm's hooves crashed down, and both of them froze.

Slowly, the tension between them bled into focus.

Mikael reached Storm first, laying a firm hand on his shoulder. Storm flinched but stayed.

Shana moved in carefully, her hands trembling slightly as she reached for the twisted halter.

"I'm not trying to fight you," Mikael said quietly, still holding Storm. "I'm trying to keep you whole."

"Then don't push me away," she whispered. "Let me be strong with you."

The halter slipped free. Storm snorted and dropped his head, the panic melting away like snow in the spring sun.

Mikael looked at Shana, his face pale beneath the windburn. "You could've been kicked."

"I know," she said, breathing hard. "But he needed someone. And… so did you."

Mikael didn't answer right away. He simply reached out and cupped her shoulder, steady and warm despite the biting air.

They led the horses back to the end of the enclosure away from the gate, rechecking every latch and tie. By the time they returned to the house, the wind had died down again, as if nothing had happened.

Inside, the fire was still burning, the stew now lukewarm. But no one complained.

They sat together in silence for a while, the weight of the moment settling over them like another kind of snow.

Mikael finally spoke. "We're close. But we can't forget that they're still wild at heart. Like the journey ahead."

Shana nodded. Her hands still trembled faintly, but she curled them into fists on her lap.

"I don't want to forget," she said quietly. "I want to remember. So I'm ready."

Outside, the horses stamped and snorted and were safe again for now.

Chapter 46

THE STILLNESS BETWEEN

Winter continued with a fury, wrapping the land in a silent, white shroud. The wind howled through the trees like a restless spirit, sweeping snow into drifts against the sides of the enclosure. A makeshift covering had been secured over part of the pen so the horses could shelter beneath it, though the cold still nipped at their flanks.

That morning brought a rare stillness with no fresh snow, and for once, the sky held a pale, silver-blue light filtered through thin clouds. It was the kind of morning that hinted at hope.

Today was the day Shana would mount Beauty for the first time.

She led the young mare in slow circles, the soft crunch of snow beneath their feet the only sound between them. Her breath curled in the cold air, heart thudding louder than she wanted to admit. Beauty, sleek and restless, tossed her head but followed faithfully.

Then Mikael and Eldad stepped into the enclosure, bundled against the cold. Eldad took the lead rope while Mikael came alongside Shana, offering a quiet, reassuring smile. Without a word, both rubbed their hands along Beauty's back, warming her with familiar touch.

"You ready?" Mikael asked softly.

Shana nodded, though her fingers trembled. He lifted her swiftly, setting her on Beauty's back. For a moment, the horse stood still, ears twitching, uncertain. Then, without warning, she bucked.

Shana gasped, clutching at Beauty's mane. Eldad held the rope tight, anchoring the mare, but the motion was too wild. Shana slipped. Mikael lunged, catching her mid-fall, wrapping her tightly in his arms.

"You all right?" he asked, his breath warm against her cheek.

She clung to him for a moment, breathing in the scent of leather and firewood that clung to his cloak.

"Yes," she managed. "Thanks for catching me."

Their eyes met, just for a heartbeat, before both turned to stroke Beauty's neck, soothing her.

Shana's voice was steadier this time. "I'd better try again… I have to head in after that."

Eldad led Beauty to the center of the pen. Shana took her place once more, and Mikael helped her mount. This time, the mare danced beneath her but didn't buck. Eldad walked them forward slowly, speaking in low tones to keep the horse calm.

Shana was riding.

"I'll give you the ropes next time," Eldad called. "Come on down."

She dismounted, landing again in Mikael's arms, but this time with a triumphant smile.

"I can do this."

They watched her go, her feet crunching across the snow, a little bounce in her step.

A gentle warmth met her at the doorway, wrapping around her like an embrace. The scent of herbs and roasting roots filled the home, and the low hum of conversation blended with the crackling fire. Sarah looked up from her work and smiled as Shana entered.

They were ready to fit the woven tunic to Mikael today, to prepare it before the wedding. After the midday meal, they would finish it.

Shana slipped into the room and paused. The glow from the hearth warmed the room, its light shifting with every spark. Through the small window, she could see the men working. Tonight would be a full moon. Half of the moon phase had passed, and with it, the season of waiting was drawing to a close.

"Yahweh Elohim," she prayed silently. "I pray this is the path You have for me. We both love horses. We feel the pull toward the sunset. We want to know more of You. Guide us, lead us… Amen."

Footsteps approached the doorway. Shana turned to see Mikael standing just outside, arms folded gently over his chest. He didn't speak right away.

"Can we talk for a moment?" he asked.

She stepped outside with him into the fading light. Snow had begun to soften along the path, water glinting where the sun had kissed it earlier.

"What is it?"

He looked at her for a long moment, then said, "Before we go west, I need to go back."

Her brows lifted.

"Back to my family," he continued. "I promised my mother I would return. That I'd tell her what I'd found. I didn't know it would be you, or this place… or this faith. But I can't break that promise. I have to go home for a season."

Shana's heart fluttered. She was surprised, but not shaken. "And you want me to go with you."

"If you will."

She nodded slowly. "Then we'll go. She should see you—who you've become. And she should know Elohim."

He let out a breath, his shoulders relaxing. "I needed to tell you before the vows. Before anything else."

Shana reached for his hand. "This only makes me more certain."

The silence between them deepened. It was not heavy, but whole.

"You keep your promises," she said. "That's the kind of man I want to follow."

Shana stepped back inside. A gentle hand rested on her shoulder. Sarah.

"My girl," she said softly, her voice thick with emotion. "A woman now… ready to be married."

Shana turned and wrapped her arms around her mother. "Mother, I will miss you so much. But it will be good. Just as Yahweh showed you and Father where to stop, He will show Mikael and me the same."

That afternoon, when the men returned for their meal, they stamped snow from their leather-covered feet and dropped their snow-dusted cloaks near the door. Shana moved quickly to gather the pile, the smell of wet wool mingling with the rich aroma of stew and fresh bread. She laid the garments near the hearth to dry.

One by one, the men clustered around the fire, rubbing their hands together, cheeks reddened from the cold. Though winter still pressed heavily around them, the approaching marriage brought a hush of anticipation; something new was stirring among these frozen days.

After they ate, Shana tugged on Mikael's sleeve. "Before you disappear, we need you for something."

He raised his eyebrows, a playful glint in his eyes, but followed without protest.

Sarah brought out the tunic and slipped it over his shoulders. The wool draped neatly, though not quite perfectly. Mikael ran his hands across the fabric.

"What is this?" he asked, his brow furrowed.

Shana stepped closer. "For our marriage. And to keep you warm after."

He looked at her, truly looked, with a rare softness. "It's beautiful… like the one who helped make it. I might not want to take it off."

She laughed, easing it back over his head so she and Sarah could adjust the fit. They worked through the afternoon, their hands steady, hearts full, finishing the garment just as the sun began its slow descent.

Not long after, Johanan, Eldad, and Mikael returned again, this time with Martha and Jairus in tow. Outside, the sky blazed with streaks of orange and violet, the full moon rising behind it like a second flame. Sunset and moonrise seemed locked in silent competition for the sky's attention.

The evening meal passed with quiet conversation and occasional laughter. Then villagers began to arrive, cloaked and bundled, their breath curling in the cold night air.

Johanan welcomed them, guiding them to places around the fire. Jairus cradled a warm cup of tea in both hands. He took one last sip, then passed the cup to Martha beside him. Rising slowly, he lifted his arms, and the room hushed.

"Most of you know the story of Noah and the ark," Jairus began, his voice low and even. "But tonight, I will tell it as Noah told us, back at the time of the scattering."

The fire dimmed to a low glow as his words filled the space. They were reverent, rhythmic, and soaked in memory. When he paused, the silence deepened.

"I cannot tell the story as Noah did," he said, "not with the weight of survival in my voice. But this I remember: Elohim cares for His children. He gives promises and He keeps them. The rainbow is one of those promises. And the promise of One to come... we still await."

He glanced toward Mikael, a quiet invitation.

But Mikael only shook his head, gently. The story still rang too freshly in his spirit, too sacred to follow with speech.

So Jairus closed with a prayer.

"Yahweh Elohim, thank You for the promises fulfilled... and those still to come. Watch over us and guide us. Amen."

The villagers rose slowly, murmuring soft farewells as they wrapped themselves once more in cloaks and shawls. Outside, the full moon cast a silver sheen across the snow-blanketed earth. The cold pressed in again, but the house remained warm with what had been shared: stories, prayers, the memory of Noah, and the quiet sense that something holy had walked among them.

Chapter 47

THE VEIL AND THE VOW

The moon phase was moving on. Seven days until her marriage, Shana thought. Her heart was fluttering like a bird ready to take flight. Excitement stirred inside her, but it was braided with nervousness. So much had changed, and soon, everything would change again.

Morning light brushed the ground in golden strokes. Johanan must have stirred the fire already; the scent of herbs rose warmly to meet her. Shana prepared her tea, then bundled herself in a cloak and stepped outside, steam curling from the cup in her hand.

At the horse enclosure, Eldad and Mikael were already at work. Their voices were low, like the hum of the earth awakening. Tobiya joined them some mornings, but today it was just the three of them. Shana leaned on the fence, sipping her tea, watching as they worked the ropes onto the halters with practiced ease.

Mikael had spoken with Johanan about crafting something to help carry supplies on the horses during travel, like a wooden frame cinched beneath the belly, resting behind the rider. It was simple, clever, and today they were going to test it.

She waited until her tea was gone, then walked into the enclosure. Her breath puffed in the cold morning air.

"Are we ready to try this?"

Mikael looked up, a grin tugging at the corners of his mouth. "Are you?"

She stepped toward him, and he boosted her onto Beauty's back. The mare snorted but stayed calm.

"If there were something I could put my foot in, I could swing my leg over easier," she said, steadying herself.

"Maybe we'll need to make you something," Mikael chuckled.

He secured the apparatus behind her, Beauty sidestepping a little before settling. The cold leather creaked under his hands. Eldad handed Shana the ropes, and she began guiding Beauty slowly around the enclosure.

Mikael mounted Storm, and Eldad attached the second frame to his horse. Storm resisted—tossing his head and giving a small buck before calming. One by one, they moved together, the horses adjusting to the new weight.

"Let's try the trail to the river," Mikael said. "It's familiar."

Eldad opened the gate, and they rode out into the early light. Frost still clung to the ground, glittering like fallen stars. The quiet rhythm of hoofbeats filled the air as they rode down to the river. There, the horses drank deeply, the sound of splashing mingling with the soft creak of leather.

On their return, Eldad shut the gate behind them. Mikael dismounted with a swing of his leg. "Let me help you, Shana," he said, moving to her side. "Should I take the frame off first?"

"Yes, you'd better take it off," she said, a flicker of nerves tightening her chest.

Once it was removed, she slipped down into his waiting arms. For a moment, he held her there, the warmth of his body anchoring her. He hugged her, and she smiled into his chest.

"I have to leave again," she said softly. "But I'll see you at midday."

***

At home, the scent of honey and warm bread greeted her. Sarah and Martha were bustling— laughter and urgency in their voices. Sarah had pulled honey from a hidden store and was shaping cakes; Martha was humming to herself, concocting something new.

"What should I be doing?" Shana asked, brushing flour from the edge of the table.

"In a few minutes, let's see what we can do with your hair," Sarah said, glancing over. "Men seem to like taking women's hair down, so it needs to go up in a way that's... memorable."

Shana grinned and fetched the carved wooden comb her father had made—the twin to her mother's. She began gently untangling her hair. Her fingers moved slowly, rhythmically. There was something soothing in the motion.

Sarah stepped behind her and began weaving small braids, connecting them delicately. "Martha, what do you think?"

"I like it," Martha said, pausing in her work. "But it'll take time on the day."

"Well, many of the women are bringing food. It's not the usual way, but nothing here is usual," Sarah replied. "Maybe I should stay here, and you do her hair."

Shana's brow furrowed. "Wait! I know you'll both be busy. What if Bathshua helps? She's always doing things with her hair. She's amazing."

Sarah and Martha exchanged a glance.

"That would be very good," Sarah said, nodding. "We'll need all the help we can get."

That evening, the scent of roasting meat drifted through the air, rich and mouthwatering. Firelight danced on the hearthstones. The men lounged nearby, hands stretched toward the warmth, voices low and steady.

Mikael spoke with Tobiya and Johanan, gesturing now and then toward the enclosure. There was something about the new bag setup. A low ripple of laughter followed, quiet and genuine.

Shana caught snippets—"Storm hardly flinched today," "Beauty's smarter than we thought," "Better than goats by a mile." The talk circled back to horses—living symbols of movement, freedom, and what lay ahead.

***

As night deepened, the room swelled with warmth and life. Villagers arrived one by one, cloaks heavy with cold, feet thudding softly on the packed earth. Children peeked out, then scampered to the fire. Mothers called greetings. Someone passed warm cups, and steam was curling in the golden lamplight.

Then Jairus stood. "This is the story of how many languages came to be," he began, "as told at the gathering." He spoke of the Tower of Babel, how pride led to chaos, and chaos to dispersion. "Our journey was to the sunset. Others went north, south, east. Elohim desires His people in every land."

Heads nodded, murmurs of agreement rising like a tide. "When Mikael came," Jairus continued, "I had to speak the original tongue. But we learned each other's language. And now, we speak as one." He paused. "Let us walk with Yahweh, so our children and their children will tell the stories of *our* time, of what He has done and how His promises continue." The villagers lingered, voices weaving in the warmth. Then they began to drift homeward, the stars overhead silent and sure.

***

The morning of the celebration came.

"Finish what you need this morning," Sarah said. "Remember you're with us women at sunset."

Shana dared not leave. Her mother's voice had that tone. Soon Bathshua arrived, flanked by Tabitha and Hadassah. They brought pots of water, their cheeks flushed with excitement.

Warm water steamed in waves as Shana soaked. Bathshua combed her hair carefully, washing it with herbs and oil. Her dark curls hung in damp ringlets, reaching her hips. She wrapped herself in a blanket by the fire, cheeks glowing, while Bathshua rubbed scented oil into her skin. The scent of frankincense and myrrh filled the room.

As the sun slid toward the horizon, everyone moved with purpose. Bathshua wove small braids into Shana's hair, intertwining them with tiny threads of gold. Then came the robe—new, deep-hued, soft. Sarah approached, holding something delicate.

"This is for you."

A veil, light as breath, shimmered in her hands.

Bathshua secured it into her hair. The other women smiled. Their eyes were damp.

Outside, the smells of roasted meat, flatbreads, and honey cakes filled the air. The women gathered, waiting. A cry went up—

"They are coming!"

The men arrived, laughter and warmth rolling in like a wave. Jairus and Johanan entered first. Then Eldad and Lemuel. Finally, Mikael.

Mikael.

Shana's heart pounded like a drum in her chest.

Sarah and Martha stepped forward. Bathshua followed. Then Shana.

The world narrowed.

Jairus took Mikael's hand and covered it over Shana's and raised his voice. "A man will leave his father and mother and be united with his wife…"

"Do you, Johanan and Sarah, agree to this?"

"We do."

"Mikael, do you take Shana to be your wife?"

"I do."

"Shana?"

Her voice barely trembled, "I do."

Mikael lifted the veil. His lips met hers, soft, reverent, real. The crowd erupted in cheers. A path was cleared, and food was brought. The music rose, a harp, a lyre, a flute, and the beat of drums.

Dancing began. Shana laughed, resting her head on Mikael's shoulder. His beard tickled her skin. He traced a finger along her cheek. Their eyes locked. His sky-blue gaze was steady and warm. Her eyes were deep and brown like ripened dates, soft with wonder.

As the sky turned indigo and stars winked into place, Mikael rose. He took her hand.

Silence fell.

The villagers parted, creating a path. They walked, hand in hand, to Jairus' house. At the door, they turned, smiled, and waved.

Then shut it.

The room welcomed them with lamps flickering, cushions and blankets arranged in soft invitation.

Mikael's voice dropped low. "How does one remove this veil… and loose your hair?"

Shana laughed. "I've heard men enjoy that."

"Then let me try."

He stepped closer, reverent. One by one, he freed the pins, careful not to tug too hard. The veil floated to the floor like a feather, catching the flicker of the lamplight as it fell.

As he unraveled the final braid, her hair spilled down in dark, gleaming waves like rivers of night cascading over her shoulders and back. Mikael drew in a breath, as though seeing her for the first time. He reached out, running his fingers through the thick curls, slowly and gently.

"It's softer than I imagined," he said in her ear, the strands slipping like silk between his fingers. "Like water and fire, all at once."

Shana's breath caught. She lifted her hand to his, her eyes searching his face.

"Let's remove these beautiful tunics and get comfortable," he said tenderly.

She smiled, shy but certain, and stepped closer, folding into him. His arms came around her, warm and sure. He lifted her chin, kissed her softly at first, then with rising passion, as the night wrapped them in its hush.

Chapter 48

HE KEEPS HIS PROMISES

Winter lingered, long and stubborn. For months, snow clung to the trees like forgotten lace, and the cold wrapped itself around the village with no intention of letting go. Slowly, the light changed. The air began to smell of earth again with wet soil, thawing roots, sap stirring in the branches.

Shana had joined Mikael in his space at Jairus's home. It made sense: practical and comforting, too. Their lives had become deeply woven together, the rhythm of their days shared in meals, in work, in quiet companionship. Johanan, Sarah, and Eldad moved fluidly between both homes. Tobiya and his family came often, his children skipping between the dwellings, their laughter echoing in the still-chilly air. They now called Jairus and Martha "grandparents."

This group, that had once journeyed westward together, had become something more: a family. And all had accepted Mikael as part of it.

Even the horses seemed to sense the peace that had settled, growing more cooperative with each passing week.

And then it was finally spring.

The snow began to recede, not in grand sweeps but in cautious trickles. Grass emerged, fragile and green. Crocuses broke through the softened soil—first purple, then yellow, then a burst of white. Hyacinths and daffodils followed, releasing a breath of perfume as if the earth itself exhaled relief.

One crisp morning, Mikael and Shana rode out to the hills. The breeze had lost its bite. Clouds drifted high and slow. Shana scanned the horizon.

"Will the herd return?" she asked softly.

They saw no sign of them yet.

Mikael drew his horse beside hers. "Soon, we'll begin our journey to the sunset," he said, voice steady but low. "Do you have your things ready?"

Shana nodded. "Most of them. We'll have to be careful. Take what we need most. Food first. Once we're out, we can hunt and gather."

He reached out and brushed her cheek, warm and lingering. She smiled and let her fingers glide down his hand, feeling the familiar strength in it.

As they rode around the foot of the hills, a figure caught Mikael's eye. He stiffened.

There, silhouetted against the pale blue sky, stood the black stallion, proud and watchful. Alone atop the ridge like a sentinel of the wild.

Below, the herd gathered quietly in the valley.

Mikael turned sharply. "We need to go. Storm's nearing the age to challenge him."

They galloped back, the wind tugging at their cloaks.

Later that day, Mikael gathered with Eldad and Johanan.

"I think we should leave soon," he said. "Before the stallions clash."

Johanan exhaled slowly, eyes resting on the horizon. "I understand, but it feels like I'm losing a son as well as a daughter." He turned to them. "What do you still need?"

Shana joined them, quiet and resolved. "Only food. Everything else is ready. But leaving… that's the hard part."

Johanan wrapped his arms around her, then Mikael too. "Yahweh is calling you. He will bless your steps."

At midday, they returned to the house. Smoke curled from the hearth. The scent of roasting meat filled the room.

Sarah looked up. "What's happening?"

"They need to leave soon," Johanan said gently.

Sarah's hand covered her mouth. "Oh." Her voice cracked on the single word.

They sat together; conversation hushed like a shared breath. When the time was right, Eldad jogged off to fetch Jairus and Martha. Soon, the room filled again with more hands, more voices, and more memories.

"We won't leave tonight," Mikael said. "But tomorrow is best."

They all helped gather supplies. They filled bags with dried meat, cheese, dried fruits, fire flints, and cooking tools. Johanan laid out the plans: "You can strap five bags behind you, the little tent, too. A bundle for each of you for what you'll need quickly."

Shana looked around. "Can we play music tonight? Eldad, will you fetch Tobiya and his family?"

"I'll run," he grinned, already halfway out the door.

That night, laughter returned, though soft and weighted. They rearranged bags, shared food, adjusted straps and bindings. Then the music came.

They sang the Creation Hymn, voices rising and falling like a prayer of memory, songs from the Gathering, songs learned in the village. The music wove them together one final time.

Afterward, they sat, sipping mountain tea by the fire. Shana leaned into Mikael. He put his arm around her.

"So many stories I have never heard," Mikael said quietly, his voice thoughtful.

Shana turned slightly, resting her head against his shoulder. "You listened well."

He smiled and whispered into her ear, "I'll tell you mine as we go."

She brushed her fingers across his lips by her cheek, warmth blooming in her chest.

Before parting, Jairus stood. "Let me pray for you."

They all rose. Hands reached out, soft, calloused, trembling, and rested on Shana and Mikael. Jairus's voice trembled as he spoke.

"Dear Yahweh Elohim, watch over them as they journey to the sunset. Make them fruitful, bless them as they go. Remind them of Your promises. Let their days be long, their hearts steadfast. Amen."

Tears flowed freely. No one wiped them away.

One by one, they embraced. Tobiya gathered his family. "We'll head out. Maybe we'll see you in the morning."

Sarah and Shana clung to each other, wordless. Eldad clasped Mikael's back. Mikael returned the gesture, tight and rough.

"Time to rest." Mikael took Shana's hand, and they stepped into the night.

At Jairus's house, Martha held Shana tightly once more.

"Thank you for praying," Mikael said to Jairus.

Jairus smiled, placing a firm hand on his arm. "Go with peace."

***

The sunrise flared in hues of rose and gold, a sky painted with promise. Mikael fetched the horses from the enclosure, their breath pluming in the morning chill. Shana, Martha, and Jairus walked across the space one last time to Johanan's.

Inside, the fire burned bright. Sarah handed her daughter a cup of linden tea.

"I saved a little... for today." Her eyes glistened.

"Eat," she said gently. "Cheese. Flatbread. Keep your strength."

They sat by the hearth, Shana leaning into her mother's shoulder.

A soft knock came at the door. Bathshua stepped in, wrapped in a thick cloak, cheeks flushed from the cold.

"I had to say goodbye," she said, crossing the room quickly.

Shana rose and embraced her, holding tight.

"I'll miss you so much," Bathshua whispered. "But I think a man will come for me someday… one who wants to stay. I've always loved this place."

Shana smiled, her eyes glistening. "Then may he find you here—with your feet rooted and your heart full."

They held each other a moment longer. Then Bathshua stepped back, blinking quickly.

"Go well, Shana. Carry the stories only you can tell, and share them in the light of the sunset."

"And you are planted deep in this place," Shana said with a soft laugh. "I'll carry you with me in my heart."

When Mikael arrived, the men began hauling the bags out with the final packs, the tent, and the last provisions. The fire crackled one more time for them.

Mikael turned to Shana. "It's time."

More hugs. More kisses. Words too thick for voices.

He lifted her carefully onto Beauty, the familiar feel grounding her. Mikael secured the bundles, then mounted Storm. And then, they were off.

The sun rose behind them. Crocuses carpeted the hillsides in violet, orange, and white, like a benediction beneath their hooves.

They wound through the hills, the village fading away behind them like a prayer already answered as they rode into a promise still unfolding.

***

The next morning, gray clouds veiled the sky, heavy with rain.

"We'll go as far as we can," Mikael said.

By midday, the rain began. First it came down in soft drips, then in steady sheets.

It baptized them as they rode. Not cruel, just insistent. The rain was a separation, a washing, and a way of goodbye.

Mikael guided them beneath overhanging trees. "No staying dry now," he murmured, pulling Shana close, their cloaks pressed together, sharing warmth.

The rain eased into a gentle drizzle. Shana's hair clung to her cheeks. Mikael lifted her gently back onto Beauty, then mounted up.

They rode.

Ahead, the sunset blazed across the horizon, bold, gold, and endless.

And arcing across it: a double rainbow. Crimson to violet. A promise written in light.

Mikael slowed his horse beside hers. His voice was soft, almost reverent.

"Do you believe He still keeps His promises?"

Shana looked up, her heart aching and full. She paused.

"Yes," she whispered. "He keeps His promises."

Chapter 49

THE PROMISE KEPT

The North Star guided them like a faint memory, constant and clear. For weeks, they followed it, riding through thawing valleys and over wind-scoured ridges, retracing the path Mikael had taken so many months before, only now, he was not alone. They moved slowly, mindful of the horses and the land.

The snow retreated by day and crept back at night. Crocuses gave way to wild tulips, birds returned in bursts of song, and rivers surged with meltwater. Their cloaks flapped in the wind like banners.

The journey was long, but it was not bitter. They were learning about each other again.

At night, they camped beneath a canopy of stars. Sometimes Mikael would speak in his language, repeating words for fire, for sky, for bread. Shana echoed them back, careful and curious. Other times, she sang in hers, her voice lilting with memories of the Gathering.

But one evening, as they reached the banks of a swollen stream and began to unpack, the rhythm snapped. Shana had led Beauty to drink, but the mare balked and was startled by the shifting current. The rope slipped. The horse stumbled and bolted uphill.

Mikael shouted sharp and fast and ran after her. By the time he caught up, both horse and man were bristling.

"Why didn't you tie her better?" Mikael snapped, breathless. "You know she still spooks near water."

"I had it under control," Shana replied, voice tight. "I've handled her before."

"You *thought* you did," he muttered, tugging Beauty back toward camp. "She could have broken a leg."

Shana's cheeks flushed. "Then say it in *my* language, not yours. Don't let your words strike me like stones I can't catch!"

Mikael stopped cold. The silence between them thickened. It was heavy and raw.

"I didn't mean to..." he began, then shook his head. "When I get scared, I go back to the language I learned first. I forget."

Shana's voice softened. "I want to learn it. But don't leave me out when it matters."

They stood with Beauty snorting between them.

Then, slowly, Mikael reached for her hand. "We'll keep teaching each other. Not just when things are calm."

Shana nodded, the heat fading. "We're not just learning words. We're learning about each other."

That night, they sat close under the trees. Shana traced stars with her finger. Mikael whispered their names in his language, and Shana echoed them back in hers, singsong and steady.

And slowly, the space between them closed again.

***

Weeks passed. The landscape changed. Mountains softened into hills, and familiar markers emerged—stones, streams, and bends in the trail. One morning, as the mist lifted from the valley floor, Mikael pointed ahead.

"There."

Below them, nestled in the crook of the land, was a small cluster of homes. Smoke curled from cooking fires. A figure led goats to pasture. Another carried a child in her arms.

Shana felt Mikael's hand tighten around hers.

They approached slowly. When they reached the edge of the clearing, Mikael dismounted and walked forward. From one of the dwellings, a woman stepped out.

Mikael stopped, frozen. "Mother."

He crossed the space and wrapped her in an embrace, careful not to jostle the baby in her arms. Shana followed, her heart full.

The woman smiled and held out her hand. "You kept your promise."

"Mother, I have returned with Shana, my wife."

"Shana."

"Peace be to you," Shana said, careful in the language she had practiced.

She was thinner than Mikael had described, with silver streaking her dark hair and weariness in her posture. Yet, her eyes were steady and warm. In her arms, the child nestled against her shoulder, dark curls bouncing with each step.

"This is Makas," Elizabeth said, cradling the baby toward them. "She came after you left. A girl, after three wild boys."

Shana reached out, gently brushing the child's tiny hand.

"Makas," she repeated. "An end… a growing hope."

Elizabeth nodded. "Yes. Mikael, she is why I was so tired when you left."

"What a surprise!" He bent to the child's level. "You have Mother's eyes…and her hair!"

Just then, Jared strode to them and pulled Mikael into a firm embrace.

"Father. It is so good to see you. I have so much to tell." He turned.

"First—my wife, Shana."

Jared took her hand. "Welcome."

"Peace be with you." Shana offered a small smile.

Mikael glanced around at the dwellings, smoke rising from hearths, children's voices echoing beyond garden walls.

"It's not just our family anymore," he said. "While I was gone, others came. There's a village now."

Shana followed his gaze. The neighbors were working side by side, a man was carving wood near a fire, a woman was pounding grain, while another tended goats. The scent of earth, woodsmoke, and bread mingled in the warming air.

Her heart settled in her chest.

"Then this is where we begin," she said.

***

They were welcomed in without fanfare, just open doors, warm food, and grateful tears. Mikah and Malaki came bounding in, their feet light, their grins uncertain but eager. The language barrier remained, but gestures and smiles bridged the space.

That night, they gathered outside beneath the summer sky, the fire crackling low at the center of the circle. Shana sat beside Mikael. The warmth of the flames reflected in the faces around them—family, friends, new neighbors.

"You kept your promise," she said softly, reaching for his hand, echoing his mother's words.

Mikael turned to her, his voice quiet and steady. "Now it's time to teach them why I left, and why you came."

She leaned into him, her gaze drifting to where baby Makas slept in her mother's arms, curls glinting like copper in the firelight. Above them, the stars blinked awake, familiar and bright. A breeze stirred through the tall grass, warm with summer and full of direction.

Hope had returned.

And the journey to the sunset still waited.

Chapter 50

STORIES BY FIRELIGHT

The days grew longer. Warm winds stirred the grasses, coaxing blossoms from the low-hanging branches. Birds sang from rooftops at dawn, and the sharp chill of morning softened into golden afternoons. It was planting season for the new villagers, and hunting season for those who still followed the rhythms of the wild.

Mikael's family worked hard, but they were watching, too. The village, though young, had settled into its own rhythm. The presence of Mikael and Shana had shifted something. Curiosity rose like heat from the earth.

It began quietly.

One evening, as fire crackled in the center of the village, Mikael told a story.

He hadn't planned to. His brothers asked about the bear Mikael and Shana had faced near the glacier, and before he knew it, one story slipped into another. Shana sat beside Mikael, with her hand resting on his arm. Her smile was warm and watchful as he spoke of the deep snow and the eerie silence of that frozen place. The massive bear had come without warning, its breath steaming white in the air, its eyes reflecting the pale light like molten gold.

"We were ready to crawl into the tent for the night," Mikael said.

"We'd set our bows and spears aside and were sitting by the remaining fire. My breath was shallow as every muscle froze. Yet somehow, a prayer rose from my lips. One I barely remembered forming."

He looked into the flames. "Then, I don't know why. I grabbed the end of a branch sticking out of the fire. The other end was glowing embers. I threw it. It hit near the bear's feet. Sparks flew. I think it even singed his fur."

He paused.

"The bear roared, reared back, then dropped and ran."

A murmur of awe rippled through the listeners

"I thought we would die," he said simply. "But we didn't. Because..."

He stared into the fire. "Elohim was there. He heard me. He saw me."

Shana's voice was soft but sure. "He heard us. And He saw us."

A hush settled. The fire popped.

Shana felt her breath catch. Something in the way Mikael said it, quiet, almost reverent, unlocked the memory of that night with the bear in comparison to the night of the confused language. Elohim was there both times.

"We don't worship the fire," Mikael said, his gaze sweeping the circle. "Or the wind, or the beast." His voice was gentle. "We follow the One who made them."

Shana lowered her eyes. His words didn't settle over her like a lesson. They rooted deeper, threading through places inside her she hadn't known were still waiting.

Mikah, fifteen and almost a man, leaned forward, eyes wide in the firelight. "That's... that's an amazing story," he said loudly. "This Elohim can really be with me?

Silence settled like a hush across the gathered circle.

Someone asked a question and then another.

And Mikael began to speak, not of beasts, but of beginnings. "In the beginning, Elohim created the heavens and the earth…"

His father listened, his brow furrowed. His brothers leaned in. One by one, others joined the circle, neighbors and friends. Shana joined in then, and together they told of the beginning, Adam and Eve, and the fall.

Unlike sages or priests, they spoke as those who had walked the path. They told stories. From memory, from wonder, from experience.

And the people listened.

***

In the morning, the men prepared to hunt. Mikael rose early, the scent of firewood and oiled leather already thick in the air. His father inspected the bows, testing their tension with practiced hands. His younger brothers bickered over spears and quivers; their energy was sharp and eager.

"You ready?" one of them called.

Mikael nodded, glancing back toward the doorway. Shana stood there, quiet and watchful. She stepped forward, brushed a hand over his shoulder, and tightened one of the leather straps on his chest.

"Come back safe," she murmured.

He dipped his head and pressed a kiss to her temple. "Always."

Laughter followed them as they set off, feet crunching over dew-laced grass. The trees ahead shimmered in the early light, leaves whispering overhead. The forest welcomed them with scent and sound, with creaking bark, birds bursting into wingbeats, and the hush of wildness all around.

They moved in practiced silence, though Mikael's presence altered the rhythm. He noticed things like fresh prints in the mud, tufts of fur snagged on bark, and a snapped reed near a water trail. His father gave a small nod of approval. His brothers followed his eyes now, not just their own instincts.

By midday, they had killed two deer. On the way back, the mood had lifted.

"Tell us again about the time the goat chased the boy through camp," one brother said, grinning.

"After he tried to ride it," Mikael replied, smirking. "Said if I could ride a stallion, he could ride a goat."

Even his father chuckled.

***

While the men were gone, Shana stayed close to Mikael's mother, Elizabeth.

They worked in quiet companionship, shaping dough, chopping herbs, and layering wild roots into clay pots. The rhythm of the kitchen needed no translation.

Later, while Makas took her nap, Shana brought out her lap loom. Elizabeth watched with interest, her eyes following the movement of the shuttle.

"You weave?" she asked.

"Yes," Shana said. "I learned from my grandmother and my mother."

Elizabeth nodded, then retrieved her own bundle of fibers that were coarse, earth-dyed, and well-used. Together they began to weave, exchanging simple patterns and laughter.

That afternoon, they hung the half-finished piece near the door. The pattern was simple with lines and diamonds, but already it held the feel of two lives stitched into one.

As they prepared the evening meal, Elizabeth crushed seeds and dried leaves into a paste that Shana didn't recognize.

She leaned closer, watching.

"Teach me that," she said.

Elizabeth quietly and warmly smiled. "You'll feed your family well someday."

Shana smiled back. The name "Mother" hadn't passed her lips, but the feeling was already taking root.

***

That night, more people came to the fire.

They brought bread, meat, and fruit. Despite no one announcing it, the circle grew. Elders leaned in. Children clung to their parents. Some sat on stones, others on woven mats. All eyes turned toward the center, where Mikael and Shana sat side by side, the firelight casting a golden glow across their faces.

Shana told of the Gathering of Noah and the ark, of the rainbow, the sacrifice, the tower, and the confusion of languages, along with the journey to the sunset. Her words came slowly at first, but she found strength as the listeners leaned in, their brows furrowed, expressions softening with recognition and wonder.

Mikael rose and stepped toward the altar—a simple mound of uncut stones set just beyond the firelight. Jared followed a step behind. In Mikael's hands, a white dove stirred, its feathers catching the glow like pale flame.

He turned to face the gathered families. "We will offer a dove tonight," he said, his voice calm but steady. "As Noah did after the flood—he offered from the clean birds, and it was pleasing to Yahweh. So we bring this now, seeking His mercy and guidance."

Around the circle, heads bowed. A few elders murmured quiet assent. One woman whispered something to her child and pointed toward the altar.

Mikael approached the stones. "This is how Johanan and Jairus showed me," he murmured to his father.

Jared nodded, letting his son lead.

With care, Mikael held the bird and pinched its neck—swift, firm, but not severing it. The flutter stilled. He lifted it over the altar, letting the blood fall in small, bright drops upon the stones. Then, kneeling, he drained the rest at the base of the altar, where the earth darkened as it drank the offering.

He remained kneeling, then lifted his voice in prayer—not loud, but clear enough to carry.

"O Yahweh Elohim, we come with what little we have. We bring this dove as a sign of what we cannot cleanse on our own. Forgive us, for our hearts are not pure. We forget. We stray. Yet still, we seek You. Lead us, even through the unknown. Teach us to walk in Your ways, and not be lost in our own."

A silence followed—deep and weighty, as if the night itself had drawn near to listen.

Then Mikael rose. Jared laid a hand on his shoulder. Together, they stepped back into the circle.

Shana brought out her harp, cradling it gently in her lap. Her fingers moved with care. The strings vibrated beneath the stars, each note rising like incense into the dark. A neighbor joined her, who was shy at first, with a carved reed flute. The two melodies twined together: simple, yearning, full of memory. A hush settled over the gathering, the crackling fire the only sound between the notes.

Shana lifted her voice. She sang part of the Creation Hymn, her voice unsteady at first, then swelling with quiet confidence as her fingers strummed the harp. A few in the crowd closed their eyes as they joined in the singing. One woman pressed a hand to her chest. A boy mouthed the words as if he already knew them. The melody lingered long after the last chord fell still.

Mikael leaned in and kissed her temple.

Mikah groaned, breaking the silence. "Really? Right after the sacred song?"

"Do we have to watch this?" Malaki wrinkled his nose.

Mikael chuckled, the tension easing. "Maybe you'll fall in love one day, too."

"Do I have to go on an adventure first?" Malaki made a face.

Laughter gently rippled through the circle, familiar and unforced.

Shana blushed, but her smile didn't falter. Mikael pulled her closer, his hand resting warm at the small of her back. Around them, the villagers remained gathered. The warmth of the fire reflected in their eyes, and they were no longer just curious but moved.

After the others had gone, Mikael and Shana lingered by the embers, their fingers laced together. The flute and harp were silent now. Something still stirred between them. There was an afterglow of music and meaning that hadn't quite faded.

A warmth remained in the hush, as if the stories they had shared still hovered in the air, taking root in the hearts left behind.

Mikael brushed a curl from her cheek and kissed her gently. "I love seeing you here. With them. With me."

Shana leaned toward him, eyes reflecting the flicker of coals; blue meeting blue in the quiet glow. "Do you think they understood?" she asked softly.

"I think they felt it," he said. "And maybe that's where understanding begins."

She slipped her arms around him and settled into his lap, the firelight painting their shadows on the ground.

"Wherever you are," she whispered, "that's home."

Chapter 51

JOURNEY TO THE SUNSET

The morning was warm and clear. It was the kind of day that proclaimed change before it said a word.

Shana stirred before the sun crested the hills. She slipped quietly from the blankets, wrapped her cloak around her shoulders, and stepped outside. Light stretched slowly across the fields, painting the village rooftops in gold. The world felt hushed, as if even the birds were waiting.

Behind her, Mikael appeared, barefoot and rubbing sleep from his eyes. He crossed the space between them and rested a hand gently on her back.

"Couldn't sleep?" he asked.

She leaned into him slightly, her shoulder brushing his chest. Her hand rose to his hair—dark as the night hills they'd once crossed. He smiled and bent lower, threading his fingers through her curls, soft as woven flax. Their eyes met. Hers were as dark as ripened dates, steady and full of memory; his were like the clear blue of the open sky.

"We've changed, haven't we?" she said quietly.

He nodded. "And we're still changing."

She touched his cheek, her fingers lingering. "Then let's go forward together."

***

They ate a simple meal with Mikael's family—flatbread, cheese, berries. No one asked them to stay. No one asked for a promise to return. There were embraces, quiet prayers, and soft smiles that said: We will be all right.

Mikael bent to kiss his baby sister's forehead. "Goodbye, little Makas," he whispered. "Grow strong. Grow kind."

Elizabeth wrapped her arms around him without words. Then she turned to Shana and held her close, brushing a loose strand of hair from her cheek.

"May your journey be fruitful," she said.

Shana hesitated, then leaned in and whispered softly, just for her: "It already is."

Elizabeth drew back slightly, eyes wide. Her hand came to rest gently on Shana's arm, tender and trembling.

As they prepared to leave, Shana embraced Elizabeth one last time. The baby, Makas, was nestled against her shoulder, dark curls warm against her neck.

Shana looked into her eyes, heart full. "Thank you for teaching me," she said softly. "For welcoming me." She hesitated, then added in a whisper, "Mother."

Elizabeth's eyes shone. She reached out and cupped Shana's cheek. "You're my daughter now," she said. "You always will be."

Mikael's father, Jared, handed him a satchel that was light but full. "It's not much, but it's yours."

His brothers came last. They were awkward in their farewells, rough in their affection. Nevertheless, they showed up, every one of them.

272

***

The horses were ready, and everything secured. Storm and Beauty pawed at the earth, eager to move. Shana checked the straps once more, her fingers lingering a moment longer than needed.

She turned for one last look.

The village stood hushed in morning stillness. Thin streams of smoke rose from the shelters. Elizabeth walked slowly, Makas nestled against her hip. The baby's small hand lifted in a clumsy wave, and Shana raised hers in return, heart catching in her throat. Jared and the boys stood nearby, waving with broad, open gestures.

Mikael reached for her hand. "Ready?"

Shana nodded, eyes still on the figures behind them. "Yes, let's go."

***

They rode in the direction of the sunset.

The fields turned to hills. The hills softened into plains. Summer grasses swayed heavily with seed, and bees droned in the warmth. Wildflowers, deep gold and violet, nodded in the breeze. Before them, the way stretched wide beneath the sun.

The sun climbed higher behind them, casting their long shadows forward. Behind them lay the sea. Ahead was only the unknown.

They didn't speak often. They didn't need to.

By afternoon, the land dipped into a vast silence. The sky stretched wide and deep, the air warm with promise. Somewhere beyond it, the path would rise again. Somewhere farther still, the place Elohim would show them.

Mikael pointed to the horizon, where the light gathered like flame at the edge of the earth. As if in answer, an eagle rose into the sky ahead of them; its wings wide, steady, cutting through the stillness. It circled once, then glided west, soaring into the golden haze.

"Do you see it?" Mikael asked.

Shana followed his gaze. "Yes. I see it." She smiled, her voice low. "It's the journey to the sunset… and we're just beginning."

And they followed the path Elohim set before them, for His promises endure from generation to generation.

www.ingramcontent.com/pod-product-compliance
Lightning Source LLC
Chambersburg PA
CBHW032357310726
48973CB00007B/2055